Abby's Redemption
A Whispering Pines Mystery
Book 2

Rhonda Blackhurst

Books may be purchased in quantity and/or special sales by
contacting the author at www.rhondablackhurst.com or
rjblackhurst0611@gmail.com.

Published by Lighthouse Press, Colorado
Cover Design by: No Sweat Graphics & Formatting

Library of Congress Control Number: 2020902279

ISBN-13: 978-0-9913532-9-3
ISBN-10: 0-9913532-9-3

First Edition
Printed in the United States of America

Also by Rhonda Blackhurst

The Inheritance

The Melanie Hogan Cozy Mystery Series

❖ Shear Madness

❖ Shear Deception

❖ Shear Malice

❖ Shear Murder

The Whispering Pines Mysteries

❖ Finding Abby

To the victims of domestic violence.

And to those who help them cross the Jordan to freedom, so they can begin to heal: Advocates, Police Officers, Prosecutors, First Responders. You are all heroes.

1

The cold, gray sky hovered above the snow-capped Rocky Mountains and loomed before Abby as her green Subaru Outback bumped along the side winding road. The ominous weather matched her mood perfectly, though she couldn't pinpoint the exact reason for her mood. When she'd left her therapist's office little more than thirty minutes ago, she'd been deeply unsettled and couldn't yet figure it out. Something just didn't feel right.

She replayed the hour-long session in her mind for what seemed the hundredth time before turning up the volume on her radio to drown out her thoughts. She felt a pang of loneliness when she remembered her son, Cooper, wouldn't be home waiting for her. He was one of the few people who could make her forget everything bad. Everything other than being together. And now they weren't because he was staying with his aunt Piper in Washington. He was ten years old and hadn't wanted to go until his aunt had promised him a new Xbox and movies every night before bed. Abby called it bribery. Piper called it doing what she had to, to spend some time alone with her nephew. So while Piper spoiled Cooper out on the West Coast, Abby took advantage of the time to sneak in a couple of extra sessions with her therapist. Sessions she wouldn't need if it hadn't been for Cooper's dad, her ex-con, ex-husband, Hunter.

At least the flashbacks were getting to be less frequent the past several months, and they didn't have the tight grasp on her emotions they once had. Rather than being held hostage by the memories, now they were a mere annoyance. Thanks to her therapist. And yet ... something about today's session—and the few prior, if she was honest with herself—felt somewhat off.

She reached for her bag she'd tossed on the passenger's seat when she'd gotten in her car and rummaged through it with one hand, not daring to take her eyes off the road. Finally, she pulled off to the side and rummaged through it with both hands. "Where's my darn phone?" she mumbled. She swept a strand of long blond hair out of her face with her forearm and sat back with a deep breath. Where on earth had she left it? "Let's see," she said in the quietness of her car, the radio now off. "First I went to Dr. Miller's office, then the gas station to fill up and inside to pay..." She struggled to remember the last time she'd seen her phone. "Doggonit!" she said. Leaning back against the seat, she blew an unruly wisp of hair from her face. Her phone hadn't been in her bag when she'd pulled out her wallet to pay for gas. She was sure of it. But she'd been so focused on the odd session with her therapist that it escaped her at the time.

"So much for calling Pops to let him know I'll be late." She waited for a car to pass and pulled a U-turn, heading back into town. She stepped on the gas. The faster she got her phone, the faster she could let her father know she'd be later than expected. Since the resort wasn't nearly as busy in the winter months as during the summer, he should be okay. If she could only shake the guilt of not being where she was supposed to be when she was supposed to be there. *Catholic guilt*, she chided herself.

Abby and Cooper had inherited Whispering Pines Resort in Blue Mist Mountain, Colorado, the previous summer. Her father, still mourning the death of her mother five years earlier, had agreed to come with them. Despite his chronic drinking problem, he'd become a huge asset with his handyman skills. Her thoughts brushed over the little shed down the wooded path that he'd made into a studio for her. And the mule deer she'd seen out the front French doors yesterday afternoon when she'd sneaked a few minutes to go write.

"That's right!" she said, tapping her hands on the steering wheel. She jerked the wheel to make a quick right onto Elk Horn Drive, and the car behind her blared his horn. She'd taken her phone out to schedule her next appointment with Dr. Miller, then set it down on the side table for a moment while she took out her wallet.

When she pulled into the parking lot of the row of office buildings that housed Dr. Miller's office, she was disappointed to see a car in front of his door. If he was with a client, that meant she would have to wait for him to finish before she could collect her phone. Which meant a longer period of time before she could call her father. "What did we ever do before cellphones?" she grumbled.

Abby sat in her car until a quarter to the top of the hour. A few more cars pulled into the lot in front of neighboring businesses before backing out again. Finally, she got out to wait in the hallway of the exit door. Dr. Miller liked a waiting area for the person arriving and a back door for the person leaving to allow for privacy. *I wouldn't want to be responsible for two people who know each other running into one another. That's the way*

3

gossip begins, he'd explained to her. While it made perfect sense, it created an awkward situation for her now. Should she wait by the exit door, so she knew when the person left, or wait in the entrance waiting area? He didn't have a receptionist. He handled his business entirely on his own except for his wife, who helped him with billing from home.

Hmmm … what to do. Just as she decided it best to wait in the waiting area, the door opened and out came a striking woman, a sheet of coal-black hair on a head that hung low. She glanced at Abby, startled. The woman's bangs nearly covered her watery, red-rimmed, striking blue eyes. The woman quickly looked away after what Abby read to be a moment of panic, and escaped through the door, yanking on the belt of her ruby-red coat that had gotten stuck. She stumbled and nearly fell when the belt yanked loose. *That must have been a hard session*, Abby thought, feeling pity for the woman. Maybe her own problems weren't so bad.

Abby refocused on her missing phone and knocked lightly on the door. "Dr. Miller?" she called softly. The door swung wide, and Dr. Miller stood before her, straightening his tie with one hand.

"Abigail," he said with a smile. "I'll bet you're looking for this." He extended his hand, her phone in his palm. She reached for it, but he gripped it tight, meeting her eyes. "How long have you been standing there?"

"Not long."

"How long is 'not long?'"

Abby felt her cheeks flush, unsure as to why except it felt like she was being scolded. "About fifteen minutes. Tops."

"Hear anything?"

"Nothing." She glanced away from his eyes that seemed to pierce right through her.

"Okay, then. You know how I feel about keeping patient matters confidential."

"I do. And I can appreciate that. But I didn't hear anything. I just came back for my phone. I was going to wait in the other room, but your client came out before I—"

"She's having a rough time of things." He furrowed his thick brows and his lips turned down. "Sometimes it's one step forward, ten back, I'm afraid."

"I'm sorry to hear that. And I'm sorry for your client."

He looked at her squarely. "Of course. And I can trust you'll keep this to yourself."

"Of—of course. I don't even know her." She squirmed under his watchful eye. "If you could just give me my phone— I have to be going."

He slid the phone into her hand, his fingers brushing hers, lingering a little too long. The hair on the back on her neck prickled with unease. It suddenly dawned on her what hadn't settled well with her after her session. She snatched her phone and jerked her hand away as if she'd touched a hot stove. As she turned to leave, his fingers wrapped around her bicep. Not too hard, but firm, nonetheless. She felt a fresh wave of discomfort.

"Abby," he said, his voice low and even, "have a good day."

She met his gaze, trying to read what was there. Something different. Like a dog caught chewing apart a pillow. Or a shoe. Caught in the act.

"Yes, you, too." And she spun on her heel and left.

2

After calling her father, who hadn't been upset in the least, she decided to follow his suggestion of taking some time to meet a friend for lunch or coffee. Not the 'with a friend' part, though. Other than her sister, Piper, the two college kids who helped at the resort during summer breaks, and her boyfriend, Gabriel, her life revolved around the resort. She hadn't taken the time to step out and make new friends. And she was especially gun-shy after her fallout with Holly last summer. Holly, her fellow teacher in California and who she'd thought was her best friend, had horribly betrayed her. Holly, who had secretly been seeing Abby's ex-husband, Hunter, and who eventually lead the monster to the resort, putting hers and Cooper's lives in danger. And now that Holly and Hunter had a baby together, a half-sister to Cooper, Holly would always be part of Abby's and Cooper's lives, whether she wanted her to be or not. Abby shuddered at the thought.

She turned back onto Elk Horn Drive and followed it until she reached one of her favorite coffee stops in Blue Mist Mountain, The Coffee Hub, at the end of the row of shops. *Just because I don't have a friend to call doesn't mean I can't have coffee by myself*, she thought.

Snow had been scarce this year. Large patches of brownish-green grass scattered the ground, and the roads and sidewalks were clear. Despite being the middle of March, typically still cool and wet, the air was pleasantly warm. The sun was even beginning to peek out, providing a light haze in the air. It was stunningly beautiful.

"Hey, Abby," Travis called out from behind the counter with a grin. "Your usual?"

"Is there anything else?" she asked, smiling at him.

"Let me make you something different today. I promise you'll like it."

"Yeah?" she asked, giving him a sidelong look.

He laughed. "Come on. Live on the edge a little. Trust me."

Trust me. Two words she trusted less than anything in the world. Had it not just been coffee they were talking about, she would have turned and run like the wind.

"Yes? No?" He asked, still grinning and waiting for her answer.

She shrugged and laughed lightly. "Sure. Why not?"

Like a kid who won a video game, he pumped his fist in the air and exclaimed, "Yes!" before spinning around to begin his magic.

"So what is it you're making that's so important to you that I try?"

"Trust me."

Again? Really? "Not happening, my friend," she said.

He turned his head to look at her, his hands still working their magic on her drink. "I'm crushed."

"I can tell," she said, laughing again, happier more than ever that she'd decided to make this stop. Nothing like coffee and laughter to help lighten the ping of unease she'd been feeling most of the morning.

"Ta-da!" Travis sang, producing the most delicious looking, albeit fattening, cup of something, topping piled high.

He even served it in a blue ceramic mug that said, *Speak Your Kind* in white Windsong calligraphic script. "I know what you're thinking," he said.

She shook her head, eyes fixed on the mug. "No, no, I don't think you do."

"Sure, I do," he insisted. "You're thinking, 'How did Travis know I wanted this delightful, delicious piece of art this morning?'"

Abby tossed her head back and laughed again. "No, I'm pretty sure that's not what I was thinking. First, I thought 'What in God's name is this?' Next, I thought, 'Guess I'm not sitting outside today unless I can take this most awesome mug with me.'" She slid some bills across the counter and put a healthy tip in the jar alongside the cash register.

Someone stepped up behind her, patiently waiting to place an order, so she turned to walk away.

"Go ahead and take it outside, Abby," he called. "I know you'll bring the mug back in. Unlike you, I trust people." He winked at her.

"You're still young. You'll learn," she said, winking back at him.

She started walking toward the back of the shop, intending to leave through the back door that led to the Riverwalk. Instead, she planted herself on an oversized chair in the back corner, a large window behind her and one to her left, giving her full view of the river sparkling in the sunlight that had by now pushed the clouds out of view. Partial ice glaciers hung over the river, the water beneath trickling through. The sun shone through the window and on her shoulder, spreading warmth over her.

She closed her eyes for a moment, tipped her head back, then side to side. She pressed her fingertips against the back of her neck and shoulder, wincing when she'd applied too much pressure on an overly tight muscle. Eyes back open, she gazed at the water. The mountainside rose behind it, squirrels scampering, birds flitting.

Pulling her phone from her purse, she absently took a sip of her coffee, startling at the unusual, delightful flavor. She looked at Travis, who happened to glance her way and gave him a thumbs-up, producing another fist pump in the air.

"I knew it, girl!" He called over. "Someday you'll learn to trust me." He winked at her again.

Abby looked at her phone, bringing Dr. Miller back to mind, front and center. She opened the Internet. First things first. Something hadn't felt right. She needed to trust her gut and find a new therapist. Or did she? Maybe she was just overreacting like she sometimes did. Like when Hunter got out of prison last time. But as it turned out, she reminded herself, her overreacting had actually turned out to be justified.

Out of sheer curiosity, she opened a search engine and typed in, *female therapists near Blue Mist Mountain, Colorado.* It produced only three names, none of which had any reviews. She removed the word *female* and searched again. A few more names popped up, even some with good reviews — Dr. Miller's name among them. Maybe her gut had been wrong. He had, after all, come as a recommendation from Gabe, who heard good things from a friend of his. And Gabe was one of the few that she *did* trust. He would never lead her astray or give her the recommendation if he hadn't trusted the person who gave it to him.

She glanced up from her phone and out the window toward the river. She spotted the woman in the red coat sitting on a large rock beside the water. Abby couldn't see her face, but that coat and sheet of black hair was a dead giveaway. Fighting the urge to go over and talk with her, she forced herself to stay put. By the looks of things earlier, the poor woman was having a terrible day and probably needed some time alone.

"Hey, Travis?" she called out after the only other customer had left through the front door.

"Yup? Want another one?"

"No. Do you know who that woman is out there?" Travis skirted around the counter and over to her chair. Abby jerked her head toward the window. "That one."

He squinted as he looked through the glass pane. "Susan?"

"The woman in the red coat. Her name's Susan?"

"I'm pretty sure that's her. Why?"

"What do you know about her?" Abby watched as the woman appeared statuesque, not moving a muscle. Was she even breathing?

"All I know is she's not a very happy person."

"Why do you say that? That she's not happy?"

"For starters, she goes to the coffee shop three doors down instead of coming here."

Abby shot him a look, and he put his hands up.

"Kidding! Geez!" He chuckled, sounding more pubescent than the age she guessed him to be.

"How do you know her name if she doesn't come in here?"

Travis looked at her as if she'd just fallen off the turnip truck. "It's a small town, Abby. The locals pretty much know everyone's business."

"Everyone's?"

"Yes. Even yours." He shrugged. "Sorry. You probably didn't wanna hear that."

She shivered. "No, I didn't." She paused. "So what is it people know about me? Or *think* they know?"

"That you and your son moved here from California when you guys inherited Whispering Pines Resort from some guy who died there."

"That's not exactly true. He didn't die there." She looked out at Susan again then back to Travis. "And? What else?" she asked.

"That your ex wasn't exactly a nice guy and your best friend got knocked up with his kid."

Her eyes bulged out of her head. "Are you kidding me?" she squeaked. "How?"

"What do you mean, how? I'm sure I don't need to give you a talk about the birds and the bees. You have a kid."

She narrowed her eyes at him. "Very funny. I mean how do people know all these things. I haven't told anyone any of that. It's personal."

"Nothing's really personal in a small town, kiddo."

Kiddo? She wanted to laugh but couldn't. She figured she had at least ten years on him.

"Anything else?" she asked, afraid of the answer.

"That your dad lives there with you, and he likes to tip the bottle."

"Holy cow!" She shook her head slowly, trying to digest all of it. She felt exposed. Like she might as well be sitting there stark naked.

"Sorry you asked, or sorry I told you?" he asked. He sounded sorry he'd told her.

"Both," she sulked. "Feels like I should hibernate and never show my face around town again."

"Everyone knows your face anyway. They all think you're hot." He smiled, his cheeks pink.

She squirmed in her chair and looked back out the window. Susan was gone.

"You never answered my question," she said, looking back at Travis. "How do you know her name if she doesn't get her coffee here? Other than being a small town, I mean."

"Cause she's involved in a nasty custody battle over her four-year-old. That kind of thing spreads fast. The only thing that people don't seem to know is who the dad is. People assume he must be a high roller with big bucks. Otherwise, how could his information stay a mystery? So far as anyone knows, she's been a good mother."

"Does she have custody now?"

He shook his head and turned for the counter when a customer came in. "Nope. The guy does. Whoever and wherever he is. It's all real hush-hush."

That explains why she was so distraught when she left Dr. Miller's office. And it also explains why Dr. Miller was so protective of the woman's privacy, making sure Abby hadn't overheard anything she wasn't supposed to. She couldn't imagine hearing other people's pain all day every day. She'd decided she had probably been too hard on Dr. Miller. He was more than entitled to a bad day here and there.

Abby picked up her coat and tossed it over her arm, not bothering to slip into it since sitting in the sun warmed her through and through. She brought her empty cup to the counter.

"Thanks, Travis," she said as she opened the front door. "See you next time."

He lifted a hand and waved. "Counting on it."

As Abby walked to her car, she scanned the area, hoping to catch another glimpse of Susan. Knowing what she'd been through with Hunter, her heart was heavy for the woman. She slipped her sunglasses on and tucked her phone in her purse, slipping the strap over her head and across her shoulder. The purse bumped against her hip with each step.

When she reached her car, she pressed the key fob to unlock the door. It beeped at the same time as the car next to it. She glanced over at the blue Honda CRV and caught a glimpse of a red coat disappear behind tinted windows. She looked closer and met eyes with Susan. Abby waved and smiled, neither of which Susan returned.

Abby got in, slammed her car door shut, fastened her seatbelt, and stayed put, giving Susan the first move to back out. She watched as Susan's SUV turned onto Elk Horn Drive, followed by a gray Prius, close on her bumper, windows tinted darker than Susan's car. Too dark for Abby to see who it was. She hadn't missed, however, Susan's display of her middle finger at the Prius following her.

3

Back at the resort, Jeremiah stood behind the counter swapping fishing stories with one of the guests.

"Sharing about the one that got away, Pops?" Abby teased as she slipped the strap of her purse over her head and dropped it on the stool behind the counter.

"Yup," he said. "The two-foot trout." He grinned around an ever-present toothpick sticking through his lips.

"Uh-huh." She laughed, then looked at the man on the opposite side of the counter—tall, unkempt black beard, and a gut that said he probably drank more than a few beers in his life.

"Conrad," the man said, extending his hand to Abby.

She reached for his hand, shook, then put an arm around Jeremiah. "Abby. I'm Jeremiah's daughter."

"So he said," Conrad answered. "In fact, he said you're the brains of the family."

"Is that so?" Abby smiled and playfully punched her father's shoulder. "Pops, you never told me that."

"Didn't want you to get a big head."

"Well, with all these brains, and all, I can't promise that."

Her father grunted his amusement. Conrad gave a hoot.

"She's got the humor in the family, too, huh, Jeremiah?"

"Not so much," Jeremiah said. "Her sister has that one. Abs is my serious one."

"Pops, that's not true."

He simply shrugged and gave her a light squeeze. "Conrad's staying another night. His cabin was available."

"Great!" Abby said, training her eyes on Conrad. "Do you have something special you're going to do? Or just need another day of paradise before heading back home?"

"Both. I'm gonna take a short spring mountain hike and see if I can find me some elk."

"I heard they calve in the springtime, so be careful. From what I hear, the females can get pretty aggressive."

"Seems I heard someone say that's a bit later in the spring. Say May and June. Anywho, another night in the hot tub'll be good, too."

"Ah, yes," she said dreamily. Each cabin had their own private hot tub. "Early mornings are the best time in the hot tub, though. As the sun is rising on the mountaintops, everything is wrapped in still silence..."

She'd stayed away from the hot tub for months, for no other reason than not taking the time to relax. But when her outdoor yoga sessions in the little secluded wooded area by the lake ceased because of the cold and snow, she tried the hot tub on the back of her wrap-around porch. Once was all it took to be hooked. Nearly every morning, no matter how cold, she snuck out at dawn before she opened the store.

"Earth to Abby," Conrad said in his baritone voice.

She jerked her thoughts back to the present. "You enjoy yourself, Conrad. Pops, I'm going to make us a late lunch. I'll be right back."

"Heard from the boy today?" Jeremiah called after her.

"No. I'll call him now."

She took the two stairs up into the living room in one step, pulling her phone from her back pocket. "Call Cooper," she said into her smartphone.

"Calling Cooper," the robotic woman's voice said back to her from her phone.

She waited as it rang and rang, finally rolling into voicemail. "Hey, this is Cooper. You know what to do. If not, it's time you learn."

Abby sighed and rolled her eyes. "Cooper, this is your mom. You need to change that message. It's rude. Anyway, just calling to see how you're doing. Miss you like crazy, buddy. Looking forward to having you back home. Hugs and kisses."

She clicked the off button and chuckled. She could only imagine his reaction at the hugs and kisses part. Over the past couple of months he'd gotten to where hugging and kissing his mom was not the cool thing whether his friends were there or not. He was only ten for Pete's sake. She thought she'd have at least another couple of years. As much as she wanted to blame it on his best friend, Johnny, she couldn't. Johnny had a horrible home life and didn't have a mother to hug and kiss. Only a grandmother who wore a perpetual scowl. But that was probably because she'd gotten mad at Abby last summer. Maybe she was one to hold a grudge.

She dug out the sandwich meat—roasted turkey—from the back of the refrigerator, mustard, mayo, lettuce, tomato, and a loaf of 7-grain bread. Next, she pulled a butter knife from the silverware drawer, fished out four slices of bread, and began slathering mustard and mayo on one and just mustard on hers. Abby couldn't stand the taste of mayo. It reminded her of when her mother used to put it on her hair when she was a little girl with hopes of detangling. Just the smell of it turned her stomach.

She looked up and out the kitchen window in front of her, and startled. Conrad's face was just inches from the window pane as he stared back at her. The knife clattered to the floor, and her hand flew to her chest. She tapped on the glass then shouted through the closed window.

"Conrad! What are you doing out there?"

"Wanted to see what we're having for lunch," his voice boomed back as he laughed. "Scared ya, huh?"

Abby swallowed her retort and said instead, "Next time use the door, Conrad."

He turned and walked away, still laughing.

"Glad you're so amused with yourself," she said under her breath. "Because you're the only one who is."

"Talkin' to yourself, Abs?"

She jumped at the sound of her father's voice, dropping the knife she'd just picked up.

"Pops!" she scolded. "What is it with you guys?"

"Why're you so jumpy, Pipsqueak?"

"Your buddy Conrad thought it would be funny to plaster his nose up to the window, scaring me half to death."

"The man's just lonely. Cut him some slack."

"Well, he's going to stay lonely if he pulls stunts like that." She slapped the last sandwich together, plopped it on a plate, cut it diagonally, tucked a handful of chips and a dill pickle on either side, and handed it to her father.

"Where's the beer to go with it?"

She shot him a look. "At the liquor store where it belongs. Far, far away from your little paws."

He shrugged and chuckled, enjoying ruffling her feathers entirely too much.

She could tell the winter cold was beginning to get to all of them. Springtime teased them, but winter wasn't quite ready to let go yet. As beautiful as the wintertime is up in the mountains, pristine white snow blanketing the earth, she missed the warmth of summer. She even loved the chaos of the resort in the summertime. She longed for days she could go barefoot or wear flip flops instead of boots, and t-shirts or tank tops instead of piling on layers of clothing every time she stepped outside.

She looked longingly out the window, knowing dusk would be moving in all too soon. These days of limited daylight were beginning to wear on her. Despite Daylight Savings Time a couple of weeks ago, giving them an extra hour of daylight, she longed for the days of summer when it stayed light well into the evening hours.

Her black lab, Gus, ambled up beside her and started licking the floor where the knife had been just a moment ago.

"Lunchtime for you, too, Gussie?" She reached down and patted his head, then ran her long fingers over his short, thick fur.

"Have a good time this afternoon?" Jeremiah asked. He cleared the newspaper from his place at the table, sat down, and took a bite of his sandwich.

"Yeah."

"That good, huh?"

"Yeah."

"Somethin's got you," he said around a mouth full of sandwich. Abby set a glass of water in front of him, and he took a long swallow. "What is it?"

19

"I'm not sure."

"Is it cause Gabe's gone? He gets back day after tomorrow, not?" He took another bite.

"Yeah, but it's not that. I talked to him this morning, actually. Sounds like he might be getting home tomorrow night. Either way, I can't see him until the weekend. I miss my boy, though." She sat on the chair beside him and toyed with the chips on her plate. "I called him just now, but I got his voicemail."

"Your sister will have him spoiled by the time he leaves. She needs one of her own."

"I don't see that happening, do you? The kid part, I mean." She looked at him with an arched eyebrow.

"Not unless she hurries."

"Well, maybe things will work out between her and Slider."

Her father grunted in response then popped a chip into his mouth.

"What was that about?" she asked. "You don't like Slider?"

"Verdict's out. Don't know that I trust the man. Who has a name like Slider anyway? His momma hate him or something?"

"Motorcycle accident. Slid across the highway, just missing an oncoming car. His motorcycle crew started calling him Slider after that. Or so he said." She popped a chip in her mouth and shrugged. "Anyway, given the fact that you don't know him very well and he's dating your daughter, I think not trusting him is warranted."

Slider was a guest at the resort last summer. Physically, he was the stereotypical biker, but from what she could tell and from what Piper told her, the rest of him couldn't be more different. Abby was sure there was a history there that she wouldn't mind knowing, for her sister's sake more than anything. But he seemed to be a genuinely good guy. Not to mention ruggedly handsome.

"You trust him?" he asked. His chewing suddenly halted.

Abby shrugged. "I wouldn't say I *trust* him, per se. That shouldn't surprise you. But Piper I trust. And if she trusts him, then I think we need to." She nibbled on another chip, then said, "At least make an effort. He did save our lives, don't forget." Last summer it was Slider who came to their rescue when someone had been intent on ending their lives. Hers specifically.

"The devil'd spare a life, too, if it'd benefit him."

"Pops!" she exclaimed, laughing.

"Nevertheless, it's not like they get to see each other often enough to make anything happen anyway."

"It doesn't take long for that to happen," she said and chuckled. She knew that would drive him up the wall. His grumble proved she was right. She laughed again. "Sorry, Pops. That was mean."

He stayed silent and took another bite. Finally, he said, "What about you? Maybe you should think about having another little one."

"Me?" she squeaked. "I'm thirty-six years old."

"Your sister's thirty-eight, and you're talking about her having one."

"I actually wasn't; you're the one that mentioned it. We're not young anymore, Pops."

"It'd make your mom happy to see you both happy with little ones. She always loved babies."

She could almost see him transporting back in time. "I am happy. And the last time I checked, Piper was, too."

"With that tattooed biker, Sly."

"Slider," she corrected him, laughing. "And just because he has tattoos and rides a motorcycle doesn't make him a bad person."

"Maybe not."

"Pops," Abby said with a sigh, "no man is going to be good enough for your girls."

"I like Gabe."

She chuckled softly and shook her head slowly. "Do you know anyone by the name of Susan who's going through a nasty custody battle?"

He stopped chewing and looked at her, frowning. "Why would I know that?"

She nibbled on another potato chip. "Seems everyone knows everyone's business here. They seem to know ours, too."

"Who's everyone?" He took a bite and wiped his mouth with the side of his hand.

"Travis from the coffee shop in town."

"Maybe this Travis fella is a busy-body and no one else actually knows anything. Ever thought a that?"

She shrugged and took a small bite of her sandwich. "Maybe. But according to him, people know about Hunter and me, and they know about you and—"

"Me and what?" He casually watched her, seemingly unconcerned about what she might say.

"Nothing." She took a swallow of her water. Telling her father people knew about his drinking wouldn't benefit anyone. "You're right. It's probably just Travis being Travis. I mean, a coffee shop could be like a bar or a hair salon, right? I'm sure he hears a lot of gossip."

"Don't waste your time with gossip." He leaned forward, eating his lunch in earnest. Conversation dismissed.

Abby suddenly felt like she was twelve years old. But not because of anything her father said. Simply because she knew she'd gotten caught up in the town's gossip. And there was nothing she disliked more than gossip.

Her father finished his lunch and pushed his plate out of the way. Abby shoved her chair back, legs squeaking on the floor.

"Stay put and eat. You're going to blow away. I'll get the dishes when you're finished eating."

She smiled at the familiar phrase. When she was younger, she actually feared she'd blow away if she didn't eat and was frightened by strong winds. What if she blew all the way to the land of Oz? The memories relaxed her, and she began to pick away at her sandwich.

"Why did you ask me about this Sarah or Susan? Whoever it is. And, no, I'm not engaging in gossip," he added.

"Susan." His chattiness this afternoon surprised her. He was typically a man of few words. "It might be nothing. I just ran into her at Dr. Miller's office and then again downtown. She just looks so sad, is all. And then Travis said she's going through a nasty custody battle. I feel bad for her. What if the father of her child is another Hunter?" She remembered the vacant look in the woman's eyes, the smeared mascara, and the bright red coat, then shrugged. "Guess I feel like I should help her but I don't know how. How can I help if I don't know the problem?"

"Don't go assuming every woman's story is the same as yours."

"I know, but—"

"Hunter's the exception, Pipsqueak."

"He's not the only one. This world is crawling with people just like him. In fact, I think I saw a bruise on her hand as she pulled her belt out of the door."

"A bruised hand doesn't mean she's been abused."

"And it doesn't mean she isn't," Abby argued.

He met her eyes, searching her out, then picked up the paper and began reading.

She finished her lunch in silence. Her father, true to his word, picked up the dishes and put them in the dishwasher, wiped the table, and reached for the paper.

"You can leave that, Pops. I'm going to scan through it while I make a cup of tea. You go ahead and do your thing, whatever that is. I've got the store."

He leaned over and kissed the top of her head. "I'll be out by your studio fixing the door on the facilities." And he was gone.

Her studio had been an old run-down shack when they moved in, but Abby saw the beauty and the promise in the old dilapidated building. Her father, the handyman, rebuilt it for her as a surprise. And what a surprise it was. It had everything she'd ever dreamed of. She finally had a space to get away and cultivate her passion for writing. And lately she'd begun painting again, something she'd given up since she quit teaching art back in California. She'd even begun dabbling in watercolors, a new medium for her. And sometimes, she'd steal away and just sit there and dream, enjoying nothing but quiet nature, deer and elk passing close to the French doors in front. The facilities her father referenced was the bathroom and sink around the back of the building, which he'd managed to restore, complete with running water. It was, in one word, perfect.

Pushing in her chair, she scooped up the newspaper and wandered through the living room and down the two steps into the adjoining store. She skirted around the counter to the cappuccino machine and made herself a cup of Chai tea.

She perched on the stool behind the counter, lay the paper on the countertop, and looked at the front page. More political disturbance and drama. *Shocking*. The current president was a magnet for attracting scathing comments and opinions. She shook her head, shaking off the yuck she felt every time she read about his scandalous presidency.

She scanned further down. The physical therapist of a popular actress had been accused of sexual abuse and now more victims were coming forward. "Why, oh, why, do people even read this stuff," she said in clear disgust. She looked up and around to be sure no one had snuck in unknowingly. They'd think she lost her mind talking to herself like that. Seeing no one and feeling a wee bit silly, she wrapped her hands around her large mug of steaming tea and took a sip.

She looked ahead and out the window over the little lake at one edge of the grounds. There were patches of open water here and there, but it was mostly frozen over. She reached for the binoculars she kept under the counter and looked closely at the bald eagles that frequently visited. Today there were four of them, sitting on the edge of the ice near one of the open patches of water. Abby caught her breath at the sheer beauty of it.

Having her fill, she tucked the binoculars back beneath the counter and flipped open the front page of the newspaper, hoping for something lighter. She skipped ahead even further to the local section, hoping to catch up on the town's goings-on. It seemed the entire population of Blue Mist Mountain was up in arms about a plan to rezone the streets so the one going through town was a one way rather than two, hoping to ease traffic jams. Businesses were afraid of losing business if they carried out the plan, but several locals were fighting for it, hoping to alleviate some of the congestion. A satisfied smile crossed her lips. At least she wasn't completely in the dark and had heard some of the news around town. She skimmed through the article in case something had changed from the last article she'd read. Nothing. Just a new spin on the same story.

Someone walking by the front window caught her eye and she looked up. Conrad again. He hadn't made it very far if he was still planning on hiking. He looked in the window and waved at her. She waggled her fingers back at him.

She took another sip of her Chai and looked down to grasp the corner of the front page to flip it open when a photo at the bottom right-hand corner stopped her. Her breath caught as she read the description below the photo. *Susan Ramirez, mother of four-year-old Ryan Ramirez, leaves the office of Dr. Collin Miller. Ryan remains in the temporary custody of his father.*

Who is his father? Abby wondered. It had to be somebody famous or it wouldn't be such a huge deal. And how could they keep it away from the media? If the media knew, surely they would mention it. Wouldn't they? But if they didn't know, it wouldn't be such a big story.

The mystery of it intrigued her until her mind came up with all kinds of scenarios. She stared absently out the window, looking out at the lake, the eagles all but invisible to her now. Maybe the father was filthy rich and he was buying the media's silence on his identity. And maybe Susan has a dark history that's the reason the boy was taken from her. Whatever that could be, she was obviously remorseful.

Abby remembered the smeared mascara as she came out of Dr. Miller's office, the scared but vacant look. And yet, maybe Abby was way off-base. After all, Susan's hair had been partially covering her eyes, and she looked away so quickly after spotting Abby, that maybe Abby hadn't seen anything at all.

But wait a minute! She slapped her hand on the counter and took another look. The paper was from this morning before she'd even seen Susan. The date of the photo wasn't identified. Was the voyeur in one of the vehicles in the parking lot that very morning? She desperately tried to remember the other cars she'd seen but was unsuccessful. *Darn it!* She'd become so accustomed to being vigilant of her surroundings, and because of being so worried about her phone, she'd let her caution slip. Someone was obviously following Susan. Again, her heart went out to the woman she didn't even know. Abby knew what it felt like to be followed, stalked, and terrorized. She sincerely hoped Susan wasn't going through what Abby herself had gone through. If so, Abby felt it was her responsibility to help in some way. But how?

She closed the newspaper and pushed it off to the side, drumming her fingers on the countertop.

The bell above the door rang, startling her, bringing her back from the dark tunnel her thoughts were traveling down.

"Welcome to Whispering Pines Resort," she said, pasting on a welcoming smile. A man standing at nearly six feet tall and a woman barely reaching his chest in height stood before her. She bore a striking resemblance to Susan, though smaller in stature.

"We're here to check in," the man said.

"Your name?" Abby asked, mustering as much enthusiasm as she could and sneaking another look at the woman before looking down at the reservation book.

"Lopez. Bob and Judy." His voice was baritone. "Beautiful place you have here."

Warmth spread throughout her. "It is. We love it here."

"How long you had the place?" he asked, looking around.

"Not even quite a year."

"Simon and Margie were the owners the last time we were here," Judy said, now looking at Abby. Even though she resembled Susan, at least Judy appeared genuinely happy. Her blue eyes shone brightly beneath a straight line of silky black bangs.

"Maggie," Abby corrected. "Simon and Maggie. They didn't own it; they were the caretakers for the prior owner, Henry Lancaster."

"Well, I couldn't imagine selling a place like this," Judy said. "I think I would be hard-pressed ever to leave if I owned this." Bob snaked his arm around Judy's shoulders and squeezed. He bent low to kiss her. Abby averted her gaze, looking at the reservation book.

Bob filled out the credit card information as Abby and Judy made small talk.

"Have you come here often?" Abby asked.

"No, not so much," Bob said, pushing the slip of paper toward Abby, followed by the pen. "Judy's little sister lives here, so we come to see her once in a while. She's gotten herself in some hot water so we came to see if we can help."

"Yeah?" Abby asked, snagged by curiosity. "You don't stay with her? Not that I'm complaining," she added quickly. "We love to have you stay here at the resort."

"Judy and her sister aren't the best of friends," Bob said. "Let's just say it's in everyone's best interest if we don't stay with her when we visit."

"I'm sorry to hear that," Abby said. She couldn't imagine Piper staying somewhere else when she visited. Or vice versa. "My sister is my best friend, so—"

"You're lucky, then," Judy said, the corners of her mouth turned down. "I've tried, I really have. But there's something—well, let's just say I've tried and leave it at that. We're here to have fun, Bob and me. So let's talk about happier things until we go see her tomorrow, shall we?" Judy said, looking up at Bob, her eyes pleading.

"Who is your sister?" Abby asked. "Maybe I know her." She sincerely doubted it. She didn't know many of the locals. If they didn't stay at the resort, she didn't know them.

"Susan Ramirez."

4

Abby shook her head, clearing the confusion, yet uncertain *why* she was confused. This woman was a dead ringer for what she'd seen of Susan. "I'm sorry, you said Susan?"

"You know her?" Judy asked. "Of course, you do," she answered matter-of-factly. "It's a small town."

"I met her today. I mean, we didn't actually meet. I saw her when I was in town." Abby hoped they didn't ask where.

"Where?" Judy asked as if reading her thoughts.

Abby cringed. "By one of the local coffee shops," she blurted.

"I don't suppose she had a child with her?" Bob asked.

"No, she didn't." Abby was dying to ask about it but thought better of it, relieved when she didn't have to.

"Her little boy was taken away from her. Supposedly, Susan hasn't been making the best choices."

"Supposedly? You mean you don't know for sure?"

"No, I haven't talked to her about it yet," Judy said. "That's what we're here for. See if we can talk some sense into the woman."

Bob squeezed Judy's shoulder gently, lovingly. "My wife and her sister aren't very close. They haven't seen or spoken to each other in quite a while."

"Then maybe she has a legitimate, valid story and we should wait to see what that is before making a judgment."

Abby bit her lower lip before she could say anything else. She was quickly disliking this tiny, petite woman who stood before her, but she was still a guest.

Judy chortled. "You don't know my sister."

Do you? Abby sighed, her heart heavy. Perhaps she was being too presumptuous. "No, I suppose I don't. It's just that—well, I hope that if it were me, my sister would hear me out first before thinking the worst of me."

"Yes, but you're not my sister. And I should hope you wouldn't do the bonehead things she does."

"Well, she's very beautiful by any means," Abby said, smiling to calm any feathers she might have ruffled. She just couldn't help feeling a strong connection with Susan. Abby had a deep suspicion that, as she herself had once been, Susan was an abused woman desperate to keep her son and their lives together. "You two look a lot alike," she said, looking at Judy.

"We should. We're twins."

Abby tipped her head. "I thought Bob just said she's your little sister."

"He did. I was born first. And she acts like a moody teenager. It's true what they say, though, one is always mom's favorite. And it wasn't me." Bitterness dripped from her words. "That girl had mom wrapped around her little finger from the get-go."

Abby tried to remember if she or Piper had been their mother's favorite. She supposed it was different since they weren't twins. "I'm sorry to hear that," Abby said. "It must have been tough." She thought of her mother's twin sisters. One was happy and fun to be around. The other had a chip on her shoulder that caused the people around her to scatter as if she were a drop of oil in a bowl of water. Those kinds of people are hard to love. And yet—

Abby's phone rang, and Bob and Judy turned toward the door with a wave. "Thanks," Bob said. "We'll be back in a bit for a few supplies."

Abby waved and put her phone to her ear.

"Whispering Pines Resort. This is Abby."

"Hi, Abby. This is Dr. Miller. I just wanted to check and be sure the Lopez's got there okay."

Abby's mind whirled with questions at the odd, out-of-the-blue inquiry. She cocked her head to the side, eyes squinted. "I'm sorry, but I can't give out that information."

"I assume that means they've arrived."

His arrogance hadn't gone unnoticed. Discomfort rippled in her stomach, but she couldn't put her finger on why. "How do you know the Lopez's?"

"Guess you could say they're family friends."

She thought about that for a moment, deciding she was making something out of nothing. "I guess it's true what they say about small towns. Why didn't you just call one of their cell phones?"

"Well, I don't know them *that* well. Just from Susan's sessions, more or less. And with that," he said with a deep breath, "I'm afraid I've said too much. Say, listen, about earlier—"

"You don't have to worry. I already promised you I wouldn't say anything."

"Thank you, Abby. I take the whole patient confidentiality thing pretty seriously. As you know. I would hate for Susan's privacy to be taken away from her."

"You and me both," she muttered.

"I'm sorry. I didn't hear that."

"Nothing. It was nothing."

"Cooper gets home this weekend?"

"Yes, Saturday. I can't wait," she said, smiling as she thought of his blond skater hair, as he called it. And he worked so hard on it.

"—before he gets back?"

The question jerked Abby back to the conversation at hand. "I'm sorry, what?"

"Should we schedule another session before he gets back? You left in a bit of a hurry today. We can discuss what it was we worked through that put you in such a state."

"Um, yeah, that would be good."

"Friday morning? Say, ten-thirty?"

"I'll have to check with my dad to be sure he's available to cover the resort, but it should be fine. I'll call you if it doesn't work."

"See you then. And Abby?"

"Yes?"

"I take your confidentiality just as seriously as Susan's. Whatever happens or is said in my office stays there."

"Thank you, Dr. Miller. I appreciate it. I saw her by the river this afternoon. I was going to talk with her but decided against it." He was so silent she thought maybe he'd already hung up. "Dr. Miller?"

"Yes, sorry. I was just writing your appointment in my book." He cleared his throat. "Talking with her isn't in either of your best interests."

"I wanted to help is all."

"That's what I'm here for," he said.

Abby had no sooner hung up and Conrad came through the door to the store.

"Conrad," she said, shaking her head, laughing. "For a man who stayed another day to get in some more hiking, you haven't made it very far."

"No, ma'am. Getting some of my packing done first so I don't have to worry about it in the morning. In fact, maybe I could just settle up with you now. I promise I won't incur any more expenses between now and then. If I do, you know where to find me." He grasped for his wallet from his back pocket. "I see the Lopez's are here. How long they staying this time?"

"You know them, too?" She didn't know why on earth she was surprised.

"Most of the people that come here aren't first time people."

"I realize that. But—"

"Everyone's kinda like family. The Lopez's and me were here at the same time a couple of times. One of those times was back when I was newly divorced. Fact, Bob tried to set me up with his sister-in-law."

Abby looked at him sideways. "Susan?"

"Yup. She's quite a looker, but it didn't work out."

"How long ago was that?"

"Oh, a few years back now already." He jerked his thumb in the back of him. "Went out a few times, but nothin' came of it. She was hung up on some other fella. That usually doesn't make for a good time."

"No, I suppose it doesn't." Abby thought back to how she stayed with Hunter regardless of what he'd done to her, after all the abuse, until the final time when he'd nearly killed her.

She desperately hoped Susan would be as fortunate as she had been—getting out alive and winning custody of her son.

"Sounds like you're not a fan of hers."

"Ah, I'm sure she's fine. But stringing a guy along isn't the way to go. Could get a girl in trouble with the wrong man." He lowered his chin and looked at her over the rim of his glasses. "If you know what I mean."

"Hm." Abby nodded her head. "Well, you're all set. Get out there and enjoy what little time you have left. Dusk'll be settling in soon."

"Thanks, Abby. Think I'll hang around here and head out before the sun rises, do some hiking, then head home in the evening."

"Sounds like a good plan. If I don't see you anymore today, safe hiking and safe travels. See you next time."

"Yes, you will," he said, waving as he headed out the door.

A gust of cool wind swept in and caught the door, causing it to slam shut. Abby jumped.

"Geez! That man!" she muttered under her breath, hand to her chest. "He's going to give me a heart attack yet."

"Who is?" came a voice behind her.

She screamed. "Dang it, Pops!"

He chuckled, squeezing her shoulder with his warm hand.

"It's *so* not funny," she grumbled.

"Why are you so jumpy?"

"I'm just a little on edge today, okay?"

"I can tell. Want to talk about it?"

"No."

"Might help, you know."

"Coming from a man who has to be bribed to talk." Abby sighed and sat back down on the stool behind the counter.

Jeremiah walked around the other side, leaned over, his elbows rested on the countertop. He clasped his hands. Abby searched his eyes. "Do you ever get a feeling in the pit of your stomach that something bad is going to happen, but you can't pinpoint what it is? Or why you even feel that way?" Her father stayed silent, inviting her to continue. "I've just had this—this—feeling all day. Nothing happened to make me feel that way; my senses are just ultra-heightened. Like Hunter is on the loose again."

"Want to know what I think? I think seeing this Susan woman has gotten your imagination on overdrive and has dug up all sorts of things you're trying to forget." His voice was gentle, his eyes soft as he looked into hers. "Hunter is in prison. He can't hurt you. Not anymore. But you've become so accustomed to looking over your shoulder that you don't know how *not* to."

Abby looked down at her hands circling her cup, the remaining tea now cold. "It bugs me that he still has that kind of power over me, Pops. I'm a lot better than I was, but there are still things that trigger me."

"I know," he said, placing one of his hands over hers. "I know. When do you go see Dr. Miller again?"

"Friday. And Gabe comes home that evening, too."

"Now that put a sparkle in your eye," he said, smiling. "That's my girl." He patted her hand, then stood up. "Your studio is fixed. Why don't you take some time and head out there for a bit? I'll take care of things here."

"Bess must have come early today. She was gone before I got here." Bess worked part-time during the winter months cleaning cabins. Come May, Victoria and Sam would be on break from college and back working at the resort. She could hardly wait. In just one summer she'd become so fond of them that she was near tears when they headed back to college last fall.

"Only two to clean, so it didn't take long. She was in and out in a matter of two hours. Got here right after you left for town and was done right before you got home."

"Did you take money from the till and pay her?"

"Yup. Now scoot."

"Thanks, Pops." She snagged the flashlight from the ledge under the counter in case time got away from her and in case darkness fell before she came back. Once she got to writing or painting, time didn't exist. And it was exactly the escape she needed. Someday maybe, just maybe, she'd submit a piece for publication or display something in an art exhibit. Didn't hurt for a girl to have a dream.

She slipped into her parka and boots and trudged out to the studio. She moved around back to inspect her father's work. Perfect, as usual.

Sliding her key into the lock, she pulled open the French doors and inhaled the intoxicating aroma of her oil paints, some left and dried in her palette from the last time she had to hurry back to the office. Good thing she had more than one palette so she could pour fresh paint into a clean one. She closed the doors behind her, and the faint ashy smell of charcoal crayon dust wafted toward the door from her sketchbook that lay open on the small desk in the corner of her studio. The open page revealed the partial drawing of a bull elk. Even the chemical smells of her brush cleaners and the linseed oil from her canvas smelled delightful.

Scooping her long blond hair back and tying it in a ponytail, tucking a stray strand behind her ear, she crossed to the radio on her desk and turned on some Bach. Next, she picked up several paint-spattered rags from the seat of her stool, poured fresh paints in a clean palette, selected a clean brush, and began to paint. Any concerns or anxieties from the day melted away with each stroke of her brush until she was so relaxed she barely heard her cell phone. At first the interruption irritated her, messing with her flow, but it quickly dissipated when she saw it was Cooper. A wide smile crossed her face.

"Hey, Coop! I miss you and can't wait for Saturday!"

"Hey, Mom."

His ten-year-old voice, despite lack of enthusiasm, was the sweetest sound she'd ever heard. In fact, it was a little more enthusiastic than she'd heard it in a while.

"So how are things at Aunt Piper's? Ready to come home?"

"Yeah. I kind of miss you and Grandpa."

Abby felt like she was going to fall off her stool and she laughed. "Do you mind saying that again so I can record it?"

"Mom," he complained. But she could hear in his voice that he was grinning.

"Well, be prepared when I see you. It doesn't matter who's around, I'm swooping you up in the biggest hug you've ever had."

"Great," he said, trying to complain but failing. "Johnny said you told him he could come over this weekend."

"Yeah, but not until Sunday. I want Saturday with you alone. Well, I guess I'll have to share with Grandpa and Piper. I don't know why with Piper, though. She's had you for a week."

"She bought me the coolest video game ever!"

Abby groaned and rolled her eyes. "I'm sure she did. You're leaving it there, right?" She held her breath, hoping.

"Yeah. She said I have too many at home the way it is, and this way I'll come back to stay with her again."

"Agreed. You do have too many. Maybe it's time to go through them and toss the ones you don't play anymore." His gasp was unmistakable. "It's not like you have the time to play them like you did when we lived in California."

"I do in the winters. It's stupid cold in Colorado."

"But it's beautiful, yeah?"

"Whatevs."

"By the way, after looking at your last report card, you'd do well to play less and focus on social studies class a bit more. We'll need to come up with some ideas when you get home."

"Mom..." he whined.

"Relax," she said, chuckling. "We'll think of something fun." She'd need Gabe's help on this one.

"Mr. Miller pulled me outta class—"

"Mr. Miller?"

"Yeah, he—"

"Who's Mr. Miller?" Abby asked, interrupting again. "Your social studies teacher is Ms. Cornwell."

"He's one of the shrinks who fills in at my school when the regular shrink is gone. Supposedly he has a minor in history or something. He's gonna help with Cornwell's class when she's gone having a baby."

"Ms. Cornwell. Calling her Cornwell is disrespectful."

"Ms. Cornwell," he said, dragging out the Ms.

"What's Mr. Miller's first name?"

"I dunno," he said, annoyance clear. "Curt, Connor, C something or other."

"Collin?"

"Yeah, that sounds right. Why?"

"No reason." Her instincts told her something was odd. Why would a licensed psychologist fill in for a teacher? She took a breath. Now wasn't the time to let her imagination run wild. "Has he worked there before?"

"Yeah. I told you he's the backup for the school shrink." A wave of relief swept through her. Yes, he had said that earlier, hadn't he? One of her moments of overreacting. She shook her head. "I'm sorry, sweetie, what were you saying before I interrupted?"

"That he pulled me out of class the week before I left to see if I needed a tutor to help get my grade up. Said he's really good at social studies. That's when he told me that was his minor in college."

"What'd you say to the offer?"

"No."

Why hadn't Dr. Miller mentioned this to me? she thought. "Don't you want him to help you?"

"No. My grade isn't even a D."

"Darn close, buddy. It's a C-. You're capable of much better than that."

"You and Gabe can help me."

She remembered her own social studies grades. Her strength was language arts. "We'll talk to Gabe."

Piper's voice sounded in the background.

"Gotta go, Mom."

"Tell your Aunt Piper to cool her jets. Moms trump aunts."

"Sons trump both," he said.

"Yeah, that's not funny. Or true."

"Then why are you laughing?"

"Hey, buddy?"

"Yeah?"

"I'm beyond excited to get you home. I've missed you a ton."

"Thanks, Mom. Missed you, too. Bye." The line went dead.

"Was that the kid?"

She startled at Jeremiah's voice behind her. "How long have you been standing there?"

"Long enough to know you have no concept of time. It's dark outside, and I was getting worried." He looked at her paintings propped up against the wall on the far side of the studio. "My daughter. The most talented painter out there."

Abby tipped her head back and laughed. Her mood had dramatically brightened after talking with Cooper. "You're biased, Pops."

"Ready to head back? I can wait for you."

"Who's watching the store?"

"Locked it to come out here. It was dead anyway. Starting to snow."

Abby looked out the window toward the lake. The mountains beyond were black overhead, not a star or sliver of moonlight in view. "Looks like the spring storm they predicted might actually hit us." Despite the frequent warnings on the news and in the paper, she hoped beyond hope that they were wrong and it would miss them. Looking outside now, she knew that was about as likely as a tsunami in Arizona.

"Looks like it," Jeremiah agreed, picking up Abby's coat. "Come on." He held it up as she slid one arm in at a time.

"I hope it doesn't delay Cooper from coming home. They were planning to leave in the morning, spend the night at a hotel, and finish the last leg of the drive Saturday, putting them here about noon."

"If we get hit with as much as they're predicting, they won't be coming so soon."

"Coop goes back to school Monday." Abby paused, zipped her coat, and looked out the window again at the ominous darkness. Her brows furrowed. "I wonder if I should try to find a flight for him instead. Airlines assign someone to fly with children so he wouldn't be alone."

"If the storm packs the punch they're expecting, flights will be delayed. It's safer for Piper to drive him, staying back a day or two if they need to."

"But school—"

"Will still be there whenever he's able to make it back," he interrupted her. "It's not going anywhere. Fact of the matter is, they'll cancel school anyway."

She sighed. "You're right, I know. I just miss him so much."

"An extra couple of days isn't going to hurt. Them driving when it's not safe will. Last I saw on the news before coming out here is it's supposed to start flurrying tomorrow 'bout noon. Hard snow starts tomorrow evening."

Abby frowned. "Hm. Maybe I should call Piper and give her a heads up." As if on cue, Abby's phone rang. "Hey, Pip. Pops and I were just talking about you."

"All good, I'm sure."

"Of course. Hey, there's supposed to be—"

"An enormous snowstorm moving into the mountains," she interrupted. "Blue Mist Mountain is in its direct path. We're going to hold off a couple of days before coming out."

Tears stung Abby's eyes. "That's safest, I suppose." She brushed a rogue tear away with the palm of her hand. "What about work?"

"Are you kidding me? I have so much vacation time they're practically pushing me to take it." There was a pause, before she added, "Hey, little sis, you okay?"

Emotion sprang up on Abby, and she felt her father's hand on her back. "Just missing my kid is all."

"Most parents would take advantage of a little free time, Abs."

"I'm not most parents."

"No, that, you're not," she mumbled. "But listen, he'll be there before you know it. And so will I in case you miss me, too. Just sayin'."

Abby laughed through her tears. "Sometimes I do. Miss you."

"We'll keep in touch, yeah? Let us know how it's going on your end. Weathermen aren't always accurate. It's the one profession you can always be wrong and still keep your job."

"I'll call you tomorrow. Is Coop there? I just want to say goodnight one more time."

"He's in the shower. I'll have him call you when he's out."

"Thanks, Piper. For everything."

"My pleasure. Love you, sis."

"Love you, too."

Abby tucked her phone in her pocket. "Well, let's head on back to the house."

Jeremiah followed Abby after he closed and locked the doors behind them. Both were silent as snow crunched beneath their feet. The impending storm held heavy weight, making Abby feel pounds heavier. She aimed the flashlight on the path in front of them, tiny black squirrels scampering off to the sides, chirping their disapproval at the disturbance.

When the overhead lights from the resort greeted them, she clicked off the flashlight.

"I can stay downstairs and listen for any customers if you want to go upstairs to hibernate and read," Abby said as they climbed the three stairs on the porch.

"There's a good Western that comes on soon. Maybe I'll go watch that."

Jeremiah had always loved Westerns. Sometimes he'd turn them up so loud it sounded like the shootout was right there in the house. "You been writing at all, Pops?" He shot her a look that was all the answer she needed. "Mom would want you to, you know. She'd be devastated if she knew her death was the death of your writing, too."

"You don't need to tell me what your ma would or wouldn't like," he grumbled.

"I'm just saying—"

"Well, don't say."

She shook her head slowly. "Go watch TV. Night," she said, knowing he would more than likely turn in for the rest of the evening. She watched as he fetched a fresh glass, filled it with water, and headed for the steps. "Oh, Pops?"

"Yup," he said, turning to look at her.

"Think you could take over Friday morning for a while again?"

"Sure. What's goin' on?"

"Dr. Miller."

He tipped his head. "Got it covered." He turned and disappeared up the stairs to his room and to whatever Western she would hear coming through his door in a few minutes.

She made a cup of chamomile tea, nabbed her book from the table, and headed out to the store. Perched on the stool behind the counter, she opened her book and began reading. No more than two minutes into the book, the bell alerted her to a customer. She looked up and saw Bob, slightly disheveled. His hair was askew, his shirt partially untucked.

"Hi, Bob."

"I know what you're thinking," he said. "But it's not that." He ran a hand through his hair, making it stick up more than before. "I was settled in for the night, hoping for a little something, if you know what I mean, and Judy decides she needs bacon for the morning."

Abby felt her cheeks flush. She shrugged her shoulders. "At least that means she plans on cooking in the morning, right? That's good for you in the long run."

"Yeah, yeah. Whatever." He reached into the refrigerated section and withdrew a pack of peppered thick-cut bacon, plopped it on the counter and reached for his wallet from his back pocket. "You getting ready to close for the night?"

"Pretty soon." Abby lay her book down and punched in some numbers on the cash register. "Getting cold out there, huh?"

"Been worse."

She finished ringing him out, handing him the receipt.

"I don't need that," he said, crinkling it up and tossing it down on the counter. "Throw it away for me, could ya?"

"Sure can." She swiped it off the counter and threw it into the trashcan. "You guys heading into town in the morning?"

"Not too early. Not meeting Susan till eleven."

"So you'll get to sleep in."

He snorted. "Yeah, right. Judy doesn't sleep in. The crack of dawn she's up. Usually before." He turned for the door, one pant leg haphazardly tucked into the back of his boot. "See you tomorrow, I'm sure."

"Take care, Bob."

She watched the door close behind him and stared for a moment not sure what to think of the conversation. Finally, she chuckled, shook her head, and took a sip of tea. She opened her book again. Five minutes into the book, and again the bell rang. She looked up to see Conrad, Judy right behind him. She raised her eyebrows.

"A busy night in here," Abby said, smiling. "Bob forget something, Judy? Did he get the wrong kind of bacon?"

"What do you mean?" Judy asked, frowning.

"I need some chocolate," Conrad said. "Can't sleep without it."

"You know that chocolate contains caffeine, right?" Abby asked him.

"So they say. But I say I need it to sleep."

Abby shrugged a shoulder and rung up the chocolate bar. "Want a bag?"

"Heck no. It'll be gone before I get back to the cabin."

Abby grinned. "What am I going to do with you, Conrad?"

"You could go out with me, that's what." He looked at her expectantly. "Tomorrow evening? I could stay an extra day."

She chuckled and shook her head. "I have a boyfriend. You might know him since you've been here before. He's got a fifth wheel permanently parked here."

"You're not talking about Gabriel."

Abby nodded, the sound of Gabe's name making her smile wide. "I am. He'll be here Friday evening."

"Well, I'll be," Conrad said, shaking his head slowly. "You know how many women fall all over that one and he doesn't give 'em the time of day. And you caught him, huh?"

Abby grinned, and her heart flopped. "Guess I did. Lucky me, huh?"

"Lucky him," he said.

"Yeah, yeah, ya'll are lucky," Judy griped. "Just ring up my cereal so I can get the heck back." She set a box of Cheerios on the counter.

"Cereal? Aren't you cooking breakfast in the morning?"

Judy looked at her as if she were a card short of a deck. "Cooking? You crazy? I don't eat breakfast at all. Bob can have cereal."

"What about the bacon?" Abby asked, suddenly wishing she hadn't when she saw Judy's eyes study her.

"What is it with the bacon?" she asked.

"Just confused and discombobulated with the whole impending storm probably," Abby said.

"Better get used to these spring storms if you're living in Colorado."

"I'll walk you out, Judy," Conrad said, saving Abby from any further explanation. Bob obviously didn't want his wife to know something, whatever that may be. "Make sure you get to your cabin okay."

Abby watched the door close behind them and shook her head. What could she make of that? No matter how she tried to put things together, they didn't fit. Finally, she gave up and went back to her book. Her phone rang the minute she did. Reading was not to come, she decided. With a sigh she looked at her phone, instantly perking up.

"Hey there, handsome," she said, her voice low.

"Well, hello there," Gabe said, his voice matching hers. "Had I known I'd get this reception I'd have called sooner."

Abby's chest filled with joy. "Ready to come home?"

"Oh, man! More than ready. You have no idea." He continued to fill her in on the details of his trip then asked, his voice low and sexy again, "So tell me, Ms. Sinclair, what have you been up to?"

"You know, the usual." She didn't say anything further and knew it was driving him crazy. Finally, she laughed.

"You're evil. You know that, right?"

"Coop is enlisting our help in getting his social studies grade up. You know what that means, right? It means I'm deferring to you so his grade actually does go up. My strong suit is English and Art."

"So he needs a tutor. Tutors cost. What will you give me?"

Abby chuckled, tingling clear to her toes. "I'll make it worth your time."

"Yeah?"

"Yeah. I'll make you a fabulous dinner."

"Abigail Sinclair, you're such a tease."

Laughing together felt good, even if it was just over the phone. She missed him. So much so that it frightened her. She was in this with both feet when not long ago she'd promised herself never again. She filled him in on the incoming weather.

"What if you're not able to get back tomorrow night?" she asked.

"I will."

"But what if—"

"There's no 'what if.' I will make it back."

"I'm just saying, Piper and Cooper—"

"Don't have a four-wheel-drive truck."

She giggled. "Are you going to finish all of my sentences?"

"If I have to, yes," he said.

The banter continued, neither wanting to end the call.

"Hey, do you know a Susan Ramirez?" she asked.

"Hmmm...the name sounds familiar, but I can't place it. Why?"

"No reason, really. I just ran into her today after my appointment with Dr. Miller. Then I saw her in town by the coffee shop. Travis said—"

"Wait. Who's Travis?"

Abby chuckled. "Gabe, are you jealous?"

"I admit to nothing of the sort. Just trying to keep everyone straight."

"Uh-huh. Right."

"Okay, maybe a little. I've been gone, so one never knows," he teased her.

"Travis from the coffee shop. The same one who's all of twenty-five years old."

"A simple thing like age never stops a man."

"Apparently. Conrad asked me out tonight. In fact, this Susan I asked you about, her sister, Judy, set them up. Judy's husband, Bob, said he knows you."

"I hate to say it, but it sounds like you're living a soap opera there. I leave for a week and look what happens."

She could almost see the twinkle in his eye, the smile playing on his lips. "Hey, I didn't go looking for all of this. It came to me."

The banter continued again until Gabe stopped mid-sentence. "Oh! That's why the name sounds familiar. Bob and Judy Lopez?"

"Yes."

"Last winter Bob was telling me about Judy's sister. Said she's hot but a mess. Wanted to set me up with her but I passed."

"Well, between Judy trying to set her up with Conrad and Bob trying to set her up with you, they obviously don't think she has a mind of her own. I'd be super mad if Piper tried to set me up with everyone."

"She did. She pushed you toward me. Are you saying that was a mistake? Choose your words carefully."

Abby laughed at the memory. "No. I'm glad she did."

"Me, too. Or I'd still be pathetically pining after you. Cause there isn't anyone else out there who can hold a candle to you, my love."

She smiled, feeling her cheeks flush. "Back at'cha." The line fell silent for a moment before she spoke again. "Why do you suppose it's such a secret? And why do you suppose it's such a big deal the media is involved?"

"Because it's a small town, first of all. It's coming back to me now, though. She was the wife of some big, high-profile guy in the oil industry. It turned out he wasn't such a nice guy from what I heard. She ended up in a psychiatric treatment facility somewhere before she moved to Blue Mist Mountain. Geez!" He whistled softly. "I'd forgotten all about her until now."

That helped Abby understand why she was seeing Dr. Miller. "Was her ex-husband abusive?"

"Bob never really outwardly said that, but that's the gist I got."

"Who's the friend who told you about Dr. Collin Miller?"

"Ironically, I think it was Bob. He was saying how good he's been for Susan. Her situation with the father of her baby has been a mess."

"Did he ever say who the father was?"

"No, I don't believe he did. But I didn't ask, either. There wasn't a reason for me to. Why, babe?"

"My gut is just telling me something is wrong. I can't pinpoint what it is, though."

"I think you should follow your gut then. It's more reliable than word from a third party," he said.

"I'm going back to see him Friday morning," said Abby. "I'll see what kind of vibe I get and go from there."

"Good idea. Friday night when I get up there, I want to hear about it."

"You think it's safe for you to be driving if there's a snowstorm?"

"I'll put a plow on the front of my truck if I need to. I'm getting there."

A small smile crossed her lips. "I miss you, Gabe."

"Miss you too, Hermosa. I'll see you soon."

"Bye."

She held the phone in her hand after he hung up. She looked around the room, and emptiness engulfed her. Her father was upstairs, but with Cooper and Gabe both gone, it was as if part of her world was missing. She skirted around the counter and walked to the door, flipping the sign to *closed*. Snow had begun falling softly beneath the outside lights, and everyone appeared to be tucked in for the night. She glanced at Gabe's fifth wheel, dark and empty. Despite having an electric RV furnace, if the weather was cold enough, she wouldn't hear of him sleeping out there. She insisted he use the fold-out sofa in the house. Friday night would be one of those nights. With the snow moving in, it would be silly to sleep out there. Especially since the bulk of the predicted two feet would already be on the ground. That and she looked forward to staying up, snuggling by the fire and catching up.

Chilled now, she wrapped her arms around herself and shivered. Time to slip into a nice warm bubble bath, perhaps use one of the bath bombs she bought at the bath store in town and then slip into Slumberland. She was already looking forward to an early morning hot tub.

She flipped off the light and stopped when she heard something or someone outside. She hoped desperately that no one wanted anything from the store. She'd already dropped the money from the till into the floor safe. She heard muffled voices, looked out into the night and saw Conrad walking one way, Bob the other. Conrad turned and said something to Bob before Bob lifted a specific finger and raised it high. Conrad threw up his hands and walked to his cabin. Hm. Nothing like an impending storm, whether it be a thunderstorm or snowstorm, to get people riled up. And tonight was no exception. Maybe they'd all be back to normal come morning. One could only hope.

5

Morning dawned and Abby stretched, yawned, opened one eye and looked out the window. The snow was falling slow but steady. The last report stated the storm was ahead of schedule. *Ya think?* She groaned and covered her head with the blankets, until she remembered the hot tub. She flipped the covers back, swung her legs over the edge of the bed, and stretched one last time, reaching her arms high above her head. She slipped into her swimsuit, then her fuzzy robe, tying the belt tight. Snagging a towel as she passed by the bathroom, she headed downstairs, absently looking in Cooper's room. She couldn't wait until he was back home and life was back to usual.

A glance out the window revealed soft white flakes dancing in the air before they reached the ground. It mesmerized her for a moment. The grounds were silent, nary a life in sight. All was just as it should be at this time of the morning. Especially at the beginning of a snowstorm. She imagined the guests, all here on vacation, not a care in the world, cozily tucked in their beds, either sleeping or watching it snow, grateful they didn't have to go to work. And the animals? Well, they'd be out eventually, too. Especially the deer, and perhaps an elk or two, looking for food. Her father had strategically placed salt blocks in the woods for the deer. *Deer crave salt in the springtime and summer when there's plenty of water and other minerals,* her father had told her.

She started a pot of coffee and watched as the birds flitted around the many feeders scattered throughout the yard and edge of the wood. They busily fed on the food her father had put out for them last night, including peanuts in the shell for the jays. She spotted a few black-capped chickadees, the pink of a rosy-finch, some juncos, the fluorescent blue of a jay in a nearby tree, and a few nuthatches. A pair of mourning doves perched on the edge of one of the feeders. The beauty of the colorful birds against the white snow was breathtaking. Even the magpies, which most locals didn't appreciate, were beautiful. She spotted a northern flicker on a pine at the edge of the wood, pecking away. Her gaze slipped to the rare appearance of the downy woodpecker busily pecking at a pole that held one of the food tables, enjoying the pole more than the sunflower seeds that had been put out for him. Nature at its finest.

The coffee pot gurgled its last, letting her know it was done. Usually, her father was up and had coffee made already but he must have stayed up later than usual watching television. At least she hoped that's all it was and not that he was hung over. Her stomach churned at the thought, and she tried to push it away, but it nagged at her.

She headed up the stairs and to his room, quietly putting her ear up to his door.

"Need somethin'?" He said from behind her. She startled and he chuckled.

"You just love that, don't you?" she grumbled.

"Maybe just a little."

She turned and saw the smirk on his face. "It's not funny."

"To you."

"I was just checking to be sure you were okay," she said.

"You mean if I was passed out?"

She felt her cheeks get hot. "N-no." She was so busted.

"Well, I'm not. I've already been outside. Made sure the hot tub was up to temperature for you and put more food out for the birds."

"That's why there were so many this morning," she said with a small smile. Her father was doing so much better here than she'd even hoped for. Now if he could just kick the drinking binges. "You didn't make coffee like you usually do so I just assumed you were still asleep." *Not totally a lie.*

"Was just going to do that. By the smell of it, you beat me to it."

"Sorry, Pops." Shame swallowed her. "I shouldn't have—"

"It's okay. Can never trust a drinker, I s'pose."

"There's the problem. I never know when I can. It's the weirdest times when I do and find out I shouldn't have. You have no pattern. You're so frustrating."

"Keeps you on your toes." And then he was down the stairs.

"I'm going to take my coffee and head out to the hot tub," she called after him.

"Figured you would."

"Thanks, Pops."

She swirled her hair into a ponytail, piled it on top of her head, fastened it with a clip, and headed downstairs. Grabbing two cups from hooks she'd hung beneath the cupboards, she filled one for her father and one for herself.

"See you in about twenty minutes," she said over her shoulder as she left the kitchen.

As she unlocked and opened the side door just feet away from the hot tub, a gust of wind blew snow in her face and down the front of her robe. "Brrrr!" she squealed, shivering. She closed the door behind her and as fast as she could, lifted the cover of the hot tub, folding it over on itself so half of the tub remained covered. She stepped up on the stairs to get in, dipped one foot in then quickly slipped out of her robe, piling it and her towel on the side of the tub for easy reach when she was ready to get out. She put the other foot in and stretched her legs out in front of her, startling when her knee bumped up against something. She peeked beneath the part of the tub that was still covered and in one split second screamed and jumped out of the tub.

"What in God's name—" Jeremiah said, stopping short. "Abs, go in the house," he ordered.

Abby stayed frozen in place, her gaze stuck on a body that now floated from under the partial covering until it was fully in view, arms splayed wide. Even though she was face down, Abby knew exactly who it was. The red jacket and the black hair spread out around her was a dead giveaway.

"P—p—pops, th—th—that's Su—Susan."

Jeremiah circled his fingers around Susan's left wrist. "Go call 9-1-1, Abby. I'll put the lid back down until they get here."

"You can't!" She said, horrified. "You can't close her in there!"

"Abby, she's already dead. Don't want any of the guests runnin' to see what the commotion is all about and see the body. Go. Call 9-1-1," he ordered.

She snatched her robe and wrapped it around her, a chill it couldn't even begin to warm. Shaking, she searched for the phone, finally reaching for the one on the wall. Her fingers were trembling so violently she could scarcely touch the right buttons. After what felt like an eternity, she called through.

"9-1-1, what's your emergency?"

As she spoke, it sounded like a voice outside of herself was rambling, bordering on hysteria.

"Are you sure the victim is deceased?"

"Yes."

"Did you feel for a pulse?"

The woman's voice annoyed her. "Yes!" Abby said, exasperated. "How else would we know she's dead?"

"Ma'am, I need you to take a deep breath."

Abby, an odd combination of panic and numbness, felt it nearly impossible to put together a coherent thought, much less a sentence.

"Ma'am? Are you there?"

"I'm here," Abby answered, taking several slow, deep breaths.

"We've got police and an ambulance on the way."

"She's dead. We need the coroner."

"We'll take care of that, ma'am. Right now I just need you to try to stay calm, okay? I need you to stay with me. Can you do that?"

"Yes. But Susan—"

"You know who the victim is?"

"Yes. I think so. I mean, I didn't turn her over. She was face down. But I recognized the coat and her hair and—"

"Who's out with the body now?"

"My father."

"What is your father's name?"

"Jeremiah."

"Jeremiah what?" the woman asked.

"Jeremiah Jordan."

"Abby—you said your name is Abby, right?"

"Yes."

"Abby, what is your last name?"

"Sinclair. Abby Sinclair."

"Is there anyone else there, Abby?"

"No. Yes—"

"Are you in danger?" The woman's voice suddenly filled with urgency. "Who else is there?"

"A lot of people. I mean they're not *here* here, but they're here." Abby felt hysteria rising in her throat again. "Who could have done this?"

"Abby, listen to me. I need you to take deep breaths, okay? Stay with me until the police arrive. Don't hang up. Stay on the line with me."

Abby fought for control, clutching the phone with one hand, fanning her face with the other.

"Abby?" Urgency filled the woman's voice again.

"Yeah. Yeah. I'm here," she gasped.

"Honey, who else is there?" The woman's voice was calming now, reminding Abby of her mother.

"I own a resort. Whispering Pines Resort. So there's a lot of people here. But who would do this?"

"That's what we're going to find out. Just stay on the line with me. You said a lot of people are there. Can you give me some names?"

Her mind began to clear as her attention shifted from Susan to the guests. "Um...yeah...there's Jim and Sadie Wilcox. They're from Omaha, Nebraska. And Nancy and Tim Connolly from Denver. Um, let's see..." Her mind was flitting from place to place, trying to remember who was in each cabin and once again trying to push from her mind the vision of Susan floating face down in the hot tub.

"Honey, who else is there?"

"Um, Bob and Judy Lopez from New Mexico, Roxanne and Cody Stanley from Kansas, John and Carrie from Ontario, Canada, and Conrad Schmidt. He's from—oh, let's see—I can't remember. Do you need me to go find out? I can go ask my dad, just a minute."

"No!" she exclaimed before Abby could move. "No, just stay put. You're in the house, right?"

"Yes."

"Stay where you are until the police arrive. They should be there in just a few minutes. Are any of the guests by the body now?"

"No. I don't know. Maybe. I screamed when I found her so they may have heard and come over. I can't see them from where I am. I'm on a stupid phone with a cord. Who even has those anymore these days? I don't recall where I put my cell phone." She knew she was rambling but couldn't stop. She started shaking from the depths of her, chills radiating throughout her body at an alarming rate. "Oh, my God. It could have been me. I could have been the one."

"The one what? What do you mean it could have been you? Did you do something to the woman in your hot tub?"

"No. I don't know. I should have stopped it and I didn't. It's my fault."

"Ma'am, what do you—"

"I have to go. I need some answers."

"No! Abby, stay on the line with me. Just—"

She disconnected and dropped the phone back in the cradle. She made it as far as the sofa when her legs gave way and she collapsed. Her ring tone sounded from between the sofa cushions, but she didn't answer. This was all her fault. She knew she should have helped Susan. She knew it! Why hadn't she done something? If Hunter had his way, she could have been the one floating face-down and Cooper would be without a mother. The possibilities wormed their way deep into her mind, refusing to let go, suffocating any potential positive thought.

She fought for control, taking forced long, deep breaths until oxygen worked its way back to her brain. She had to call Dr. Miller. To let him know about Susan as well as needing a debrief. She dug her phone out from between the cushions just as it rang again.

She dug it out and looked at the display before answering. "I was just going to call you," she said.

"Are you okay?" Dr. Miller asked.

"No, I'm not." Sirens were getting closer, now screeching toward the house. If the guests hadn't been up already, they would be now. Blue, red, and white lights flashed through the windows, lighting up the house. "I found Susan in my hot tub. Dead."

"That's terrible," he said, followed by a shallow gasp.

She noted the odd lack of surprise in his voice, then quickly dismissed it. Of course he wasn't going to be freaking out like she was. He was a psychologist. They're trained to keep emotional situations under control. *Right?* "Thank God Cooper's not home."

"I'm coming out there. I can be there in fifteen minutes."

"Are you in town?"

"Yes."

62

"What are you doing in town so early? Your office doesn't open for a couple more hours."

"I spent the night at my office. But that's unimportant right now. What is important is that you're okay. I'll be right there."

"Thank you."

She dropped the phone back onto the sofa and walked tentatively toward the side door. She saw her father talking to two police officers, one of them the same that was out there last summer when Hunter pulled his shenanigans. As if sensing her presence, he looked up and through the window. Their eyes met briefly before she looked away. *Now's not the time to be a coward*, she scolded herself. *Susan needs you to be brave for her.*

She took a deep breath and strode toward the door. The snow and the cold snapped her to her senses in a hurry when she stepped outside. She realized she was still in her robe, swimsuit underneath. Doing an about-face, she took the stairs two at a time up to her room.

Now dressed in a pair of jeans and a sweatshirt, she'd turned the corner at the bottom of the stairs and bumped into one of the officers. She stumbled backward. He reached and grabbed her arm, steadying her.

"Sorry." Beads of perspiration rolled down the center of her back.

"In a hurry to go somewhere?" he asked.

"I was in my robe. I needed to get dressed."

"I'll need your robe if you can please get it for me."

"Why?" Humiliation crept in. Was he some kind of pervert?

"It's Abby, right?"

"Yes."

"I'm Detective Robles. Can you tell me what happened this morning?"

She looked into his brown eyes finding some needed warmth there. The casualness of his jeans, black turtleneck, gray tweed jacket, and black cowboy boots made her anxiety calm the slightest bit. She focused on the spot of turquoise in his silver bolo tie. "I don't know what happened. I was doing my usual morning routine of enjoying my hot tub before starting my day and found Susan."

"You know the victim?"

"Yes. No."

"Which is it? You know her or you don't?"

"I don't know her, but I've seen her."

"Where?"

"In town. She was..."

"She was where?"

"Um...I don't think I can say."

"Ma'am—Abby, the woman is dead. I think it's okay to tell me where you saw her. It's important."

"At Dr. Miller's office. Dr. Collin Miller."

"The shrink?" He turned toward the door and hollered, "Hey, Johnson?"

An officer poked his head in the door and said, "Yeah?"

Detective Robles motioned him over with a finger and Johnson strode over, putting his ear close to Robles.

"We may be looking at a possible suicide," Robles mumbled quietly.

"No, it wasn't suicide," Abby said.

"How do you know that?" Robles asked.

"I just do. She was going through—"

"Abby!" Collin's voice sounded behind her. "Gentleman, I think that's enough for now." Collin appeared beside her in two long strides, wrapping a protective arm around her shoulder.

"And you are?" Officer Johnson asked.

"Collin Miller. Dr. Collin Miller."

The two officers exchanged a look.

"Sir," Detective Robles said, "my partner here has some questions for you. Could you go with him please?"

"Now's not a good time for me to leave Ms. Sinclair."

Once again, Johnson and Robles looked at each other, each raising an eyebrow.

Johnson said, "I assure you, she'll be in good hands with Detective Robles."

"Gentleman," Collin said, "Can you give us a few minutes?" When they didn't move, he said, "Please."

"You can have a few minutes after we're done getting statements," said Robles. "First you need to go with Officer Johnson."

Collin leaned in close to Abby's ear. "Remember patient-doctor confidentiality. I will, too." He gave her a curt nod before Johnson grasped his right bicep and led him into the kitchen.

"Ms. Sinclair, what can you tell me about the victim?" Robles asked her.

Remember patient-doctor confidentiality. I will, too. Dr. Miller's words rang in her head. It sounded more a threat than a request.

"Ms. Sinclair, I understand this is upsetting for you, but I need you to tell me about the victim. How did you know her?" Robles asked.

"I just saw her in town today is all."

"And?"

"That's all."

"If that's all it is, why would she end up here, of all places, at your resort, in your private hot tub?"

Abby looked toward the kitchen then back at Robles who scribbled on his pad before looking back at her.

"Her sister is staying here." Her eyes flew open, her hand to her mouth. "Judy! Oh no! Someone has to tell Judy. She and her husband, Bob, are staying in cabin three."

"Hey, Johnson?" he called toward the kitchen. Officer Johnson poked his head around the corner. "The vic's sister is staying in cabin three. Can you let someone outside know that so they can go there? Also, we'll need a victim advocate out here ASAP."

While the two of them talked, Collin stood in the doorway, looked directly into Abby's eyes, and put a finger up to his lips. Abby merely nodded and turned her attention to the floor, shifting her weight from one foot to the other.

"Sure thing, Detective," Johnson said before he said something to Collin and left the room. Collin hovered near the living room entrance, well within hearing range.

"So, Abby," Robles said, "if you only saw the victim in town today as you claim, how do you know her name?"

"Um...well..." She glanced sideways at Collin, watching her closely. "I heard someone call her by name."

"Who was that?"

"I have no idea who it was." Heat crept up her neck to her cheeks.

"You sure that's the truth, Ms. Sinclair?"

"Of course, I—"

A scream, followed by loud sobs, sounded outside the door, jerking their attention to the side of the house. Collin was but a blur as he ran past them, the door slamming behind him. Robles followed, Abby behind him.

Judy's gaze fixed on Abby, her eyes wide, filled with accusation. "You!" she huffed. "My sister was found dead in *your* hot tub! What did you do?"

6

Judy became more hysterical by the moment, and Abby increasingly humiliated.

"I didn't do anything," Abby said. "I came out to use my hot tub and found her."

"Sure you did," Judy said, venom dripping from her words. "Talking about how beautiful she was. You were jealous of her. I knew it."

"Why would I be jealous?" Abby asked, her tone rising. "I didn't even know her."

"Right," Judy said as she stepped toward her, shoulders squared.

"Ladies," Bob said, putting an arm around Judy and pulling her toward him. "Abby, please forgive my wife. She's distraught, as I'm sure you can understand."

"Bob, I didn't do anything to Susan. I would never. I didn't do this," she said, flinging her arm toward Susan, who was still floating face down in the tub.

"Sir," Collin said to Detective Robles, "I would recommend getting your crime scene under control."

"Why don't you help with that, Dr. Miller? Take yourself back into the kitchen where Officer Johnson asked you to wait." He jerked his head toward the house. He addressed the small crowd that had begun gathering. "Ladies and gentlemen,

I need you each to go back to your cabins until an officer comes to speak with you."

"I'm not going anywhere," Judy said, chin thrust outward. "You can't make me leave my sister."

"The best thing you can do for your sister is let us process the scene so we can find out what happened to her," said the detective. He looked at one of the officers that remained on the perimeter of the scene. "Holland, get Mr. and Mrs. Lopez out of the cold and get their statement. Carter, take the other folks back to their cabins." He looked at the people who weren't moving an inch. "People, please. Go with Officer Carter. Give him your names and someone will come for you soon."

"We're leaving," one of them said. "Obviously someone here is a killer. It's not safe for us to be here."

Murmuring broke out over the growing crowd. Abby was sure that every person at the resort had now gathered at the scene.

"People!" Detective Robles broadcasted. "We don't know if this was a homicide. The sooner you let us do our jobs, the sooner we'll know."

"What else could it be?" someone asked.

"Suicide."

Abby looked at Collin, eyes wide. His voice was quiet, but not quiet enough. "Certainly you don't believe that," Abby said.

"Why would you think it was suicide, Dr. Miller?" Detective Robles asked.

"I'd like to think we don't have a killer in our midst. Nothing less, nothing more," Collin said.

"I don't believe that for a second," Abby said. "She had a son to live for." She looked at Detective Robles, now jotting something on his notepad.

"A son she was losing custody of," Bob said.

"And now that poor little boy lost a mother," Abby said. "No, I don't buy it. She wouldn't have done this to her son."

"What do you know about my sister?" Judy said, resentment looming large. "You don't know anything about her situation. How dare you pretend to know our lives! Unless I'm right and you know her better than you're letting on. She was found in your hot tub after all. Which I'm still trying to wrap my head around."

Abby stared at Judy, trying to get a read on her hostility. She was hiding something. She was certain of it. Abby sought out her father, noting him quietly reading the situation.

"Go on, people," Detective Robles said. "Officer Carter will walk you to your cabins. Holland, take Mr. and Mrs. Lopez."

"Where's Conrad?" Judy asked, scanning the area.

"Who's Conrad?" Officer Johnson asked.

"From cabin one," Abby answered. She looked around. "I don't see him." She sidled up beside her father, leaned in and whispered. "Pops, have you seen Conrad?"

"Nope." His voice was low, flat. "Reckon he could have left already. He was planning on leaving first thing."

"Maybe I'll go check on him to be sure he's alright. If there's a killer on the loose..."

"You stay. I'll go," he said.

"You both stay and I'll go," Johnson said. "Cabin one you said?"

"Yes."

"The two of you go back inside the house and wait there. A victim advocate is on the way, and Detective Robles will be back with you in just a moment, Ms. Sinclair."

Being in the house wouldn't have been so bad if Collin hadn't done what he was told, that being to go back where he was supposed to wait. He paced the kitchen floor, looking at his cell phone every couple of seconds. Abby stayed where she could keep an eye on him. He was a complicated man, and she wanted answers. Both he and Judy were hiding something. She could feel it from deep within her.

"Abby, can I talk to you for a minute?" Dr. Miller asked, now standing in the doorway to the living room.

"That's not a good idea," Jeremiah answered.

"Mr. Jordan, your daughter has suffered a terrible experience."

"And I'll take care of her."

"How about I take care of myself, gentleman. I'm not a child," she said, then turned to her father and said quietly, "Sorry, Pops. But I'm a thirty-six-year-old woman. I've gone through much worse than this."

"It's because of what you went through that—"

"I'm stronger than you think I am."

"When your boy is thirty-six, you tell me you won't worry."

Rare, raw emotion filled his voice, and guilt took up residence. "It's just that—well, I'm used to taking care of myself. I need to know I always can."

"I've no doubt you can." The firm set of his jaw, the narrowing of his eyes, she knew he was remembering Hunter. "But I thank God every day for Henry the one time you couldn't."

Henry popped up in her mind. Her neighbor from when she lived in California who, over time, became like a grandfather to her son and a savior to Abby when her ex-husband tried to kill her. He was also the man who left her and Cooper the resort when he died. Yes, she, too, thanked God for Henry every single day. She only wished Susan would have had a Henry. A fresh wave of sadness washed over her. *Oh, Susan, I will find out what happened to you. I promise.*

"I'm headin' upstairs for a bit," Jeremiah said. "The cops are probably gonna want to talk with you."

"Yup. Imagine they will. I'm not going any further than my room."

She watched as he trudged upstairs, fighting the urge to run up behind him and throw her arms around him. Instead, she felt chained to the floor, her feet unwilling to move.

"Abby," Collin said, standing again in the doorway. "Are you okay?"

"I'll be fine. But I can promise you this, I will find out what happened to Susan."

"Stay out of it, Abby. It's not your fight."

"That's where you're wrong, Dr. Miller." She squared her shoulders. "You of all people should understand why I can't just sit back and let this go. That could have been me when Hunter was around."

"The police will figure it out. It's not for you to be the hero."

"It's not for me to sit idly by and let a monster go free, either. That could have easily been me at Hunter's hands."

"But it wasn't. Just remember that Susan being a patient of mine isn't open record. Her death doesn't change that."

But it did, didn't it? Didn't death forfeit that rule? A gust of wind blew a swirl of snow in the door as Detective Robles came back in. "Johnson will be with you in a few minutes, Mr. Miller. Abby, let's pick up where we left off."

Abby watched Collin jam his fists in his pants pockets and retreat from the doorway but stay within listening range.

"I get the feeling you knew the victim better than you're letting on," Robles said. "Why don't you start from the beginning and tell me how you knew her?"

"I told you."

"The truth, Ms. Sinclair."

Abby sighed. "Look, I'm not sure what it is you want me to tell you. You say you want the truth. That's what I'm giving you, and you don't believe me." She sat on the edge of the sofa, glanced down at the floor to avoid his piercing stare. She leaned forward, resting her elbows on her knees, clasping her hands together to still the shaking.

"If you only saw her, as you claim, how did you know about her child?"

"From a newspaper article I read. That, and word travels fast in a small town," she said, copying the words she'd heard all too often lately. "Fact of the matter is, it seems everyone knows about her and the custody battle. How did you not know it?"

"And the outburst from the victim's sister about you being jealous of the victim? How do you explain that?" he asked, ignoring her question.

"I have no idea. You'd have to ask Mrs. Lopez." She dared to look at him ever so briefly before picking a piece of dog hair from her pants. *Gus. Where was he?* As if sensing her need of him, Gus ambled up beside her and touched his nose to her hand.

She absently stroked his head as she glanced out the side window. The coroner was now beside the hot tub. There was a knock at the door, followed by a stocky middle-aged woman who now stood beside Robles.

"I'll be done in a minute," he told her. He fished out a business card from his front pocket and handed it to Abby. "If you think of anything else that you may have forgotten, please give me a call. I'll be in touch. Where's your father?"

"Upstairs in his room."

"Can you get him for me, please?" He looked at the woman standing beside him. "She's all yours."

When Abby got back from letting her father know Robles wanted to speak with him, she sat down on the sofa. The woman sat beside her, and Abby scooted over. More than anything, she just wanted everyone the heck out of her house. Including Dr. Miller.

"Hi Abby," the woman said. "My name is Tonya. I'm a victim advocate, and I work with the Blue Mist Mountain Police Department." Her voice, though soft, grated on Abby's nerves. "I'm here to offer support and resources that might be of help to you during this time," Tonya said. "How are you doing?"

She had a couple of pamphlets in her hand, which she now extended to her. Abby didn't move, so Tonya lay them on the coffee table.

"I'm fine," Abby said. "I don't need an advocate. But the victim's sister probably does. She's in cabin three."

"I've already been there. She said she doesn't need any services."

"That makes two of us then." She stood and walked toward the door. "I appreciate you coming out, Tonya. Truly, I do. And I appreciate what it is you do. But right now I just want my house back." She looked at Tonya, who stood rooted in place. "Please," she pleaded.

"Of course." Tonya patted the pamphlet on the coffee table. "My contact information is in here. Call if you need anything."

Abby watched as Tonya walked toward the door and outside. She closed it behind her and rested her forehead against the cool wood. She spotted Dr. Miller from the corner of her eye, approaching her.

"It will be okay, Abby," he said, resting his hand lightly on her shoulder. Her stomach twisted at his touch, and she shrugged his hand off of her. "You will be okay. Just remember what we've talked about in your sessions."

"I know I'll be okay. I'll be even better once everyone is gone and I get someone out here to sanitize the hot tub. The crime scene investigators drained it. The detective said they need to check for hair, fibers, and stuff like that." She shuddered. "Don't think I'll fill it again for a while. If ever."

"Probably not a bad idea."

"They'll find something linking it to me," Abby whispered.

"Why do you say that?" Dr. Miller asked, his tone sharper than she could ever remember. Suspicion?

"Because it's my tub. I'm the only one who uses it. Mostly, anyway."

Dr. Miller exhaled through pursed lips and ran his hand through his hair. "Oh, that. They'll take your DNA to rule you out."

Officer Johnson breezed in through the door. "Dr. Miller, just a couple more questions and then you can go. Can you step over here, please?" Officer Johnson stepped into an adjoining room.

"You can ask me right here," Dr. Miller said, not moving an inch. "I'm bound by doctor-patient confidentiality, so I probably can't answer your questions, anyway. Technically, I can't even tell you whether she's a patient of mine or not."

Officer Johnson glanced at Abby, turned his back toward her then asked, "Can you tell me if the victim had any suicidal tendencies?"

The officer tried to keep his voice low but Abby heard anyway.

"Officer, I told you, I can't talk about a patient."

"The woman is deceased, Doctor. The confidentiality agreement no longer applies. We're looking at possible murder here." He looked at Collin, skepticism written all over his face. "Unless it's suicide as you suggested earlier."

"I wouldn't know, sir. I just like to think the best of people and choose to believe no one here is a killer." He looked at Abby, his right eye twitching slightly. "Wouldn't you agree?"

Abby remained silent. At this point, she was all talked out. She had no words left to say. Not to mention the less she said at this point, the better. She just desperately needed everyone to be out of her house, and Susan's body gone. She shivered and wrapped her arms around herself.

The bell above the door to the store jingled, and she was never so happy to have a distraction. She turned to help whoever it was, surprised to find the Wilcoxes and Carrie standing at the counter. Before she could say a word, Judy opened the door, with Bob right behind her.

"We're here to check out," Sadie Wilcox said.

"Us, too," said Carrie. "We're sorry, Abby. But we just don't feel safe here."

"Did the police say it's okay to leave?" she asked.

"We gave our statements. Unless they arrest us, they can't keep us here."

"Let 'em try," Judy said.

"You're leaving, too?" Abby asked.

"No reason to stay now," Bob said. "We were here to see Susan. We just hadn't anticipated it would be this way."

"We'll arrange to have her transported back home," Judy said. "So we'll need to get back and start funeral arrangements." She paused, stared out the window, then at Abby. "Sorry I was a witch earlier out there." She nodded her head toward the side of the house as a tear rolled down her cheek. "It just really threw me for a loop. At least she's out of her misery now. There is that, I suppose."

"Judy, do you know who the father of her little boy is?" Abby asked.

"At this point, it doesn't matter much, does it? The fact is she wasn't fit to take care of Ryan and he is."

"Says who?"

"The filed documents. I was able to obtain a copy of them. My sister was a sweet girl, but she was messed up."

Renewed energy to solve the crime spurred Abby to question further. "Hm. If you don't mind my asking, who wrote up the reports?"

"A doctor who evaluated her."

"And who was that?" Abby pressed.

Judy looked around them, Carrie's and the Wilcox's interest were apparent. "This isn't the time or place. Our personal lives are not up for display."

"Of course not," Abby said. Her cheeks warmed. She wasn't only disappointed but felt like a child caught in a lie. She'd been so close to finding out some crucial information. But it wasn't too late. The Lopez's were the last ones through the door to check out. First come, first served.

"Jim and Sadie, I can check you out." While going through the routine, Abby apologized profusely for the turn of events that caused them to cut their vacation short.

"It's not your fault," Sadie said. "We know that. And we'll be back. We're booked for next fall already."

That means they're not the killers or they wouldn't plan on coming back, Abby noted. *Or would they? Maybe they were the killers, which is why they're comfortable making a return.* As soon as they turned to leave, she said, "Carrie, looks like you're next. Where's John?" She looked around the small store, over the tops of the isles.

"Loading the car. Best to get a move on with the weather moving in. Looks like you might be on the edge of it though, aye? Not at all what they first predicted. That's weathermen for you."

She looked out the window at the steadily falling snow. It seemed so calm and peaceful. If there hadn't been a body in her jacuzzi that morning, it would have been a beautiful day. A jacuzzi would never hold the same appeal ever again.

When it was just Bob and Judy left in the store, she fought for the nerve to ask one more time. "Judy, I have to ask. Is the father of Susan's child from Blue Mist Mountain?"

"For God's sake, Abby, let it go." She sighed, exasperated. "That's not for me to say. It was my sister's demon to fight. Her story to tell. And now it needs to be put to rest with her. Maybe she'll find some peace knowing that."

Abby opened her mouth to object, but Collin came down the steps from the living room. "Well, ladies—and gentleman," he added, looking toward Bob. "I've been given the green light to go. Come on. I'll walk you out."

Officer Johnson was right behind him. "All parties have been approved to leave. I've gotten everyone's contact information except Conrad."

Abby's eyebrows raised. "He wasn't in his cabin?"

"Nope. Clean as a whistle. Doesn't even look like anyone was in there."

She watched as Bob, Judy, and Collin walked toward the door. Bob said something to both of them. Officer Johnson waited for the door to close and said to Abby, "I have to ask you not to do anything with cabin one. We need our investigators to go through it first."

"Conrad's cabin?"

"I don't know where he was staying, ma'am, but it couldn't have been in cabin one."

"But that's the one he checked into. Why do you say he couldn't have been staying there?"

"Because nothing's been touched."

7

By the time the police left and the crime scene was cleaned up, it was one o'clock. All the guests had checked out except for Cody and Roxanne. "Everyone's gone now," Cody had said. "That means the killer is too." Oddly, that gave Abby peace. It meant they didn't think of her or Jeremiah as the killers.

The hot tub maintenance company was scheduled to come out the following morning to completely dismantle it. Abby pleaded with them to make it sooner, but the man insisted he was already overbooked for the day. The crime scene crew completed their work in Conrad's cabin, and when Abby tried to call the number he had listed on the check-in form she received, the robotic voice said the number had been disconnected. She couldn't find anything on Conrad in the papers left by the prior resort managers, Simon and Maggie. Abbie scowled. First thing tomorrow, she was going to figure out how to computerize all the records Simon and Maggie left behind. They had been old-school, and Abby wasn't even sure they had owned a computer, much less have a database for customers and Whispering Pines Resort business.

She rifled through the paper records once again that they left but couldn't find anything for Conrad Schmidt. Or Bob and Judy Lopez, for that matter. Hadn't all three said they'd stayed there before? Conrad and Judy both said they knew

Gabe. And Gabe finally remembered them after some additional thought. She thought about Conrad's behavior the previous day. It was more than a little odd, staying an extra day, saying he was going hiking then not going, coming in the store at the same time as Judy at closing time last night. The argument with Bob that she witnessed. Could he be the father of Susan's child? But where was the little boy while Conrad had been at the resort? Not with Susan, that much was certain.

As she processed all the loose ends, she remembered another. Her eyes flew open. She flipped the sign on the store door to *closed*, indicating with the red hands on the little clock when she'd be back. Not that it mattered. Cody and Roxanne were the only other people on the property. But just in case someone decided to stop by unexpectedly, it wasn't a bad idea. She slipped into a coat, boots, hat, and mittens, and went outside to find her father.

She tried to find tracks to see which way he had gone, but any prints were quickly filling in with fresh snow and drifts from the wind that had picked up.

"Pops?" she called, holding her coat tight around her and looking on all sides of her.

"Here!" he said from around the side of the house.

She trudged around the corner. "What are you doing? Haven't you had enough of this side of the house for a while? Like forever?"

"Shoveling for the maintenance crew tomorrow."

"It'll be all drifted in by that time. Hey, Pops? You said you turned up the heat on the jacuzzi for me this morning, right?"

"Yup." He continued working, his back covered in white powder from bending over as he shoveled.

"What time was that?"

"'Bout five."

"How can that be? You would have seen Susan's body. That means someone had to have done this after you checked the temperature. Were there any tracks in the snow?"

"Didn't pay attention. The porch awning hangs over the tub, and I didn't look for prints below the patio on the ground."

"Pops, someone had to have killed her after you were out there."

"I didn't lift the whole cover. Only the one side. Enough to see the temperature display."

She thought about this. The tub cover was one piece but folded in the center, so half of it opened at a time and flipped over on the other half. Susan's body could have been wedged under the closed half of the cover until Abby opened it to get in. Turning on the jets would have pushed the body to the front half. She shuddered.

"Don't tell the police that, okay? You didn't already, right?"

"They didn't ask."

"Thank goodness. I don't want them reading into something and making you a suspect."

"Too late for that. We're all suspects at this point." He stopped shoveling to glance at her briefly, then got back to it.

"I'm gonna find out who did this. I have to for Susan."

"Go on back in the house. I'll be in shortly."

Her stomach complained its neglect. She hadn't eaten a meal since last evening. While in the throes of a murder, the last thing on her mind had been food. But now that she had some downtime, if one could call it that, she realized she was starving. "I'll whip together a late lunch. You hungry too?"

Without waiting for a response, Abby brushed off the flakes from her coat and went inside. She took her hat off and shook the snow from it. The path her father had shoveled was already filling in. It would be easier for the maintenance crew to follow the patio around and not have to follow the shoveled path at all. She suspected it was his way of keeping his mind busy and off the disturbing events of the morning. He wasn't one to sit still for long to begin with unless he was watching one of his Westerns.

She flipped the sign back to *open* and went about putting together some soup and grilled cheese. Comfort food for a cold, snowy day. She was buttering the slices of bread before placing them in the griddle when her cell phone rang. She glanced over at the number displayed on the screen. Dr. Miller. She wasn't in the mood to talk to anyone that had anything to do with the morning's events. All she wanted to do was forget about it and pretend life was business as usual. She especially didn't want to think about telling Cooper or Piper and hoped she could find a way around telling them at all. That, however, had bit her in the hind end last summer when Cooper found out she hadn't been honest with him about his dad. The problem was, the only people she wanted to talk to right now were Cooper and Piper, but the Catholic guilt was already settling in her bones about keeping the secret from them. But was it really a secret? She stopped, considered the options, and sighed. *Tell yourself anything you want, Abigail. Either way, you'll have to deal with it.*

The grilled cheese was golden brown when she took them out of the pan and slapped them onto plates next to two steaming bowls of soup. She carefully placed each in front of a chair at the table and poked her head out the door. "Soup's on!"

Seconds later, Jeremiah came in, brushing off his coat as he did. "The bulk of this storm is going around us."

"Thank goodness. It's kind of culture shock coming from California. Last spring was so mild."

"From what I hear, this is more typical than not."

She took his coat from him and hung it over a chair. "Well, it's going to take a while for me to get used to this. Beautiful as it is, I miss summer."

"The boy call today?"

"No. I'm going to call him in a few minutes."

"Don't tell him about this morning."

Abby raised her eyebrows in question. "You're the one who tarred and feathered me for not telling him the truth about Hunter."

"Don't see how you can even compare the two."

"You don't think he's going to find out eventually? And Piper will crucify me if I kept a secret this big from her."

He took a slurp of his soup and looked up at her. "Who said anything about not telling Piper?" He went back to pulling up another spoonful.

Silence engulfed the space between them until Abby thought she would explode. She scooped up her phone and listened to her voice mail then set her phone on the table.

"Dr. Miller said he needs me to come in at nine tomorrow morning instead of ten. Does that work for you?"

"Yup."

"Stop talking so much. It's hurting my ears." She saw him smirk.

"Someone needs to get out of the house," he said.

She lay her spoon on the table and poked at her grilled cheese with her finger. "Sorry. I'm still rattled from this morning. Think I'll go up and take a long hot bath after I wash up the dishes."

"Good idea."

She watched him eat for a few minutes, then asked, "Pops, what do you think about all of this? Do you think it could have been Conrad? He was acting so weird yesterday. And he said Judy and Bob set him up with Susan a while back, remember? Maybe he's the child's father and was harboring ill-will toward Susan so he decided to take care of it."

"That's a stretch."

"Well? It's possible, right?"

"The man didn't strike me as a killer."

"Why did he leave so early, then?"

"He said he was checking out early. That's why he settled up last night."

"But what about the police finding his cabin unused?"

He shrugged a shoulder. "Yup, that's odd."

"And what about Bob and Judy? They were pretty upset with Susan."

"Being upset with someone doesn't make them a murderer. If it did, you would have murdered me a long time ago."

She chuckled. "True story."

"Do you know I can't find any record of them staying here before?" She pushed her plate and bowl away. "I'm going to spend some time getting everything electronic. What do you think of that?"

"Hadn't thought about it." He tore off a piece from his grilled cheese.

"Aren't you curious about any of this?" She pushed her chair back and picked up her dishes, bringing them to the sink. "I expected you to be a little more concerned."

He finished the last spoonful of soup and popped the last piece of grilled cheese in his mouth. He turned serious eyes on her. "I'm worried as hell. All I've been doing is wondering who could have done this and why. And when. What if the monster would have been out there at the same time that you were sitting in the hot tub? *What if?*"

Guilt stabbed her. Of course he was worried. And he was processing the information the same way he always did—by running scenarios inside his head and by keeping busy, and not by talking about it. Why would she expect this time to be any different? She rubbed the back of her neck and sighed.

"I'm gonna get out of your hair and take a cup of tea up to the bath. Think I'll call Gabe, too."

"You go. I've got things covered down here."

She stepped toward him and leaned over, giving his shoulders a light squeeze. "Thanks."

The bell above the door to the store jingled. She glanced that way as her father got up from the table. "Go," he ordered. "I've got it."

Instead of tea, Abby heated a cup of milk in the microwave and listened to the muffled voices from inside the store. Tempted to see who it was, she fought the urge and gave in to the greater temptation of the hot bath. As she climbed the stairs, the voices faded to nothing by the time she was at the top. She snagged her remaining robe—the one Detective Robles hadn't confiscated—from the hook behind her bedroom door, slipped out of her clothes and into the robe.

She should have told him it was this one and given it to him, she thought. The one he took was her favorite.

She crossed over into the bathroom and started the water, dropping in a bath bomb she'd picked up in town earlier in the week. While the tub filled, she selected a fresh pair of yoga pants and a hoodie, setting them on the chair beside the tub, and then pulled up the music app on her tablet. She piled her ponytail high on her head and fastened it with a clip.

As she slid down, the blue water up to her chin, the scent of the Caribbean Crush bath bomb filled her senses. She closed her eyes to blot out the ugliness of the morning. But the harder she tried, the more invasive it was. Susan's body, her red coat, and coal-black hair spread out around her. Judy's angry outburst at what Abby had done to her sister. Conrad's empty cabin. Jim and Sadie, John and Carrie, and Nancy and Tim leaving nearly three days early because they didn't feel safe. And what was that she saw in their eyes? Suspicion? And she hadn't even seen John, only Carrie. A faint feeling of sweet relief pinged against the wall of ugly when she remembered Roxanne and Cody. *We don't think there's a threat here, Abby. The threat is gone.*

She slid down further, fully submerging her head, silencing all sound, including the classical music playing on her chosen Pandora station from her tablet perched on the vanity. She stayed under until she couldn't hold her breath any longer, then burst back up from beneath the water, taking a huge gulp of air. The gulp that Susan was never able to get. The breath that she no doubt fought for but was brutally taken from her. Abby prayed Susan fought back hard enough to leave some of her attacker's DNA under her fingernails or somewhere else on her body. Despite the hot water, she shuddered at the thought of what Susan may have endured not only in those last moments but the fear that no doubt was a large part of her life. Abby herself had lived with that fear for far too long.

As she recalled vividly the intense fear of Hunter coming home from work the muscles in her neck contracted. She pressed her fingertips deep into her neck muscles, then ran her fingers along the ribs that he'd once broken. Usually all it took was a glance to see the look in his eyes when he walked through the door at night. And sometimes, it didn't matter what she did—or didn't do. It was the evenings he went out with co-workers after work for a drink that she feared most. When he drank, even if it was one beer, as he'd often claimed he had, it transformed him into a monster. Like the night he almost killed her because she wouldn't get him another beer. She'd had the nerve to refuse his demand. It was then, as he was beating her senseless, that she knew she had to leave. If not for her, then for Cooper. If Hunter ended up killing her, and he would have had she gone back to him after her lengthy hospital stay, Cooper would have been left alone with him. "Over my dead body," she whispered, her voice shaking. And it almost was. Over her dead body, that is.

On the evenings Hunter went out after work, Abby made sure Cooper was in bed before he got home. She didn't want Hunter's foul mood to be aimed at Cooper. And it had been more than a couple of times. He'd never hit him, but the verbal lashings were just as bad.

Tears burned her eyes. *Is that what you went through, too, Susan? Feeling like an utter failure for not being able to protect your little boy from the evils inside the walls of your own home?* She burned with humiliation and shame at the memory. Felt suffocating sadness for Susan.

It was then that she realized what she needed to do. She took a deep breath of relief from finding peace that had been lacking not only today but for a long time. Peace that silenced the inner demons. Peace that came from purpose. She was going to start a support group for victims of domestic violence. A group that would help alleviate the shame, the guilt, the aloneness that she felt when she was struggling through it. She would give them a place to feel safe and understood. Blue Mist Mountain might be an upscale mountain town, but domestic violence holds no prejudice. She knew full well it crossed every boundary, every race, religion, and economic status.

She made a mental note to ask Dr. Miller at her appointment tomorrow morning if he had any suggestions on how to get started. First off, she would need a location. She didn't want to use the resort. Keeping any disgruntled domestic partners away from her home, Cooper, and her father was critical. For the first time that day, she smiled, resting her head back against the vinyl pillow affixed to the tub. She was going to make sure she did everything she could, so the hell both she and Susan lived through didn't happen to more women.

And I'll find out who did this to you, Susan. I will. I promise.

8

Abby woke Friday morning remembering the plans she'd been making before she fell asleep. Sleep brought unsettling dreams of Gabe, who somehow morphed into Hunter, as Susan tried to tell Abby a secret but there was no sound coming from her mouth. And try as she could, Abby couldn't lip-read what Susan was saying. The sound of the alarm was a welcome relief.

Snowflakes danced quietly outside the window, tapering to nearly nothing at all. The trees were still, the sun was rising, its light creeping higher and higher on the mountainside. Birdsong filtered through her window, chirping their anticipation of the beautiful day.

Jumping up and slipping her robe over her worn-too-thin nightshirt, she grabbed a pair of faded jeans and a long-sleeved Coffee Hub t-shirt and headed for her bathroom. She had rinsed the blue bath bomb from her hair yesterday. Despite that, she looked forward to waking up in a proper shower.

She stood under the pulse setting of the showerhead. The water pounded on her shoulders, and the hot steam awakened her senses to full alert. Awake now, her mind traveled at lightning speed as she planned her group. What to call it? *Blue Mist Mountain Support Group*? No, that's too generic. People would assume it's a drug or alcohol support group. But if she used the term domestic violence, she was afraid it would keep women away. She knew women didn't like to think of their situation as domestic violence. It somehow made her feel 'less than.'

The pulsing water massaged her left shoulder. It was there she carried stress the most. It was that shoulder Hunter had once dislocated. Her muscle finally loosened, clearing the way to think more clearly. Maybe Dr. Miller would let them use his office space one evening a week. He closed at five most evenings anyway.

Aha! The name came to her in a flash. *A Future Without Violence.* Yes! That offers hope, the precise thing women didn't feel at that time in their lives but desperately needed.

As she cruised along the road to her appointment, she was deep in thought about her new mission. Her phone rang at the same time that two elk lumbered up on the side of the road, startling her. She slowed, swerved just enough to avoid getting too close, and grasped for her phone from the front passenger seat.

"Hello?"

"Hey, gorgeous."

An instant smile spread across her lips at Gabe's voice. She'd called him yesterday after her bath but didn't catch him, so she had left him a voicemail. "I never tire of hearing that, you know."

"I hope you never do."

His calm, husky voice sounded close. It felt as though he was sitting right there with her. She wished he was. She pictured his flannel shirts he loved to wear, his brown hair messed up from being outside in the wind. He loved being outdoors even more than she did.

"Are you still coming back today?" She crossed her fingers, worried the snow might keep him away longer.

"Already home. Can't wait to see you tonight."

Her smile broadened. "Me either. Can't wait to see *you*, I mean." She felt like a teenager with her first crush. Yet, she knew without a doubt that it ran so much deeper than that. She'd never felt so deeply about a man. And so safe. She had never known before that it was possible to have both in the same man. It felt almost too good to be true. When she'd mentioned that to Piper, her sister set her straight in a hurry. *None of us liked Hunter,* she'd said. *We all love Gabe. There's a big difference. Dad and I would never steer you wrong.*

"How are you doing?" Gabe asked. "It makes me sick that I wasn't there with you."

"There's nothing you could have done. Unless you could have brought Susan back to life."

"Still. It tears me up that you had to go through that alone. I should have been there."

"Gabe, stop that right now. I know you want to take care of me, but you have to know I need to take care of myself."

"I do know that. And I have to admit you're good at it. But it makes a guy feel good to be able to take care of the woman he loves, ya know?"

"You knew what you were getting into when we made it official," she said.

"It?"

"Us," she said, chuckling. "I'm healing, in large part thanks to you—"

"How in thanks to me? I haven't exactly been able to protect you from the world out there."

She laughed softly. "You and I both know that's not realistic."

"Realistic or not, it doesn't mean I don't want to," he said. "I'm not the weak little flower people seem to think I am."

"Oh, no mistake, Abigail Sinclair," he said dramatically, "I never said you're weak. On the contrary."

She could see in her mind's eye his wide-eyed look, hands up in the air, and laughed. "Okay, so it would have been nice to have you here. Does that make you feel better? It would have. But that scares the crap out of me."

"Because you're human? And a human being wanting support when she's going through a traumatic experience is somehow a sign of weakness?"

"These, my dear Gabe, are reasons I'm seeing a therapist. Which is where I'm going now. Trying to learn how I can be a survivor, a normal person, and open to a new relationship without sabotaging it right out of the gate because of baggage and fear—well, that's what I need to re-learn. Or learn. I'm not sure I ever had it down to begin with. I just need you to be patient with me."

"I'll give you the rest of my life if that's how long it takes, Hermosa. How's that for patient?" His voice was low, sexy.

"A girl could never ask for anything more." And yet fear tried to weasel its way back in. Was it too good to be true? "Why don't you stay in the house tonight when you get there? That way you don't have to worry about starting your heater. It's cold and snowy."

"Or you could stay in my camper and keep me warm."

She smiled to herself, fear melting away to nothing. Lying in his arms, warm, safe, a haven from the past twenty-four hours, nothing but pristine white silence outside the walls of the tiny camper, sounded like heaven. "Hmm. Maybe I could."

"Yeah?" he asked.

"Yeah."

By the time she reached Dr. Miller's office, Abby was thinking again about the women's support group. She'd planned on telling Gabe about it when he called but decided to wait and tell him that evening. She wanted to see what he thought about the idea rather than hear it in his voice over the phone. This would, after all, affect him, too. Their time together was limited as it was. Bringing a new project of this caliber into the mix, meeting weekly, being available to women who may inevitably need more time, would undeniably have a negative impact on the small amount of time they had to spend together now. But the compulsion to do this, to help women find hope when they had none, drawing on her own experience, well, that was something she had to do, regardless of Gabe's input. It would make it easier if she had his blessing, but she was prepared to move forward, easy or not.

After silencing her cell phone, she dropped it into her purse and moseyed on in. She still had ten minutes to spare. She camped out on one of the chairs in the incoming waiting room and rifled absently through a magazine for a few moments before tossing it aside. She pulled a notepad and pen from her purse. At the top she wrote, *A Future Without Violence*. She drew a line underneath it and scribbled back and forth a few times while she pondered further. She tapped the pen on the paper then scribbled *To Do* and began a bulleted list beneath it.

Find Location.

Plan advertising.

Men allowed? Will need to think about this. May make women feel unsafe, but some men are victims of domestic violence. She thought about it then scribbled it out. Nope, women only. Abused women would feel threatened if men were in the group. Men can have their own group.

Meeting structure. Speakers? Round-table style?

*Brochures with critical numbers? (Safe house, National DV hotline, National Coalition Against DV, Emergency Shelters, Legal Advocacy.) **Come up with more.*

Facilitator training?

Come up with a set of rules to promote group cohesion, respect, stability.

"Ready?" Dr. Miller said from the doorway.

"Oh!" she exclaimed, stuffing her notepad back into her purse. "I didn't even hear the door open."

"Come on in." He stood aside for her to enter his office. The overhead light was off, as usual, the soft glow of a lamp on the table between the two dark upholstered chairs on the opposite side of his desk. "Thank you for coming a little earlier. I'm trying to move all of my appointments up so I can spend the afternoon with family."

"Of course. I didn't realize you had family around here. That's wonderful."

"For what you went through yesterday, you're looking better than I've seen you. Ever, actually. What were you working on so hard out there?" He jerked his thumb toward the waiting area. "It must have been something good."

She took a seat and smiled at him. "I feel better than I have in a long time. In years."

He took the chair near hers. He'd mentioned before that the desk between him and his client could create a distance that hindered progress. She turned sideways in her chair to face him, tucking one leg underneath her.

"So what brought this new Abby out into the world?" He jotted something on his notepad, then looked at her.

"I'm going to start a support group for victims of domestic violence. Women only." She saw surprise register in his eyes, and he paused before replying.

"Abby, that takes training."

"I realize that. I'll do whatever is needed to implement this. It's a needed service."

"Do you think you're strong enough to carry that out?"

A sliver of irritation pricked her. "Why does everyone think I'm so stupid weak? I'm not a victim, Dr. Miller. I'm a survivor. A survivor who wants to give back."

"I understand your desire to help," he said tentatively. "You're a helper. But it takes a lot to run one of those groups, much less start it from scratch."

She took a deep breath as she watched him smooth a non-existent wrinkle from a perfectly pressed pant leg then cross one leg over the other, the ankle resting on the knee of the opposite leg. She hadn't expected to be met with resistance from him of all people.

"Again, I realize that," she finally said. "I've started doing some research, and it's something I have to do. I'm willing to jump any hurdle to do this. As my therapist, it would be nice to have your support. I need to do this."

"For you or for the other women?"

She felt as though he'd slapped her. Hard. Her face felt warm. "That's an ugly thing to say."

"It's a question that begs some thought."

"Helping other women get through the most horrible, hope-crashing time of their life is important to me. I can honestly relate to them. You know that from what I've talked with you about in my sessions. I can help them see there's a way out. I'm at the point in my healing where I need to give of myself to come full circle. To fully heal."

His eyes held a steady gaze on hers. He hardly blinked. "So it's for you." There was the slightest pause between each word.

Her cheeks burned. Beads of perspiration formed on her forehead. "It's for everyone involved."

"It sounds like you've got your mind made up."

"I do." She felt her shoulders square, her chin jut out ever so slightly. "I was hoping I could use your office. I would make sure it doesn't interfere with your schedule. I'm hoping to meet weekly. And of course, it wouldn't start immediately. There's too much I need to do first." Her adrenaline pumped as she thought of the possibilities. The promise.

"No," he said quietly.

Surely she misheard. "Excuse me?"

"I said no."

"But it would be a win-win for both of us. The women of Blue Mist Mountain and the surrounding area could receive a service they need, and it would draw attention to you, bringing you more business."

He shifted in his chair. "Abby, I'm not looking for new business. I have all I can handle."

"Then think about the women out there who need help. I could pay you rent if that's what your concern is."

"Money has nothing to do with it."

"Then what?" Her eyes were large as she struggled to understand.

He stood and walked to the other side of his desk. *Distance?* Pink crept up his neck just past his collar. "I'm afraid I have to strongly discourage this. In fact, as your therapist, I forbid it."

"*Forbid* it? No offense, Dr. Miller, therapist or not, you can't *forbid* me to do anything." Anger sparked through her like electrical jolts. "I'm doing this with or without your approval."

"It will be without."

His voice had an edge to it she hadn't heard before. "I'm sorry to hear that," she said.

"Have you heard anything new with Susan's death?"

The sudden change of topic was apparent. "Not that I've heard." Her words felt tight.

"Surely they've found something out by now," he pressed.

"As I said, if they have, I don't know about it." *And why am I paying you a handsome hourly rate to press me for information?* she thought bitterly.

"Could you let me know the minute you do? Please." He met her eyes. "With her being my patient and all."

Abby remained silent for a moment, trying to read his sudden change in mood.

"Dr. Miller, you know who the father of Susan's child is. You must. Don't you think you should give that name to the police? He might be the killer."

"What makes you think I haven't?"

"So you have?" she asked.

"I can't talk about it. My conversations with the police about a client aren't public knowledge."

"And yet you expect me to disclose what they may have told me? Not that they have told me anything, just that—"

"Abby," he said, his voice even, thick with forced control, "your desire to know what happened to Susan is out of sheer curiosity. I need to know what happened so I know if there's something—*anything*—I could have done for her."

"Nothing can bring her back. But you have the opportunity to help other women like Susan by allowing my group to meet here. You can help Susan that way."

He slapped his hand, palm down, on his desk. She jumped and let out a gasp. "Why in God's name are you so certain it was a domestic situation? How do you know it had anything to do with that at all? Why couldn't it be suicide or some other menacing situation? There are crazy people out there, Abby. All over. You know that. Not every unhappy woman has the same history as you."

Her eyes flashed at him and she stood. She looked into his eyes and saw what appeared to be regret. He knew he'd crossed a line. She was sure of it. *Too late.* "You know, I don't think this is a healthy business relationship for either one of us. I think it's best if we sever the relationship effective immediately. I'll look for a new therapist."

"Abby," he said, his tone doing an about-face. "Abby, sit down."

He walked around the desk and put a hand on her shoulder, encouraging her to follow orders. She flinched at his touch. She would not submit to his—his demands. This relationship hadn't felt right for several days. And today's meeting cinched it. She remained firm, refusing to follow his lead.

"No." She hung her purse over her shoulder, fished her keys out of the front pocket, and started for the door, stopping when she reached it. She turned toward him and said, "I realize every unhappy woman doesn't have the same history as me.

But you want to know how I know Susan did? It was the look of terror I saw in her eyes when she was leaving your office. The loneliness and hopelessness that enveloped her when I saw her by the river. It's the fact that a mother who is in a custody battle for her child is riddled with devastation."

"Not every mother is a good mother."

"No, they're not. But intuition tells me Susan was. And intuition tells me the bully of a father was terrorizing her."

"You don't know anything about it. Leave it alone."

"That's the problem, Dr. Miller, I'm not like you. I can't leave it alone. And I won't." She turned on her heel and left, closing the door firmly behind her.

9

The moment Abby was out of sight, she pulled into the nearest parking lot. She was shaking so badly she could hardly drive. *Pull it together, Abigail!*

She rolled her window down a bit for some fresh air. The snow had stopped and a thick layer of pristine white snow blanketed the ground. And yet it felt tainted by her interaction with Dr. Miller. The snow was already melting on the roads. A four-wheel-drive truck inadvertently splashed a man on the sidewalk. The man stiffened and turned, giving the old stink-eye to the truck that was now waiting at a red light.

Thanks to years of practicing yoga and meditation, she drew well-practiced slow, deep breaths to clear her mind. The excitement she'd felt earlier about starting her women's group dulled in the shadow of her disappointment of Dr. Miller's reaction. She thought he'd be happy. That he would be eager to help other women. He didn't even have to *do* anything, just lend her the space. She would do everything from there. And what business didn't want additional clients? True, maybe his plate was full, his time taken with the clients he already had, but if one had the opportunity to help others without expending any additional time or resources, wouldn't one take that on? Apparently not.

She unscrewed the cap on her water bottle and took a long swig. The anger was subsiding, but her gut was still telling her something was terribly wrong with the whole picture. No, she told herself as she started her car back up. No, he would not diminish her enthusiasm to help other women like her. He would not stop her from doing something useful, something she felt so strongly about.

She backed out of her parking space, glanced left, right, left again, and pulled onto Elk Horn Drive. Pulling into the turn lane to make a left onto Fall River Drive, she absently glanced around as she waited for the light to turn green. Straight ahead, coming out of Rocky's Burgers, were John and Carrie Appleton who had just that morning checked out of the resort. A little boy in snow boots, a cap, and mittens, his coat unzipped and flapping open in the breeze, trailed behind them, his parents right behind the boy. She watched as John and Carrie made their way to their car, the little boy absently following while playing with the toy he'd no doubt just gotten with his kid's meal. He whooshed his arm around in the air with the toy, apparently a helicopter or action hero of some sort.

She pictured Cooper at that age, and her heart ached for him. He'd always loved going to Rocky's when they lived in California. Almost as much as she hated it. But every once in a while she'd put aside her fear of all the germs crawling through the play area and the lack of nutrition in food saturated with fat and grease and take him there.

The boy's parents were now talking with John and Carrie near their car. They had seemed like such a nice couple, and she was sad when Carrie came in to check out early. She wondered where they were staying now.

The car behind her honked its horn and she jumped. "The light doesn't get any greener, Abigail," she mumbled. She stepped on the gas and waved at the car in back of her, mouthing the word *sorry* as he zoomed by in the lane next to her.

Fifteen minutes later she pulled into her driveway as the man who plowed their driveway finished the last swipe through, making one long snowbank along each side of the drive. If she hadn't known better, she'd think her life was the same as every other day. But a dead body in her jacuzzi and the strange behavior of her used-to-be therapist made her life anything but normal.

She opened the door to the intoxicating aroma of freshly brewed coffee. "Hey, Pops," she called. "I'm home."

"Coffee's fresh," he said from the living room.

She stripped out of her coat, scarf, and boots, and wandered on over to where he was sitting in a chair reading the paper. She plopped down in the chair beside him.

"Seems odd to have it so quiet around here, huh?"

"Yup."

"What are you doing?" she said. He lowered the paper and raised his eyebrows. "Forget I asked."

"Okay." He lifted the paper, then lowered it again. "Why are you home so early?"

"You know that women's group I told you about? The one I want to start?"

"Yup."

"Turns out Dr. Miller was less than thrilled. In fact," she said, leaning back and folding her arms in front of her, "he said he forbids me to do it. Can you believe it? How does he get off saying he forbids me to do anything?" She was angry again just thinking about it.

Jeremiah lay the newspaper in his lap and stared at her, his brows furrowed. "That's disturbing."

"Right? That's exactly what I thought. I told him he has no authority to forbid me to do something and told him it wasn't a good idea to see him as my therapist anymore."

"You fired him?"

"Yes. And it feels right. Because something about him feels terribly wrong."

"What is it?"

"I'm not sure. But something about his behavior today gave me the heebie-jeebies. I couldn't get out of there fast enough."

"Well, I'm glad you left when you did then."

She unfolded her arms and tucked a strand of hair behind her ear. "Have you seen Cody or Roxanne this morning?"

"Came in for some bait."

"Bait?" she asked, surprised.

"Said they're going fishing since the ice is gone a ways out from the shore."

"Hm." She chewed on that for a moment before getting up to fetch a cup of coffee. "Gabe called," she said from the kitchen. "He's going to be here this evening."

"That's good. He staying in the camper?"

"I told him he could stay in the house, but he said he'll stay in the camper. I'm going to stay out there with him." She stood completely still, waiting for his response. She half expected him to say no before realizing that was ridiculous. She was thirty-six years old. When he didn't say anything, she slowly walked back toward the living room and poked her head through the doorway. He was back to reading the paper. "Did you hear me?"

"Yup."

"You didn't say anything."

"Didn't realize I was supposed to."

Abby chuckled. "Of course you didn't." She walked over to the door that led to the hot tub and looked out the window where it was now void of the big tub. The vision of Susan came rushing back. "Looks like the maintenance guys were here." Her voice sounded hollow.

"Yup."

"They say anything?"

"Nope."

"Hm." She stood still, staring. "I'm not sure I would ever have been able to use that thing again. I'm glad it's gone."

"Ditto that."

"Maybe we can do something completely different with that space. I'll think of something."

"Ok."

"You sure you don't mind?" she asked.

"Why would I mind? Never used it."

She shrugged. "Yeah, guess not." She went into the kitchen and began washing the few dishes in the sink, thinking about what they could do to that side of the deck. But soon she was once again planning her support group. "Hey, Pops?" she called as she rinsed the suds from the sink. "Would you mind if I run back into town this afternoon? I'd like to look at some locations for my group. Maybe visit a real estate office to see if they have anything cheap. I can stop at the coffee shop and talk to Travis, too. He seems to know a lot about what goes on around the town."

"Fine by me. It's good for you to keep busy."

"Thanks." She wiped her hands on the towel, then folded it in half and hung it on the towel bar. "Piper's bringing Cooper home Monday. Every time I talk to him, it sounds like he's a year older. I sure miss my boy."

"Reckon you do. I do, too."

"Well, I suppose I'll get a few things done around here then head into town."

"What needs done? The house is clean and the only two guests are off fishing somewhere."

Abby looked around her, hands on her hips, and scrunched her face. "Geez! It's like a ghost town around here with everyone gone. Literally everyone except you and me." She shrugged her shoulders. "Guess I'll just head into town, then."

He nodded and stood. "Let's hope it's not a ghost town. We don't need no ghosts here."

Abby grimaced. "Bad joke, Pops. Besides, we have enough of that business in cabin five." Sam and Victoria, the two college kids who worked at the resort during the summer months, managed to sway her into believing in ghosts when strange things happened in cabin five last summer.

"I'll get started looking for a buyer for the jacuzzi," Jeremiah said.

"Where'd they put it?"

"In the shed by the lake."

She shuddered. "How will we find a buyer? Don't we have to disclose what happened in it?"

"It's a hot tub, not a house." He shook his head, one side of his mouth turning upward. "It'll sell fast."

Thoughts of what they could do with the vacant portion of the deck filled her thoughts on the drive to town. She loved her mornings out there. Cooper enjoyed it, too. That was all it took to make up her mind. They would get another one, but this one would have a hard top that locked. And a design as different from the last as she could find.

Her mind traveled back to the support group. *A Future Without Violence.* When she reached the first stoplight in town, she tugged out her notepad and jotted down another item on her to-do list: *Visit a couple of other groups in the Denver metro area.* But wait. Would they even allow her to do that? It's not like they're not protected. She'd have to find out how to make that happen.

She pulled into one of the public parking lots nearest to the real estate office she'd gone by a time or two. No matter the season, tourists flocked to Blue Mist Mountain for its shopping, food, and nature's breathtaking view surrounding it. More often than not, orange lit *No Vacancy* signs adorned the entrance to all of the places renting condos and cabins. And most of the time, hers was no different. This wasn't one of those times. But who could blame her guests this time? Not knowing who the murderer was among them, suggesting it was one of them at all, well—*Wait! Cody and Roxanne hadn't seemed in the least bit concerned about staying on.* Could one or both of them be the killer? Or were they simply comforted by the fact that everyone else had gone, so the threat had, too, as they had claimed?

Either way, she needed to call her father to warn him. She tapped his name on her list of recent calls. He answered on the fifth ring. "What'd you forget?"

"What if Cody and Roxanne aren't afraid to stay because they know who killed Susan? What if it was them? Pops, I think you should stay in the house and keep the doors locked. Close the store."

"Simmer down." His voice was calm. "First of all, if they did, it wouldn't have been random. Second of all, they're not here. They're fishing."

"But what if—"

"Pipsqueak, if the police would have had any indication that they thought either of them was guilty, they'd a had them at the police station."

Her phone beeped, indicating a call was coming through. She pulled her phone away and looked at the incoming call and frowned. "Speaking of, I think the police are calling through now. I'll call you right back."

"How do you know that?"

"Because I programmed the police department's number into my phone last summer. Pops, I gotta go!" And she clicked from one to the other.

"Hello?"

"Ms. Sinclair?"

"This is her."

"Detective Robles, here. Got a minute?"

"Did you find something out about Susan's murder? The water—did you find evidence in it?"

"We're doing everything we can. Can you come to the station?"

The breath went out of her lungs, and she felt the color drain from her face. "Am I under arrest?"

"No, no," he quickly assured her. "We just have a few more questions that we didn't ask at the scene."

She scrambled to put it all together, hoping it wasn't some trick to get her to the police department and then arrest her. Should she call Gabe? No, her father. Or—

"Ms. Sinclair?"

"Um—yes. Uh, sure. When?"

"Today."

"Well, I'm in town now. I could stop by this afternoon, I suppose."

"Do you know what time?" he asked.

"I just got here and have to make one stop first. Half an hour?"

"Great. See you then."

She took a moment to slow her breathing before she got out of the car. She pushed the crosswalk button on the light pole, pulled her coat tight around her, and waited. Down the block, coming her way, was Collin Miller and John Appleton. She recognized John right away but if she didn't know Dr. Miller as well as she did, she would have missed him. He had a hat pulled low over his eyes and a hood over the hat, shielding most of his face. His hands were shoved into his coat pockets. Sunglasses hid his eyes.

The two men were deep in conversation and didn't notice Abby. She flipped the hood of her parka up, huddled over slightly, and looked at the ground. They passed behind her, voices low. Abby heard Collin's voice say, "What'd you tell Mom and Dad?"

Her head snapped around, her gaze following their backs as they retreated down the sidewalk. They crossed the street diagonally toward the Coffee Hub.

Mom and Dad? Collin said he was meeting family this afternoon. Were John and Carrie his family? And if that was the case, why hadn't anyone mentioned it before now? Strange!

The people milling around her began crossing the street and she followed without so much as looking up to see the little white lit up guy on the pole telling them it was now safe to cross. Her mind was traveling in so many different directions, bouncing between her thoughts of Cody and Roxanne, John and Collin, the request to go to the police department, and the real estate office she headed toward. She knew Henry would approve of her using some of the money earned at the resort to pay small rent at a building if she needed to. That, in its own way, pushed her forward even more.

She looked up and saw the real estate office on the upcoming block, then turned, absently glancing at her reflection in the window of the Dairy Queen, doing a double-take. She stopped and looked closer. Sitting there was Carrie with a little boy of about four. The same one she'd seen trailing after them in the Rocky's Burgers parking lot.

She stepped around the corner and pulled open the door. When Carrie looked up and saw Abby, she stood and took a few steps, standing in front of the boy who was eagerly licking his ice cream cone.

"Abby? I hadn't expected to see you here."

"You and John decided to stick around for a while, huh? Did you find another place to stay?'

"Uh, yeah. We're staying with an old friend."

"Oh, who's that? Maybe I know them."

"I doubt it," she said quickly. "They don't live in town. They live in the next town over. We just thought we'd take advantage of the shopping since we're here."

"You probably picked the worst day of your trip for that. I mean, it's melting and all, but the snow makes it pretty messy." She looked around Carrie and the woman did a little sidestep, blocking Abby's view. Abby did one of her own and looked at the boy. "Who's this little guy?" she asked, smiling wide. "Hey, buddy, enjoying that ice cream cone?"

The little boy turned to face her, white ice cream dripping from his chin and onto his hand, reaching the cuff of his sleeve. She reached down to roll his sleeve up, looked into his eyes, and caught her breath. "Oh my." She affectionately touched the top of his head, her hand resting on the warmth of his coal-black hair. She wanted to scoop him into a hug but knew it would frighten the poor little guy. After taking a moment to regroup, she looked at Carrie, whose cheeks were flushed. A child caught with her hand in the cookie jar.

"Abby—" she said, then stopped.

"Is there something you want to tell me?"

"You don't know—"

"You couldn't be more wrong, Carrie," Abby interrupted. "On the contrary." She looked at the little boy then back at Carrie. "Now I *do* know."

10

Abby squatted on the boy's right as he continued to lick his ice cream cone.

"Hi, Ryan," she said.

He turned to look at her, his tongue dipping past his lower lip to reach the ice cream smeared on his chin. From the corner of her eye, she saw Carrie fish her phone out of her purse.

"Hi," the boy said, glancing at her before going back to his ice cream.

"How are you?" Abby asked gently.

"Who are you?" the little boy asked.

"A friend of your mommy's." It wasn't exactly a lie. Susan just hadn't been aware they were friends, she thought, rationalizing the fib.

He stopped mid-lick and turned to look at Abby, fascination filling his eyes.

"You are?"

"Yup," she said, the smile belying her heartache.

"When can I go back to my mommy?"

He laid his cone on the table and turned in his chair to face her, his eyes big, shiny, round saucers. Abby fought back tears of her own as she looked at this miniature, beautiful version of Susan Ramirez. Carrie whispered into the phone, her hand covering her mouth.

"Ryan, sweetie, where's your daddy?"

"We need to be going," Carrie said, dropping her phone into her purse and grabbing Ryan's arm. She scooped up the cone from the table and tossed it into the trashcan, leaving the melting heap of white ice cream on the table. "Come on, my little man," Carrie said, her voice sounding panicked as she pulled him toward the door.

"My ice cream," he cried, tears spilling between thick, dark lashes.

"Auntie Carrie will get you something better, honey," she said, stooping to give him a quick hug before tugging him toward the door again.

Carrie turned toward Abby, paused, and shook her head slowly. "You're really something, you know that? Look what you've done. Thanks for nothing."

"Thank you for answers," Abby said, her heart breaking at the site of the little boy who missed his mommy so much, not knowing he'd never see her again.

Carrie planted a kiss on the little boy's head and pulled him out the door.

"Can I help you, ma'am?"

She turned to see a kid no more than sixteen years old behind the counter. She brushed away her tears with the palms of her hands and wiped them on her jeans. "No, thank you," she said. After another second, she turned and left.

As if she hadn't had enough confrontation for the day, she ran smack into Dr. Miller five feet from the door of the realtor's office. Anger surged through her.

"You!" she said, her cheeks feeling hot.

His fingers grasped her bicep, and he pulled her around the corner, away from the streams of people on the sidewalk.

"Rumor has it you found Susan's son," Dr. Miller said, his fingers tight around her bicep. "Why would you upset him by mentioning his mother?"

"Susan's son?" she asked incredulously. "How about your son, too? What did you do to her?" Any lingering respect she had for him dissolved. Melted like the pile of ice cream on the table at the Dairy Queen.

"I didn't do anything," he said, his voice calm. Too calm. The tiniest twitch of his lower lip betrayed his attempt to make her think he was in complete control. His gloved fingers on one hand curled into a fist. "Why would you say he's my son? Exactly what are you suggesting?"

"I'm not simply suggesting anything. I finally know."

"You're talking nonsense. What is it you think you know?"

It was clear he was trying to get information from her. After all, he couldn't refute or deny what he didn't know. Playing the options in her mind, she finally blurted. "Heterochromia." She ripped her arm from his grasp, winced and rubbed it with the opposite hand. "And if you ever touch me again, you can bet you'll be sorry."

"I don't know what you're talking about. And neither do you."

Abby's eyes widened, her jaw dropped. "That's how you're going to play this? Although I don't know why I'm surprised." She shook her head in disbelief. "Heterochromia. Surely you know what that is. Don't play dumb." He simply stared at her. "One blue eye and one brown. Ryan. He has one blue eye and one brown."

"What does that have to do with me?"

"Everything. It has everything to do with you. A portion of your left eye is brown. Heterochromia is hereditary."

"To think I'm the only person in the country with heterochromia is ludicrous. And sheer ignorance on your part."

He kept his voice low. But beneath the exterior, she could sense his fear of being found out. Especially by her. She felt it. He knew her well enough from the sessions they had that she wouldn't remain quiet about this. That she would feel a sense of obligation to help other women like her. Like Susan.

"How long, Dr. Miller?"

"How long what?"

"How long were you her therapist before you took advantage of her? Probably while she was in a weakened mental state?"

"It wasn't like that."

"No? So you don't deny that you slept with one of your clients. That you're the father of her child. A beautiful child, by the way, who looks exactly like his mother."

"I'm not admitting anything." He sighed and looked toward the sidewalk and back at her. "Listen, Abby, I know what I did was wrong," he said, apparently deciding denial was no longer working. "But you have to believe me when I tell you that it was never my intent for things to turn out this way."

"You kept a child from his mother!"

"A mother who wasn't fit to be one. Susan needed to get herself, her life, in order before she could be capable of raising a child."

"Says the man who took advantage of her, no doubt messing her up even more. You're the cause of her issues. Did you even once stop and think about what taking advantage of her would do to her? Does your wife know?"

"Leave my wife out of it," he growled. "And it's not what you're portraying it to be. It was only one time."

"Right. Like I'm going to believe that."

"It doesn't matter what you believe. It's true. You've made up your mind about me without all of the facts."

"She was your client. She trusted you."

"And I was there for her."

Abby gasped. "Can you hear yourself? You took advantage of a woman who trusted you for help. Whether or not you had anything to do with her death, you could very well have contributed to her demise. You know that, right?" She shook her head slowly in disbelief as she studied his left eye through the lens of his sunglasses.

"It's a good thing Ryan was not with her. I shudder to think what might have happened to him if he had been with Susan," he said.

"Had he been with Susan, none of this probably would have happened at all." She squirmed from under his scrutinizing gaze and then scowled at him. "How many times?" she asked.

"How many times what?"

"I would guess Susan wasn't the first time you crossed that line." He remained silent. "For God's sake, you're a marriage and family therapist." Still, he said nothing. "I can find out, you know. And you can bet I will."

"Just twice."

"*Just* twice?" she asked, mouth agape.

"In all fairness, those women presented themselves to me."

Abby's mouth dropped open. "So you're the victim in all of this." She shook her head again. "If you'll excuse me, I have an appointment I need to keep. Especially now."

He reached for her arm, and she yanked it out of reach. "Don't touch me."

"What do you mean by *especially now?*" he asked. "I haven't harmed anyone. I didn't kill Susan. My guess is she committed suicide. You yourself saw how miserable she was."

"Well, there are two things wrong with that theory. The first is that, what, she jumped in the hot tub and closed the cover down on top of herself? And second, she chose to do it out at my resort why? There is no reason whatsoever she would come to my place over everywhere else in this town."

"Her sister was there."

"Nice try. But Judy's not the one who would have found her in my private hot tub."

"No, but she would have seen her body, which would have driven home quite the point, don't you think?"

"And what point is that?"

"Maybe she wanted to hurt Judy. To get back at her for not supporting her."

"I don't buy that, and you don't either. You're trying to rationalize with me like a child. Or like one of your clients. Which, by the way, I'm not anymore, remember?" She took a deep breath and briefly looked away from him. He made her skin crawl. She turned toward him again, her eyes meeting his. "Excuse me; I have somewhere to be. I need to find a location to hold this support group, which I am going to do. Appears to be a dire need for it."

"I'll deny it," he said. When Abby didn't say anything, he said, "If you say anything about our conversation, I'll deny it to my grave. Who will they believe, a doctor with a good reputation or his prior client who just happens to be crazy?" She narrowed her eyes. "You disgust me." She abruptly turned to leave, turning the corner by the brick real estate business.

"Hey! That's the lady that knows my mommy!" she heard a little voice exclaim excitedly just before the door closed behind her. Ryan's little voice broke her heart and propelled her forward at the same time.

After speaking with the receptionist at the real estate office, she met with one of the realtors. Short of telling her exactly what the space would be used for, she told her exactly what she needed: A single room with electricity—coffee was almost as great a requirement as lights—access to facilities, and heat. Air conditioning wasn't necessary, and neither was furniture. To begin with, she could just bring in some folding chairs and a card table or two. She left the office with a handful of pamphlets and a business card for an agent who was more than happy to help her find something that would suit her needs. It had to be as private as possible, not a public facility. *Although a church could work*, she thought. Other anonymous groups meet in churches. Yes. She would talk to someone at each of the two churches in town.

She walked to the crosswalk. A throng of people had already gathered there, waiting to cross. Instinctively she looked up and down both sides of the street for any sign of Dr. Miller, John, Carrie, or Ryan. Nothing. As much as her heart broke for the little guy knowing he would grow up without his mommy, at least it appeared as though he were loved. She noticed how Carrie doted on the boy. That brought her some degree of comfort, however small it was.

The crosswalk sign lit up, and she moved along amid the people surrounding her, turning left to walk the half block to the police department, which was tucked behind the town library. As her hand pulled open the door, she glanced around one last time, seeing only a handful of people on this side of the building. But lo and behold, Dr. Miller was one of them. Standing off in the distance, on a sidewalk that skirted the backside of the building's parking lot, partially hidden by a parked patrol vehicle, he stood by himself, hands jammed into his coat pockets, watching her. She stared back at him, straightened her back, and went in through the door. He was not going to intimidate her. No way was she going to give him that power. He'd already proved what he did with his power.

Abby looked around the small lobby, the black and white photos of the past Chiefs of Police on the wall to her left, the photo of the present chief in color. On the wall to the right was a large drawing that spanned the entire wall, depicting the town's history. Next to the drawing was a photo and description of an officer who lost his life in the line of duty back in 1965. Behind the front desk, which consisted of a counter that blocked the public from walking on back, was a door with windows that revealed more offices. Two officers were deep in conversation. One turned and looked at her. Detective Robles. He smiled and put up a finger indicating it would be just a moment.

Directly behind the front desk was an elderly woman with glasses perched on the end of her nose, a beaded chain attached to the glass's temples and draped around her neck. She looked up. Her graying hair was tucked up into a loose bun on top of her head, wisps straying haphazardly around her face. Bright orange lipstick stood out against pale skin. A smile revealed an orange smudge on her front tooth. Abby liked her already.

"Help you?" she asked, her tone as colorful as her lipstick and the blouse she wore.

"I'm here for Detective Robles, but he already saw me, so he knows I'm here."

"Well, help yourself to a cup of coffee." She leaned forward as if to whisper a secret and wrinkled her nose. "I can tell ya straight up, though, the coffee's terrible. Don't know how these kids can drink it."

Abby chuckled. "Thank you, I think I'll pass."

"Smart lady." She winked at Abby. "The name's Pearl. And you are?"

"Abigail Sinclair."

"Oh!" she exclaimed, "you're the nice gal that bought the Whispering Pines place." Abby raised an eyebrow. Pearl waved a hand. "Small town," she said.

"Of course," Abby said, smiling. She wasn't sure if living in a small town was a blessing or a curse. The verdict was still out. "Have you worked here for a long time, Pearl?"

"Changed the diapers on some of these young whippersnappers way back when," she said. "Seen 'em grow up into some fine young men and women."

"Huh." Abby didn't know what to say. The interaction she'd had with one of the officers last fall hadn't been pleasant at all. In fact, that one interaction, combined with the experience she had with her ex-husband who had been a cop, had colored her perception of police everywhere, including here. And it wasn't a pretty color. But she had to admit, Pearl was changing that. If even just a little.

"Doesn't sound like you're a fan?" Pearl asked. "Officers can be a bit intimidating, you know. With their uniform and all. And sometimes the new ones need to be knocked down a notch or two. Sometimes ten. But they're really just people like you and me. Fact, I'll let you in on a little secret." She half-covered her mouth with one hand, her nails brightly painted to match her lipstick. "They all put their pants on the same as you and me—one leg at a time."

Abby laughed just as Detective Robles came through the door behind Pearl's desk. "Entertaining, Pearl?" He affectionately patted her shoulder and smiled at Abby. "Come on back, Ms. Sinclair."

"Don't I need to go through some kind of security?" she asked, surprised.

Detective Robles raised his eyebrows. "I don't know, do you? Something in your purse or on your person you want to tell me about?"

Taken aback at first, she saw the slight glimmer of humor in his eyes. He sure was more relaxed when there wasn't a dead body in the vicinity. His light demeanor helped put her at ease. But just as quickly, her guard shot back up. What if he was only doing his detective thing by getting her to let her guard down so she would admit to something? No sir. Wasn't going to happen. She erected the invisible wall again, feeling the shift between them.

"Come on back," he said, turning to lead the way. "Pearl," he called over his shoulder, "we'll be in interview room two."

"Interview room?" Abby asked, her breath quickening.

"It's one of the only places where we can talk without people coming in and out or passing through. Distraction free."

Sure. He was up to something, she was certain of it. She followed hesitantly. The fact that she had nothing to hide was the only thing that propelled her forward. *I'll show him.*

The interview room wasn't anything like she'd seen on TV. She expected concrete walls and floor, a metal table secured into the cement floor, metal chairs, a mirror on one wall acting as a window for others to stand on the other side and watch. Isn't that what they did on *NCIS?* Instead, he led her to a room with walls painted soft blue, blue-gray carpet, an old, rugged-looking wooden table with two mismatched chairs and one window that looked out to a mountainside. She looked up and noticed a small camera in the upper right-hand corner of the room.

"We record all interviews," the detective said. "Nothing personal. Matter of policy is all. And safety."

"Yours or mine?"

"Both," he said.

"Of course." She sat down on the chair he had pulled out for her. "How can I help you, Detective?"

"Tell me what happened the morning you found the body in your hot tub. Start at the beginning."

"I've already told you everything I know."

"Adrenaline was running pretty high at the time. Tell me again. Maybe there's something we missed. Something you didn't think of at the time. Or the answer to something I forgot to ask."

"Okay, sure." She took a deep breath before she started, to calm herself more than anything else. Reliving the event wasn't exactly on the top of her to-do list. The day had sure taken a different turn than what she'd planned or expected. He listened intently, scribbling on his notepad intermittently as she spoke. Apparently, she did have new information this second time around. When she'd finally reached the end of the tale of events, she paused, then said, "And there's something else you might want to know." She paused again, weighing whether mentioning it at this point, before she had definitive answers, was the right thing to do.

"What's that?"

"Collin—Dr. Miller—is the father of Susan's child."

11

"Collin Miller is the father of the victim's child," he re-stated as if trying to digest this new nugget of information. He furrowed his brows. "You're positive about that?"

"Yes. Well, kind of. I mean, I don't have DNA proof, but my gut knows it." She realized how crazy she sounded, but it was too late. It was already out. *Should I mention the heterochromia? No,* she thought, *not yet.* She needed to do some more research first. Find out if it could be carried from a distant relative, skip generations. Besides, there was a possibility that it was coincidence that both Dr. Miller and the boy had it. *But was it really? Do you honestly believe that, Abby?* The detective's voice startled her back to the room.

"What makes you so sure?" He jotted something on his notepad, then focused his attention back on her. "According to reviews, Dr. Collin Miller has a good reputation as a marriage and family therapist in Blue Mist Mountain and around these parts. I've never seen him before, but no one has ever mentioned seeing him with a child. He's married, and if I remember correctly, his wife can't have children."

"Geez! Things seriously do get around in a small town. Personal things." She wondered exactly how much people knew about her family situation here. Probably much more than Travis admitted to.

"The only reason I remember that is because a few people mentioned how ironic it is that he's a marriage and family therapist and he doesn't have children, nor will he ever. They compared it to a priest doing marriage counseling."

"Oh." That made sense she supposed.

"So what makes you so sure he's the father of the victim's child?" he asked again.

"Well—as I said, I don't know for certain. I mean, I *know*, but…"

"We can't run with gut feelings, Ms. Sinclair. But we can look into it. It certainly gives us another avenue to explore." His pen went busily to the paper again before he looked back at her. "Can you tell me how you found this out?"

"Not if I want to keep my personal life confidential."

His eyes met hers, kind, yet firm. Unwavering. "We're investigating a homicide, Ms. Sinclair. For what it's worth, keeping your personal life confidential isn't my main concern right now."

Her cheeks warmed. Of course it wasn't. She focused a moment on a speck of something black on her jeans then shrugged and shook her head slowly. "From listening to people talk, that's not possible in a small town anyway. Besides, unfortunately, I've already had a few visits from your department." She put her hand up in the air and quickly added, "But not because of something I did."

He smiled at her. "Relax. I'm already familiar with the dealings at your place last summer."

"Of course you are."

"It shouldn't surprise you to know that we did a background check on you after finding Susan Ramirez in your hot tub. Especially since you're the one who found her."

He laid his pen down and leaned forward on his elbows, clasping his hands loosely in front of him. "What you went through was horrific, Ms. Sinclair. I don't know the details, but I suspect I'm on the right track. Trust me when I tell you I know what you might have gone through. The nightmare of it." He studied his notebook in front of him for a time, shifted a bit in his chair, then locked eyes with hers. "My mama was a victim of domestic violence. I watched my daddy beat her senseless too many times. One of those times—the last time—he came at me when I tried to protect her. I was eight years old. My mama was down. I thought she was dead. I went at my daddy, fully intending to kill him. He snapped me up like I was a little minnow in shallow water, then grabbed a butcher knife from the knife block on the counter." He shook his head, his eyes taking on a distant look. "God, I hated that knife block there. So easy for my daddy to get to. But my mama purposely set it there to cover a burned spot on the yellow laminate Formica counter so my daddy wouldn't see it. A burn that I'd caused. She made me promise not to tell daddy. Said it was our secret." He shook his head, clearing the distant memory then looked at Abby again. "The knife was to my throat, and he was about to kill me when my mama, by the grace of God, regained consciousness and managed to grasp the gun he'd brought with him into the fight. She shot him." He shook his head slowly. "He was so boozed up I don't even think he knew what happened when the bullet hit him. Normal for him to be drunk, but that was the worst I'd ever seen him."

Abby wiped her palms across her wet cheeks. "What happened? To your mama."

"Self-defense. New Mexico—that's where it was—doesn't have a Make My Day Law like Colorado does here. But they do have a form of self-defense as a defense to manslaughter." His eyes took a far-off look as he appeared to remember. "It says homicide is justified if it's committed due to a necessary need to defend life, family, or property. She has since died of cancer which made me madder than the domestic violence itself. Mad at God. But me and God, well, we were able to work it out."

"I'm so sorry," she whispered. She was grateful, of all things, that Hunter hadn't attempted to kill Cooper. "Because of what your mom went through, you can understand why I need to know what happened to Susan, can't you? To bring her justice."

"Why are you so convinced it was domestic?"

She sat back and sighed, slowly shaking her head.

"It's not that I don't believe you." He put his hands up, palms facing her, then re-clasped them on the table in front of him. "On the contrary. I'm simply brainstorming with you here."

Abby relaxed a bit, crossed one leg over the other, loosely crossing her arms in front of her. "Some of it is a strong gut feeling. Stronger than anything I've ever felt before. But also Dr. Miller used to be my therapist—"

"Used to be?" he asked.

"Yes. I severed that relationship this morning."

"Okay. Sorry to interrupt. Go on."

"A few days ago, when I was on my way home from my appointment, I realized I left my cell phone in his office. I turned around to go back and get it. There was someone in his office so—are you familiar with the layout of his office?"

He shook his head in the negative. He slid a piece of paper and a pen toward her across the desk. "Can you draw a diagram for me?"

"Sure." She took a moment to do as he asked. When she finished, she continued. "I was waiting in the hallway"—she drew an "x" where she had been—"which I knew I probably shouldn't have been, when Susan—I didn't know it was Susan at the time because I'd never seen her before—but she came out of his office looking so distraught. Almost terrified, I remember now. When Dr. Miller realized I saw her because I was where I wasn't supposed to be, he got really upset and swore me to secrecy. Doctor-patient confidentiality and all that. Well, he called me after that, making sure again that I wouldn't say anything. He said he would hate to be forced to reveal anything about my situation. Blackmail, if you ask me."

Her eyes flashed, and her teeth clenched together.

"Your situation?"

"Yeah. The reason I was seeing him to begin with." She paused before continuing. "How much do you know? About my, uh, situation."

"I know that you're one of millions. Not to minimize your situation, but there are far too many out there who have suffered as you have."

"But do you know my ex was—"

"A cop? Yes, I know. Which makes it an even greater disgrace. Not all of us are like your ex. In fact, few of us are. Most of us get into this line of work because we want to help, not hurt."

Shame warmed her cheeks. "I didn't mean to insinuate—"

"Anyone in your shoes would have wondered the same thing, Ms. Sinclair." He sat back casually, balancing on the back two legs of his chair while he pulled his notepad onto his lap, pen in hand. "So what happened with Collin Miller after that?"

"When Officer Johnson was questioning him in my house, he kept looking at me around the corner from the kitchen."

"Officer John—"

"Dr. Miller. Dr. Miller did. When Officer Johnson left, Dr. Miller told me I need to keep quiet about his therapist relationship with her."

"You have a son," he stated. "Where has he been during all of this?"

"He's in Washington with my sister for spring break. He was supposed to be back home that same day all of this happened, but they decided to wait for the storm to pass before coming back. I was disappointed at the time but thank God they did. Wait, I mean."

"Okay. And then?" he asked.

"I came in for an appointment with Dr. Miller this morning—"

"You felt okay continuing to see him?"

"I thought something was wrong, could sense it, but assumed maybe the whole situation just had me on high alert." She shrugged. "Like maybe I was grasping at something that wasn't there."

He shrugged. "Makes sense."

"Plus I wanted to ask him if I could use some of his office space for a group I'm planning." Renewed enthusiasm pushed her toward the edge of her chair as she told him of her plan. Surely, given his childhood, he would be as thrilled about it as she was. "I want to start a support group for domestic violence victims. I want to help other women who have suffered at the hands of violent men. Men who have tried to strip them of their hopes and dreams. But he said he forbids me to start the group." She laughed bitterly. "Can you believe it? He *forbids* me. Like I'm a child or something. I mean, he was so against it and acting so strange. That's when I severed our business relationship. He wasn't happy about it. To say the least." Renewed tension began forming a knot in her left shoulder, sending a zinger up to her head. She winced.

"You okay?"

She rubbed her temple. "Yeah. Residual, I guess." She saw the question in his eyes. "I'm fine, thank you."

"Maybe I can help you out with that."

Abby frowned. "With what?"

"A place. I'll check with the Chief to see if you can use the community room here for your meetings."

Abby gasped. "You'd do that?"

"Gladly." He held a hand up and said, "Don't get your hopes up yet, though. All I can do is ask. I can't see that it would be a problem, though."

"I could pay the department if necessary."

"No, no. It's a community room. Groups can use it for free. But because of the type of group it is, I just need to make sure there's not some conflict I'm unaware of. Seems it would be a safe place to meet."

She sat back as a thought occurred to her. "So long as the women aren't intimidated by meeting here, you know? Some of them might be afraid to come to a police station in case their abuser is watching them."

"With the library being connected to the PD, I can't see that as being a problem. They could use the library entrance and enter the PD through the internal door."

"Some of them might not trust that they aren't harming their abuser. Just because they want the abuse to stop doesn't mean they want the relationship to end. Many want to keep the relationship intact, just without the abuse. The apologetic phase of the abuse cycle, with the roses and hearts afterward, can give them the glimmer of hope they need to stay in an unhealthy relationship." She stopped abruptly and shook her head. "Sorry for rambling. You probably know all about that."

"Sadly, I know the cycle of abuse. Watched my mama fall for it for years. Even as a child, I could identify it."

"Do you have children, Detective Robles?"

"One. A little girl. Amy Rae." His eyes beamed as he spoke of her. "She's eleven."

"There's nothing a mother wouldn't do for her child. Or father," she added quickly, nodding toward him. "Most of them, anyway. Except those like my ex and your daddy. When I saw Susan that day outside of Dr. Miller's office, her terror haunted me. When I saw her down by the river later that day, I could see the pain and desperation. I could practically feel it. I know that sounds strange, but it was bouncing off of her right onto me. When Travis told me she was in a nasty custody battle—"

"Travis?"

"Yes, from the coffee shop. The Coffee Hub. He said he'd heard through the grapevine, being a small town and all, that she was in a nasty custody battle and that the father had temporary custody. He didn't know who the father was, which was strange to me. It's been my experience in the last several days that nothing is secret in a small town. Like literally nothing. So how is it possible to keep the identity of the father of Susan's child a secret? Unless the father has money. Or influence." She paused momentarily. "Wait—did I tell you Conrad dated Susan briefly? It was a few years back. But I'm certain Dr. Miller is the father." She waited for him to finish scribbling his notes, then continued. "John and Carrie Appleton were staying at the resort this past week. They're from Canada. Turns out John and Dr. Miller are related somehow. I think they're brothers." She saw the question in his eyes. "I overheard them talking just a bit ago when they passed behind me as I waited at the crosswalk. Dr. Miller was trying to be unrecognizable." Again she saw the question in his eyes. "He had on a hat that covered a lot of his face. And sunglasses. With the weather being what it is, no one would have thought it odd.

"I was heading to the real estate office and walked past the Dairy Queen. I looked in the window and saw Carrie with a little boy. It was the same little boy I'd seen follow them out from Rocky's Burgers earlier that day when I was going home from Dr. Miller's office. Except at that time I assumed the little boy belonged to the couple that walked out behind him. Especially when I saw the two couples, along with the little boy, talking by one of the cars. But I was mistaken about the boy belonging to the other couple."

"How do you know that?"

"Because I saw the boy with Carrie," she said.

"What makes you so certain he's Dr. Miller's kid?" Robles asked.

"Heterochromia."

"Hetero what?"

"Heterochromia." She explained it to him, the presence in both Dr. Miller and Ryan, and that it's frequently hereditary. "I know about it because of a student I had when I was teaching back in Oakland. I'm not sure if you've ever seen Dr. Miller up close, but his left eye is half brown, half blue."

"Why couldn't it be a coincidence? What makes you so certain that it's those specific two, the child and Collin, that are related?"

"There were too many coincidences and connections between them. Also, because I confronted him."

"You what?" Detective Robles sat straight up in his chair, at attention. "You realize how dangerous that could have been for you, right? If he had something to do with Susan's death, as I'm guessing you suspect is the case, that could have been a deadly move."

"It was just now, in town. There would have been plenty of witnesses had he tried to do something. And I can't let Susan's death be for nothing. When he grabbed my arm—"

"He physically grabbed you?" he asked, his tone and eyes in sync with each other. "Do you want to file charges?"

"No. I just want him to be held responsible for what he did to Susan. The man should not be a family and marriage therapist if he's ripping people's families apart. He admitted to this happening with two of his patients."

"He admitted to it?" he asked in disbelief.

"Yes. And then had the nerve to say the women are the ones who came on to him. Can you believe it?"

"Ms. Sinclair," he said, exhaling while sitting back, clasping his hands behind his head, "I need you to promise me you're not going to get any more involved in this than you already are. Promise me you'll step back and let us handle it from here. Let *me* handle it."

"Okay." Her head spun at how quickly she gave in. Apparently, she actually trusted this man. A police detective.

It was then she realized that another step of the healing process had clicked into place like a Lego piece in a work in progress. "He was watching me as I came in here a while ago," she said.

"He was in the area, or he was specifically watching you?"

"Watching me, I think. He was standing on the sidewalk against the back of the parking lot, staring at me."

He frowned. "Looks like I need to talk with the good doctor. Today." He jotted some more notes. "Abby, do you smoke?"

Abby jerked back. "Ugh. No, I don't touch the stuff. Why?"

"Does your father?"

"Occasionally. Why?" She noticed the slightest change in his eyes.

"Crime scene techs found a cigarette butt buried in the snow by the hot tub. Appeared fresh." He seemed to wait a moment, studying her, then said, "Be careful. And keep the police on speed dial. Thank you for coming in."

She pushed her chair back, the back legs catching on the carpet, nearly causing her to tip over. Detective Robles quickly reached to steady her. He walked to the door and opened it for her, following her back out to the lobby.

"Ms. Sinclair," Robles said, "if you remember anything else, please give me a call." He extended another business card between two fingers, probably assuming she'd tossed the first one he gave her. "And if Collin Miller seems to be following you, call me immediately."

"I'll do that. Thank you, Detective." She reached out her hand to shake his.

"Call me Juan. I have a feeling we'll be talking with each other a lot."

12

When Abby left the precinct, she turned when she reached the bottom of the stairs to see Detective Robles standing at the door. She looked every which way as she walked across the parking lot and to her car. There was no sign of Dr. Miller, John, or Carrie. Other than an officer who appeared to be jotting down a license plate number from a black SUV, the only person she saw was a man sitting alone on a concrete bench, oblivious to her presence, as he read some kind of brochure, plaid cap askew on his head. She wasn't sure if she was relieved or more on alert than before. After all, the devil you see is less dangerous than the devil you don't.

Nevertheless, she was on high alert until she reached her car, looked in the back seat, and locked the door the moment it closed. She took a moment to sit still and bask in the safe silence of her car. The spring sun, which made the streets and sidewalks a wet mess, was wonderfully warm in her car. Her conversation with Collin—yes, Collin. She didn't have to call him Dr. Miller anymore. He wasn't her doctor. Their conversation when he yanked her between the buildings, replayed in her mind. His behavior reminded her of one who was cornered, who knew his days were numbered. Abby's breathing quickened a bit. What would he do to be sure that wasn't the case? Exactly what was he capable of? Would she end up with the same fate as Susan? Had she survived Hunter only to succumb to Collin's evil?

She shivered and shook her head, struggling to clear the image of the woman floating in her hot tub. *What have you gone and done, Abigail?* But then, stronger than ever, the desire to help abused women from men bent on destruction and ruin, high on control, took over. She couldn't help but wonder if her experience made her stronger or stupid. Depended on who she asked, she supposed. Gabe would likely not be pleased. Sure, he would understand and support her. He always did. But he wouldn't like that she was putting her safety at risk.

She imagined his reaction when she told him the latest events that transpired since they'd last spoke just that morning. He'd be quiet as he mulled it over, processing all of the possibilities. She imagined him pulling her toward him, holding her close, his chin resting on the top of her head. She always felt so safe in his arms. So secure. The world couldn't touch her when she was in that place. She longed to be there at this very moment. Instead, she was riddled with fear of the unknown as she made one final sweep of her surroundings before starting her car and pulling onto the road. She was grateful Cooper hadn't been able to come home yet. She needed to work fast to find Susan's killer, and if it was Collin, to be sure he wasn't around to hurt anyone else. Or worse. She shuddered.

Collin walked into the lobby of the Blue Mist Mountain Police Department and slipped off his cap and sunglasses. The woman at the front desk, elderly and flamboyant, caught his attention. He strolled across the lobby to her desk.

"I'd like to speak to the person in charge of the Ramirez homicide please," he said.

"Dr. Miller?" Pearl said.

He extended a hand over the counter. "Have we met?"

Pearl smiled. "I know your wife. Well, not *know* her, but we've met."

"How's that?" Collin tilted his head to the side.

"Same nail salon," she said. "You know how we women get to talking when we're getting our hair and nails done," she said, holding up and wiggling fingers that sported her brightly polished nails. "Don't worry, it was all good. About you, anyway." She winked at him.

He raised his eyebrows. "About me?"

"Why, sure. Usually, women swap tales of woe, but I don't have a husband to talk about. So we talked about you. Just a little bit." She held her forefinger and her thumb millimeters apart.

"Divorced?" he asked.

"Widowed," she said, sadness creeping in the edges of her eyes. He'd become all too familiar with that look over the years. The look of loneliness, no matter how insistent they were that they were fine.

"I'm so sorry," he said with all the empathy he could muster at the moment. Which at this point was pretty much zilch.

"He's in a better place now," Pearl said with a certainty he admired.

Collin wondered how she was so sure. How could anyone be sure what was after this life? He somewhat envied her that she found such peace in believing something so solidly. He, on the other hand, didn't have time to ponder it any further.

He had damage control to do because of what he was sure Abby had done. "So about the Ramirez murder, is the detective in charge of the case here?"

"Have a seat over there," she said, pointing to the row of black vinyl chairs that lined one wall, "and I'll check."

"Thank you. If he's busy I can wait," he said. "I'm in no hurry." If it was the same man that stood at the door as Abby left, the one he remembered from the crime scene, Collin knew he was still there. There hadn't been enough time for him to go anywhere since Abby left. Besides, Collin had been watching the door from his car which he moved to an empty spot near the precinct, careful to tuck it between two large pickup trucks.

He stood there long enough to watch her pick up the phone to be sure she called the detective's office without giving him some bogus excuse that he was busy or in a meeting or God only knows what else. When Collin was satisfied that she'd truly called him, he turned and walked to a row of black vinyl chairs. He chose one that didn't have a tear in the seat with yellow foam escaping. The only one, by the looks of it.

He watched Pearl talk. He tried to hear what she was saying, but she kept her voice too low. Her mouth was hidden behind the counter so he couldn't read her lips either. When she lay the receiver back in the cradle, she lifted her chin to look at him over the countertop. "He'll be out in a moment, Dr. Miller."

"Thank you."

Collin unzipped his coat the rest of the way and tucked his hands in its pockets. He glanced around the room, resting his sights on a woman standing against the far wall. *Nice.* His gaze scanned her from head to toe, coming to rest on her eyes. She had the most gorgeous hazel eyes with the longest coal-black lashes he'd ever seen. They were haunting. Her eyes met his. He quickly averted his. He had to be extra cautious since Abby Sinclair was hell-bent on portraying him as a villain. He cursed the day she'd walked into his office. Little did he know that she'd be such trouble. If she'd only minded her own business, he could have helped her heal from her past.

"Dr. Miller?" Detective Robles said, startling Collin back to the present and a sharp reminder of where he was. "Come on back."

Collin followed him through the doors behind the counter, turned left, then right, into a small rectangular room. The walls were a dreary gray, the paint chipping. There was one window high on the wall, limiting the view outside to the top of what looked to be a clump of aspen trees. Probably lent some color to the drab room in the fall, he thought. He noticed the camera up high in one corner, a tiny red light flashing. He was being recorded.

"Have a seat. I'm Detective Robles," he said, motioning to the chair on the opposite side of the table he sat down at. "Thanks for coming in. Saved me a phone call."

He was right about Abby. She wasn't going to let this rest. "I remember you from Ms. Sinclair's house on the day of—" he cleared his throat and shifted in his seat, "the incident."

The detective opened a notepad, pen poised and ready. "What can you tell me about Susan Ramirez?"

"Not much. I mean, with patient-doctor confidentiality and all."

"You and I both know, Doctor—do you hold a Ph.D. or a PsyD?"

"Ph.D. Why does it matter which I am? All you need to know is that I'm innocent of any BS Ms. Sinclair is accusing me of."

"What can you tell me about her mental health? Susan's, not Ms. Sinclair's."

"Nothing. I can't tell you anything even if I wanted to. The therapist-patient privilege survives the death of the patient, Detective. But I'm sure you know that."

"I can get a warrant for her records."

"We can revisit it at that time, when and if you get that warrant. Until then, my hands are tied. I want to help you catch whoever did this, but—"

"But you can't."

"Correct."

"Yet," Robles said.

"What I can tell you is that Abigail Sinclair had an unhealthy obsession with Ms. Ramirez."

"How so?" Detective Robles sat back in his chair, tipping onto the back legs.

"I think she wanted her to be what she was once herself. A victim. So she didn't feel so alone in her past," Collin said.

"I don't follow."

"Misery loves company. I can't get into it any deeper without disclosing confidential information. But you might want to look into Abigail's mental health. From someone other than me. I think you'll be surprised at what you'll find."

"What is it you think we'll find if we look? Aside from your records, of course."

"Abigail is trying to validate herself, redeem her reputation, by tarnishing someone else's. In this case, that someone is Ms. Ramirez. As well as myself." He swallowed hard and continued. "This is hard for me to say but trust me when I tell you that you need to check into Abigail Sinclair for the murder of Susan Ramirez."

"Why are you able to tell me things about Ms. Sinclair and not Ms. Ramirez?"

"My professional relationship with Ms. Sinclair was severed this morning. What I'm telling you isn't related to anything we discussed in our sessions but rather her behavior outside of our contractual relationship. From just this morning, as a matter of fact." He crossed his arms as he sat back in his chair.

"What happened this morning?" Robles asked, watching him closely.

"She didn't tell you?" Robles didn't say anything but waited for him to continue. Collin uncrossed his arms and leaned forward, placing one hand on the table, palm down. "Ms. Sinclair insisted my nephew was my love child with Ms. Ramirez. She was acting very strange. I don't know if she was on something or what, but it was frightening even for me, and I've seen a lot in all my years of being a therapist." Collin paused, sat back, crossed his arms again, and continued. "I'm sure she told you about heterochromia," he scoffed. When Robles didn't respond either way, Collin went on. "It's true, it is hereditary. But not only between a parent and a child. It can run in families."

Robles looked directly into his left eye, absently toying with a pen between his thumb and two fingers.

"The boy is my nephew, Detective," Collin said. "Abigail became belligerent when she used that to tie me and my nephew together as father and son. I led her out of the line of traffic, away from the eyes—pardon the pun—of the growing curiosity of passersby to spare her the embarrassment she was creating for herself. She was making all kinds of ludicrous accusations and threats. Like I said, she was acting very strange." Collin looked at the camera in the corner by the ceiling, making sure the little red light was still blinking. He crossed one leg over the other, jiggling his foot ever so slightly. "Someone has to stop her, Detective. Please. I don't know what she's capable of. Perhaps even murder." He leaned forward and breathed deep. "Fact of the matter is, after the last threat she issued me, I think it would be best if I file for a restraining order."

Detective Robles studied him carefully. "You need to do what you feel you must. But I think I can say with certainty that Abigail Sinclair is no threat."

"You didn't see or hear her this morning, sir. I did. I'm in fear for my safety and that of my wife. And I fear for the safety of my nephew. She tried to tell him Susan Ramirez was his mother. Do you know how that can damage a child? I'm not sure what else she may do to him."

Robles was silent, watching him closely. Too closely. Finally, he spoke. "I'm sure you're familiar with the restraining order process. You will need to fill out the appropriate forms from the judicial website and then call the Court to get the days or times when the hearings are scheduled. Or for any additional filing requirements. Keep in mind, though, that you'll need to give specific information about what happened, including the names of anyone else who might have been present. Including your nephew."

"I'm aware of how to go about getting a restraining order. This isn't my first go-round. I just want her to stay away from me and my family, Detective. People like Ms. Sinclair are one of the hazards of my job. I can handle it, but when it threatens my family, well, that's another matter."

"As I said, Dr. Miller, you have to do whatever it is you feel is necessary." He stood up and pushed his chair away from the table. Collin did the same. "I'll call you if I need anything else."

"Please don't hesitate." He reached out and shook the detective's hand. Collin reached the door when Robles's voice stopped him.

"Collin?"

"Yes?" he asked, turning to face him.

"Where were you the night of Wednesday, March 24th and the early morning hours of Thursday, March 25th?"

"I was home with my wife and then at the office."

"Your wife can vouch for that? The being at home part, I mean."

"Yes, she can."

"And your office? What time was that?" Robles asked him.

"I went in early. About five."

"That's pretty early. Can anyone vouch for that?"

"No." Collin's gaze rested on Robles, his voice quiet as he asked, "Am I a suspect, Detective?"

"At this point, sir, everyone is."

Collin narrowed his eyes. "As I said, you'd do well checking into Abigail Sinclair. Good day."

On Abby's way home, the words between her and Collin churned in her head over and over, creating quite the storm. She was beginning to wonder what was real and what was growing into something that perhaps wasn't at all. Fear jumbled it all up. She had a strong suspicion that whether directly or indirectly, Collin had something to do with Susan

Ramirez's death. But she had no proof. And without proof, all she had were theories the police could do nothing with.

After rounding a sharp bend in the road, she looked into her rear-view mirror. A dark-colored sedan, several car-lengths back, was the only other car on the road. For a Friday, it was odd. Several other resorts and rental condominiums she passed had vacancy signs posted by the road. Thank goodness it wasn't just hers. She suspected the snowstorm, despite being much lighter than had been forecasted initially, caused a great number of cancellations.

She looked in her rear-view mirror again as she prepared to turn left onto the road that led to her resort, and she gasped. The black sedan was right on her bumper. If she sped up, she'd miss her turn. Instead, she slowed and pulled over on the side of the road. The sedan pulled over behind her, trailing right on her bumper. She rolled her window down enough to stick her arm out, waving the car around her. But it stayed where it was. The car's dark tinted windows prevented her from seeing who it was. Her breath quickened, and she started going again, the car turning onto the same road she did. Glancing behind her, she hoped to catch a glimpse of something, anything, as the car turned, but the window tint was just too dark, even with the car close to her bumper as it was. What was this maniac's problem? The car's front license plate was covered with dirty snow so she couldn't get a plate number.

With one mile left to go, she sped up, but the car stayed on her bumper. She fished for Detective Robles's business card with one hand, steering with the other, swerving when she saw two bighorn sheep on the side of the road. She narrowly missed one of them. Finally grasping the card between her forefinger and thumb, she clutched her phone and began punching in the number with her thumb. It rolled into voice mail, so she called the main desk.

"Pearl?" she asked when the woman answered. "Is Detective Robles there?"

"Hi, Ms. Sinclair. He's in with Dr. Miller."

"Dr. Miller is there?"

"Sure is. Came in right after you left."

"He came in there?" she asked, more baffled than ever. What was he up to?

"Want me to have the detective call you?"

Abby looked in her rear-view mirror only to find the car was now gone, nowhere to be seen. Any potential threat was gone. She took a deep breath. "Nah. Thank you, anyway, Pearl."

She hung up and realized she might have a much bigger problem. If the menacing car hadn't been Collin, then who was it?

13

When Abby got home, Jeremiah was in the store talking with Cody and Roxanne. Roxanne laughed loudly at something Cody had just said, bumping her shoulder into Cody's.

"That is not a story, Mr. Jordan. I swear I caught that thing on nothing more than a bare hook, but it got away," Cody said, laughing.

Abby heard her father chuckle. Her suspicions of the two guests were long gone.

"Hi guys," Abby said, stepping down the two stairs leading into the store. She stood beside Jeremiah. "Are we telling fishing stories about the big one that got away?"

Roxanne laughed, her eyes twinkling as she looked at Cody, pointing toward him with her thumb. "He is. That's a man for ya."

"Don't take this the wrong way, Ms. Sinclair," Cody said, "but you look beat."

"You should have come with us. Fresh air and an afternoon of fishing can cure anything. Even all of what's happened here."

Shame crept up on her for even thinking the two of them could have been capable of murder. "Probably would have had more fun than I had in town. In fact I *know* I would have."

"Going again tomorrow if you want to go with us," Cody offered. "Then you can be witness to the big one that got away."

Roxanne laughed and put an arm around his waist. "Come on, hotshot. I'll fry up the one fish you did catch."

"Can I ask you both a question?" Abby asked, regretting that she had to change the subject to something so serious. "Did either of you happen to see or hear anything out of the ordinary the morning we found the body? Anything at all?"

She watched as each shook their head. "Sorry," Cody said. "Wish we could help you, but neither of us saw or heard anything. We've been wracking our brains trying to remember anything at all, but no luck."

"I'm just glad everyone else left so we could stay and not worry about our safety," Roxanne said. "Sorry if that's selfish, but..." She shrugged. "I know it's not good for business, but it looks like a couple more people checked in since you left."

"Is that true, Pops?" Abby asked.

"Yup. I lit the vacant sign and got two of the cabins rented."

"But how? I haven't even cleaned them yet. And the cleaning lady isn't due for another two days."

"We did it," Roxanne said. "Asked Mr. Jordan here where the cleaning supplies were and got 'er done. Figured it's the least we could do."

Shame washed over her again. When had she become so quick to suspect people of the worst? "Thank you both so much. I don't know what to say."

"No need to say anything at all," Cody said. "It's our gift to you."

"And mine to you is a free night," Abby said. "Thank you. Really." She stepped around the counter and gave them each a quick hug. "Enjoy your dinner. Hope it's a trout you caught. They're the best."

"It is," said Cody, smiling. "See you two tomorrow."

Abby watched as the two left, closing the door behind them.

"Talk to me, pumpkin," Jeremiah said.

"Someone followed me just after Bear Creek Drive." She continued telling him what happened. "Pops," she said when she'd finished, "if it wasn't Collin Miller, then who?"

"John and Carrie?"

"No. They had a red Ford Escape."

"I don't like this."

She shuddered. "You and me both. But I'll be darned if I'm going to sit back and let some freak scare me to death."

"It's the *death* part that worries me."

"Gabe will be here soon," she said, feeling lighter at the mention of his name. "Which two cabins are rented?"

"Two and four."

"Okay." She pushed off from the counter and said, "I need to walk off some stress. Think I'll take Gus for a quick walk around here before dinner and before Gabe gets here."

"Don't think that's a good idea." He frowned, and she gave him a side hug. If the roles were different and it was she and Cooper, she'd feel the same way. She'd do anything she could to talk him out of it. But it wasn't Cooper. It was her. And she refused to let someone get the best of her.

"I'll have Gus, Pops. I know black labs are hardly ferocious, but his size will keep anyone at bay. I'll be okay. Besides, I'm staying right around here. Gussie probably needs to get out, anyway. He's been neglected with everything else that's been going on." She held up her phone. "I'll keep this in my hand at all times."

"Be back before dusk."

"I can if I leave right now." She slipped into her snow boots, slithered Gus into his harness, his enthusiasm for a walk making it difficult. She clipped the leash on and opened the door, calling over her shoulder, "I'll be back in half an hour tops."

Her boots crunched in the snow as she walked off the shoveled path and onto a trail that led to a side road. She often saw wildlife on this particular road and kept a tight hold on Gus's leash. The air was infused with pine and the smell only mountain air can give. She inhaled deeply, closing her eyes briefly as she did. This was exactly what she needed. Her phone buzzed, indicating an incoming text message. She held it up to see the screen. Piper letting her know they'd be starting on Sunday and planned to be at Abby's by Monday evening.

She stopped and wrapped Gus's leash on her wrist. *Can't wait to see my boy,* she texted back. *You guys drive careful and keep me posted. Is he there?*

No. Slider made a surprise visit, and the two went to pick out a movie for tonight, Piper sent back.

That explains why he hasn't texted me back from earlier. Slider takes precedence.

Stop whining.

Abby laughed, her voice echoing in the stillness. *As soon as he gets back, tell him to text me. Better yet, to call me. I want to hear his voice.*

Yeah, yeah. TTYL.

Remember who's kid he is. Mine! Abby smiled, knowing that would get her sister's goat.

Stop being the spoiled little sister.

But I do it so well.

Abby watched the screen, but there was no response. Which was a response in and of itself. Abby laughed, the sound echoing in the silence.

She tucked her phone into her pocket, keeping her fingers wrapped around it, and firmly grasped Gus's leash again with the other hand. There were few tire tracks in the snow. Knowing it wasn't a well-known road made her feel safer. It wasn't a through road at all. It only linked three resorts. So unless someone was from the immediate area, they wouldn't even know it existed. Abby's phone buzzed again. She pulled it out and looked.

U OK?

Her father rarely sent a text, and when he did, it was only enough to barely understand and nothing more.

Yes. Be home in 15.

She waited for a moment to see if he would respond. When he didn't, the phone went back in her pocket.

Gus lumbered lazily beside her, sniffing here and there, perking up briefly when he saw a rabbit. But when it hopped out of sight, Gus's interest waned. He lifted his leg marking where the rabbit had just been, then continued on. Abby let him set the pace. A few steps further and a squirrel chittered from a pine branch above them as if taunting him. Gus looked up, watched a moment, the little critter getting louder. When Gus eventually lost interest, Abby looked up at the squirrel and it chittered loudly at her. "Bully," she said, chuckling.

Car tires sloshing through the melting snow behind her snagged her attention. As they got closer, she stepped off to the side to avoid the splash that would inevitably happen. She tugged Gus's leash, keeping him close to her. She turned around to look and saw the same dark sedan with the tinted windows from earlier.

Her breath caught, and her heart felt like it was beating in her throat. Her fear set Gus on alert. His body stiffened. He stopped, then looked up at her. She was torn between continuing forward to one of the resorts about a hundred yards further up or turning back toward home, which was about the same distance, perhaps a bit shorter. The problem with that plan was she'd be leading the creep to her home. That and she'd be walking directly toward his car, which was following slowly at a short distance behind her.

She stepped further off to the side, her boots ankle high in slush. Forward it was. Her muscles tensed and her breathing quickened. Maybe it was nothing. It's not as if her mind hadn't played tricks on her before, tricks that sprang from her paranoia from days past. Maybe the fact that he was going so slow was simple consideration so he didn't splash her with his tires. As much as she tried to convince herself of that, she failed.

Abby pushed the speed dial button for her father as she continued walking forward, her legs shaking. She turned to see the car keeping the same distance away until it pulled forward, slowly, menacingly, passing her. She sucked in her breath and held it as she waited, not knowing for what exactly, but waiting for something unpleasant she was sure would happen. But nothing did.

"Abby?" Jeremiah answered.

"Stay on the phone with me, Pops."

"Where are you?" he said. "What's wrong?"

"There's a car following me. It's the same one from earlier, I think."

"I'm on my way." She heard something crash. It sounded like the stool that they kept behind the counter in the store toppled over.

"Hold on..." She looked over as the car finally passed. It was so close she could have reached out and touched it with her hand. She kept Gus within a foot of her and took a good, hard look at the driver's side window, able to catch a glimpse of the driver as he passed her. She did a double take. Surely this had to be a joke. The man wore a plaid cap, mustache, and a pipe, all Sherlock style. Despite odd, it piqued her interest. And she'd noticed this same man earlier today, without the Sherlock getup. But where?

"Abby!" Her father's voice sounded over the phone, the urgency palpable. "Where are you?"

"Sorry, Pops. On Walking Stick Trail. He just passed me."

"He? Who?"

"I don't know. I saw him earlier today, but I can't remember where."

"So he's following you?"

"It would appear so. I don't know, maybe I'm overreacting. It's not like it's a private road or a big town."

"Better to overreact than to wish you had. I'm coming up on you now. I can see both you and Gus."

Abby waited until he pulled up beside her before she hung up the phone. She opened the tailgate for Gus to hop in, closed it after he settled on the blanket tucked in the truck bed, then went around and got in the truck.

"Some watchdog Gussie is," she said, fastening her seatbelt. "He was more nervous than I was."

"I knew it was a bad idea for you to go out, Abs."

"I can't imagine why someone would be after me. I haven't done anything. Literally nothing. That's what makes me think I'm making something out of nothing."

"You've upset that doctor fella."

"But he was in with Detective Robles when I was driving home. I called Pearl, and she told me he was there. This was the same car. I'm sure of it."

"Did you get a plate number?"

She sighed, frustrated with herself. "No. Earlier I couldn't because the dirty slop from the roads covered it. And just now...well, I was too worried about seeing who it was and didn't even give the plate a second thought." She slammed her hand on the armrest of the door. "Geez! How could I be so stupid! It was right there. Pops, I could have reached out and touched his car when he passed."

He reached over and briefly rubbed her shoulder. "Don't beat yourself up." He glanced over at her as they turned into the driveway. "You're a hundred percent sure that it was the same car?"

"Not a hundred percent, no. But ninety-five."

"You need to call the Detective."

"And tell him what?"

"That a car has been following you."

"Earlier the driver could have just been lost. You know how tourists are. They practically ride their brakes around here looking for a turnoff or for wildlife."

He tossed her an unbelieving glare. "And this time?"

"I'm acting stupid, I know."

"You said it."

She winced. "Ouch."

"You're full of excuses."

"I guess I'm just afraid of making something out of nothing. Of looking like an idiot. And I'm mad. So mad!" She looked out the window. "If it wasn't Collin the first time, and this was the same car—well, the man behind the steering wheel wasn't Collin."

"Someone killed a woman and put her body in your hot tub. We don't know who that was. That man is still out there."

She knew he was right. She could try convincing herself until the cows come home that it was nothing. The bottom line is she didn't *know* anything. Except that there was a killer out there somewhere. Out *here.*

"I guess it was pretty dumb to go out for a walk just to prove a point. To prove that I'm not going to let some creep intimidate me."

"Stubborn. That's what you are."

She exhaled loudly. "I know, I know. I told you it was dumb. Can we drop it?"

"As soon as you call it in."

"Fine." But her tone said it was anything but fine. None of this was *fine.* And despite her rebellious, childish objection, she knew she needed to call Detective Robles. Now. She pulled her phone out and began punching in his number. "Think I'll call Piper tonight and give her the rundown. I don't want Cooper home until the threat has passed."

"That could be a long time."

"Then I'll just have to make sure it's not."

14

When Abby walked in the kitchen door, a cold draft greeted her from the living room. She unclipped Gus's leash, tugging the harness from around his thick chest.

"Pops? Did you leave the door open back there?" She jerked her thumb toward the store.

"Unlocked, but not open," he said. "Was in a hurry to get to you."

She shivered and not from the cold. "Someone's been in here. I'll call Cody and Roxanne's cabin and see if they've been in." She reached for the phone and the laminated list of phone numbers for each cabin.

He was on her heels as she descended the two stairs. "Anything missing?" he asked.

"Not that I can tell. Looks like someone's been nosing around behind the counter though."

In one step, he was behind the till and opened it, rifling through the bills. "Nothing appears to be disturbed in here. Not that there was anything in there to disturb," he mumbled.

Abby hung up the phone. "Cody said neither of them has been in here." She looked at him. "You said no money was taken?"

"Doesn't appear so."

She strode over and closed the door, taking in her surroundings. "Can't blame it on the bottle this time, can I?"

"Never stopped you before."

His typical calm speaking pattern sounded clipped.

She stood still and looked at him, but he refused to meet her gaze. She rolled her eyes and sighed. "Look, Pops, I didn't mean anything by it. We've moved passed that," she said, referring to an incident last summer when one of his drinking binges caused her some havoc at the resort. Still, he said nothing and didn't look at her. She slapped her hand on her leg. "Oh, come on. Stop acting like the victim." She looked at him, eyes narrowed. "Just give up the booze and make it easier on everyone."

"Now what would be the fun in that?"

She shook her head slowly and ignored his comment. It didn't deserve one. "I think we're both a little hypersensitive with everything that's going on. This is a business. There's going to be people in and out. Especially in the store." She looked around once again. "Aha! See?" She picked up a ten-dollar bill tucked under the right side of the register. "Someone obviously needed something and was honest enough to leave the money." She laughed, feeling relieved. "Gabe should be here any minute. Then I'll feel better."

"Me too. Another set of eyes watching over you."

"Take a break, Pops. Go watch some TV or read a book. I'm going to go through a few things in here and make sure everything is good."

"Want me to make you a coffee first?" he asked.

The coffee bar with the fancy coffee machine had become a fast favorite for all of them. Her father even learned to use it, which surprised her. "How about I make us both a good chai tea latte?" she suggested.

"That'd be good, I 'spose."

Abby expertly worked behind the coffee bar, in no time at all producing two large cups of steaming tea.

As soon as Jeremiah left with his, Abby decided to take a thorough look around, thanks to a niggling discomfort in the pit of her stomach she couldn't quite shake. She found it more and more challenging to know when she was paranoid and when there was adequate cause for concern. The two sometimes blended together.

The laptop was left open, something she didn't do. She logged in to see if anything was out of the ordinary. Nothing was. But if a trespasser didn't have the password, she supposed it wouldn't be. "Explainable," she mumbled, trying to convince herself. "I might have been distracted and left it open. Or maybe Pops did."

Cup in hand, she walked around the store, doing a visual check through all the shelves and bins, including the bait, which was minimal at best this time of year. Nothing appeared to be missing or out of order. And yet—well, something felt out of place. She made one more run through. Still nothing. But there was something about the air. Or rather *in* the air.

She stood still, holding her tea away from her nose so it didn't distract from what she tried to smell. There it was. She sniffed again. Cologne. Faint, but present, nonetheless. Her father didn't wear cologne. And then it hit her, and she realized why it made her so uneasy. It was the same smell as Collin's office. Collin had been here. She was sure of it. Another attempt to convince her to leave things alone, no doubt. Well, she couldn't. For Susan's sake. And for the sake of Susan's little boy. But she had absolutely no proof whatsoever that he had been there, just her gut feeling and the faint smell of a cologne that many men probably wore. That wasn't enough to call Detective Robles again. If she called him for every little thing—well, the way things were going, if she called him every time something weird happened, he may as well stay in one of the cabins. Someone was in the store, that was certain. They left a ten-dollar bill by the cash register. As for Collin, she knew for a fact that he was capable of unethical, disgusting behavior, but she didn't think he could have murdered someone. *Could he?* She shook her head. No, she didn't want to believe that. There had to be another explanation.

Deciding all was okay and as it should be, she reached on the shelf below the counter for her cell phone to check if Cooper called. Her fingers brushed against the binoculars she kept there.

Seeing nothing from Cooper, she picked up the binoculars and adjusted them accordingly. She looked out over the lake, spotting two bald eagles perched on the edge of a chunk of ice. She watched them for a few minutes as they waited to snatch fish from the water with their powerful talons. She turned her sights out the window to the right toward the cabins. A man and a woman were standing outside one of the newly rented cabins, the man flipping burgers on the grill with one gloved hand, the other hand circling a beer bottle. The woman stood huddled beside him, the fur-lined hood of her coat flipped up over her head, one hand shoved deep into her coat pocket, the other holding a glass of wine.

Abby studied them for a moment. They kissed, and she quickly turned away, not wanting to be a voyeur. She trained the binoculars to the left, out the window that led into the woods. The sun had begun to set, making it appear darker through the trees. As she scanned the woods, slowly, she spotted someone staring back at her through binoculars of his own! She inhaled sharply, froze, dropped her binoculars and screamed, all in a split second. The man had been wearing a checkered cap and had a mustache, the same as the man from the car that had followed her!

Jeremiah rushed from the living room, Gabe in through the door from outside into the store. Jeremiah landed on her left, Gabe on her right.

"Gabe!" she said, breathless, as she flung herself in his arms.

"Abs, what's wrong?" Jeremiah asked, his voice panic-stricken.

"The man," she gasped. "The same one, with the hat. He was out there looking at me. He was—"

"What man?" Gabe asked, reaching for the binoculars with one hand, keeping the other arm wrapped around Abby.

Jeremiah proceeded to fill him in on the events of the afternoon. "Did you call the detective?" he asked Abby when Jeremiah finished.

"I left him a voicemail. I was sitting out here in the store waiting for him to call me back when I looked out the window and saw him. That man. He was staring back at me. He was over there!" She poked her finger toward the woods.

"What's this detective's phone number? I'm calling again," Gabe said. "And why am I first hearing about all of this now, Abby?" he asked while punching in the number from the card Abby handed him.

"I didn't want you to worry when there was nothing you could have done from the road anyway. I was going to tell you when you got here. And then *this* happened." She shivered, and he held her closer, tighter. For the first time all day, she felt truly safe.

"Detective Robles, please," Gabe said into the phone.

"Now do you believe me when I tell you these are not simply coincidences? Someone is following you," Jeremiah said.

"I believe that now. What I don't know is why." She half-listened to Gabe tell Robles what her father had just moments ago divulged to him. "I haven't done anything except tell Collin what he did was wrong," she said to no one in particular.

"He knows you enough to know you won't let it drop at that," Jeremiah said.

"But Collin was at the police department the first time, and he wasn't the one behind the steering wheel the second time. Or the man behind the binocs."

"Was it John?" Gabe asked, setting his phone on the counter.

"No, it wasn't John."

"John in disguise to throw you off?" he pressed.

Abby thought about this, then shook her head. "Uh-uh. No, it wasn't him."

"Well, it's gotta be someone connected to Dr. Miller. Could he have hired someone?"

Abby shrugged. "Hadn't thought about that." She reached for her phone. "What if it's not Collin at all and there's some other maniac out there? What if I accidentally cut the wrong person off in traffic? That's happened, right? I mean not with me, but you hear about things like that." She punched in a single number on her phone. "I'm calling Pip. I don't want my son home until the threat is gone." She let it ring until it went to voicemail. "Hey, Pip. Call me ASAP. We need to talk before you head out."

She'd no sooner put her phone down when it rang. She snatched it back up but didn't have a chance to say anything before Piper's voice sounded.

"What's wrong. Is it Dad?"

"No, it's not Dad." Abby began an explanation, skimming over anything that wasn't a critical point, making it as brief as possible. "I can't have Cooper here when I don't know who's behind this."

"For God's sake, Abby! Why didn't you tell me this before?"

"I don't know."

"That's all you got? I don't know?" she asked incredulously.

"That's all I got. I guess I was hoping it would be nothing and I wouldn't have to say anything."

"Well so much for that theory. It sounds like it's *some*thing."

"Listen, Piper, I have to go."

"Where?"

"Gabe just got here. But put my kid on first. I miss him like crazy." Her heart ached as she thought of Cooper.

"Hey, Mom." Tears filled her eyes as she heard his voice.

"Hey, buddy. You sound older." When had his voice begun to change? Her heart twisted painfully.

"Are you crying?"

"No," she lied. Gabe's strong, warm hand rested on the small of her back, comforting her. "How are you doing?" she asked Cooper.

"Good. I wanna come home though."

"Yeah?" She smiled through her tears. "Can't be soon enough for me, I can tell ya that."

"See you on Monday. Say hi to Grandpa and Gabe."

"Will do. Aunt Piper is going to keep an eye on the weather and the road conditions before you start out so it might be a little bit longer." Another lie. She tipped her head back and squeezed her eyes closed, rubbing the back of her neck.

"How much longer?" he complained.

"Hey, dude!" she heard Piper say. "It's not that bad here."

"I wanna come home, Mom."

"I know, sweetie. And I want you home. But I want you to be safe. If waiting an extra couple of days is what that takes, it'll be worth it." All true statements, even if they were misguided. Gabe wrapped his arm around her shoulders. "Talk to you soon, K? Love you to the moon and back."

"Me too." His tone told her all she needed to hear to push her into discovering who was following her and threatening the safety of her family.

Setting her phone down on the counter, she asked Gabe, "What'd Detective Robles say?"

"He headed out the door the minute we hung up. He'd just got out of an interview," Gabe said, lightly rubbing circles on her back. "Probably why he wasn't available when you called him."

She glanced at her wristwatch. "It's probably past quitting time for him."

"I'm not sure a detective has an actual quitting time," he said. "And to be honest, I don't think this should wait."

She picked up the binoculars again. "He's not there anymore anyway."

"Course he's not," Jeremiah said. "He got what he wanted. You to see him. Taunting you is what he's doin'."

"Besides," Gabe said, "he knows you have company. He's not going to hang around with us here."

"Then maybe the two of you should go so he'll show his face, and I can find out who he is and what he wants."

"Not a chance," Jeremiah growled.

"I'm not leaving," Gabe said. "It's bad enough you didn't tell me about this. I would have made sure I was here a heck of a lot faster."

"But then I wouldn't have found out what I have," she said. "I know it's not much, but at least it's something."

"Well, hopefully the detective can find more," Gabe said.

"Like what?" Abby asked, fidgeting with the strap to the binoculars. "It's not like there's any evidence to be found. And it's not like this guy did anything criminal."

"Those were the exact words came outta your mouth last summer and look how that played out," Jeremiah said. "Not so well for you."

"Point taken. I just hate—I just—well, I just hate that people have to rearrange their schedules for me," she said, exasperated. "I hate that—"

"That you have to need someone?" Gabe asked, his voice quiet. He ran a finger lightly along the side of her face. "Hermosa, we all need people. That's the way we humans were designed. To need each other."

"It's just that—well, you know what I mean."

"I know how much your independence means to you," he said, "but needing help once in a while doesn't take away from that independence."

He gently pushed a stray strand of hair from her cheek, and Abby's heart skipped a beat. The fact of the matter was, she couldn't imagine being without him, and that scared the bejesus out of her. Her marriage had crumbled, shattered into a million pieces, and she saw what her mother's absence had done to her father. It scared her far more than the mystery stalker in the deer stand.

There was a knock on the front door, saving her from having to face her greatest fear any further.

Jeremiah left the room, bringing Detective Robles back with him. Abby made the appropriate introductions. "Let's go into the living room," she said. She led the way, and the three followed. Gabe sat next to Abby on the sofa, Detective Robles on the big overstuffed chair caddy-corner from them, and Jeremiah stood behind the sofa, hands shoved into the front pockets of his jeans, toothpick between his lips.

"Start at the beginning," Robles said, pen poised above notepad.

"You really didn't need to come all the way out here tonight," Abby said. "My apologies."

"None needed," he said. "How about you tell me what happened this afternoon. Starting as soon as you left my office. Sounds like it was a pretty eventful afternoon."

Abby started with the car that followed her as she was on her way home, giving him as good of a description as she could sans license plate number. She described the car as she was walking Gus and what she could see of the driver, namely the unique hat he sported, the mustache, and pipe between his lips. After she finished describing the man behind the binoculars looking back at her, she said, "It was then that I remembered where I'd seen him before. As I was leaving your office earlier today, he was sitting on a bench along the sidewalk. He had the plaid cap on. That's what I remembered. Looked Scottish."

"Did you recognize him as someone you know?"

"No. I tried to convince myself that all of these things could be plausibly explained. Until I saw him looking back at me from the woods. It was then I realized it was much more than that and that I wasn't overreacting."

He asked Abby a few more questions. *For clarification*, he said. After she answered them, he said, "Can I speak with you privately for a moment?"

"Whatever you have to say can be said in front of Gabe and my father. I don't have anything to hide."

"It will only take a moment," he said, looking at each of the men, dismissing them without saying a word.

Jeremiah shot him an I've-got-my-eye-on-you look while Gabe locked eyes with Abby, waiting for direction from her. She nodded and squeezed his hand, watching as he and her father left the room.

"What is it that you couldn't say in front of them?" she asked, afraid to hear the answer. In the two minutes since he'd asked to speak with her privately, a million scenarios transpired in her mind.

"Collin came to see me today. Right after you left, as a matter of fact."

"I know. I called you, but Pearl said you were in a meeting with him."

"Can you tell me again what happened when you met with him on the sidewalk beside the realtor's office?"

Abby cocked her head and studied him carefully. "What did he tell you?"

"Which of you initiated the disagreement?" he asked without answering her question.

"I confronted him with what I knew. He yanked me into the alley between the buildings and threatened me. Nothing has changed since we spoke earlier today."

"Did you threaten Mr. Miller at any time?"

"Threaten him how?"

"Him or his family?"

Abby gasped. "No! Not unless he considers me telling the truth of what he's working so hard to hide a threat."

"Collin Miller might be serving you with a restraining order. Just a heads up."

"What?" she asked incredulously. "Why?"

"He said he doesn't trust you and what you're capable of doing to him or his family."

"He's getting back at me. Turning the focus from himself onto me. You know that, right? I didn't do it. I swear I didn't!" She felt panic and disbelief growing out of control. She fought to slow her breathing. Why did Collin Miller have the capability to get to her so badly? *Because he was another one you trusted, you idiot. Big mistake.*

"Detective, I fully intend to find out what happened to Susan Ramirez. And I believe Collin Miller had something to do with it, directly or indirectly. I can't have my son come back home from my sister's until this is solved. I'm begging you to look at Collin Miller for the murder of Susan Ramirez."

Detective Robles stood, tucking his notepad and pen into his front shirt pocket. "I suppose I'd be wasting my breath by telling you not to investigate this on your own." Abby remained silent. "I'll say it anyway. Stay out of the investigation. Please," he urged. "We'll get to the bottom of it,

Ms. Sinclair. You have my word." He nodded and zipped up his coat as Abby sat still, unable to move. "I'll see myself out."

15

When Juan Robles left Whispering Pines Resort, he drove slowly down Walking Stick Trail, carefully eying every car in the parking lot of the three connecting resorts. Not a single vehicle traveled on the narrow road while he was on it. The only movement was a bull elk, his fur looking like a rough wool carpet from the winter. With the help of his headlamps, he spotted Abby and Gus's footprints off the road in the deeper snow, but the tire tracks that had been on the road had melted into slush and were indiscernible. The three cars he saw that could potentially match the description of the car Abby described each had a glaring difference. Two didn't have tinted windows, and the other was spotless, the license plate clearly readable. He stopped at that one, got out of his car and looked around, shining his flashlight into the windows. On the passenger's side was a plaid cap. On the dash, in full view, lay a pipe, dottle in the bowl.

It was his lucky day. Not only did he likely find the culprit, but he also knew the owners of two of the resorts that shared the large parking lot. The office was closed, still on winter hours. He looked at his watch. Six-thirty. He'd missed them by half an hour. He whipped out his cell phone and called.

"Hello?" A woman's voice came across the line.

"Hi, Shirley, it's Juan Robles."

"Juan!" she exclaimed with her usual enthusiasm. "To what do we owe the honor? Business or pleasure."

"Business."

"Oh, dear Lord. Please tell me you haven't found another body. Tell me you discovered what happened to that poor girl found at the Sinclair place."

"No and no. Not yet, anyway. But I'm working on it."

"How can we help?"

"Wondering if I could get the name of one of your guests. I'm here now. At the resort."

"Sure," she said. "Shoulda come earlier. We only left twenty minutes ago." The sound of papers shuffling in the background gave him hope that she'd find something. "Hold on while I log into the program we use for the resort business. How's Miz Sinclair? Must be pretty rough knowing someone was killed in your personal hot tub."

"Well, we don't know it was foul play for sure, yet, but—"

"Juan, come on," Shirley scoffed, "it's me you're talking to. People don't just go somewhere and drown themselves in someone's—"

"No, no, they usually don't," he said. "But we haven't found anything to indicate otherwise yet either. We can't call it homicide based on a gut feeling."

"How about common sense then?"

Juan chuckled. Leave it to Shirley to call a spade a spade. "George is retired law enforcement. You know I need evidence to prove it. That's what I'm trying to get. Solid evidence."

"Just a minor detail. What do you got so far?"

"It's an open—"

"Investigation, I know," she interrupted. "Didn't hurt to ask. Here it is. Which condo?"

"I don't know. I only have the make and model of a car." Shirley exhaled loudly. "You're not going to make this easy on me, are you? If someone doesn't list that information, I usually don't push it. Asking people to write their license plate number on the check-in sheet is like asking them to sacrifice their firstborn," she said wryly. "What kind of car?"

"A black Mazda. Four-door. Tinted windows. Plate number BXY555." He waited for a response but heard nothing. "Hello?"

"I'm here, I'm here. Patience." Juan snickered. "I don't have that car on any of the rentals. But hold on." George said something in the background. "It's Juan," Shirley said. "He needs information on one of our guests. All he has is the vehicle description." She repeated what Juan told her just a moment ago then was silent while George mumbled something. Juan tried to hear but was unable. Finally, Shirley said, "George said he knows exactly who you're talking about. His name is Duncan O'Shea."

"Is there a specific reason he remembers him?"

Shirley asked George and waited for him to finish his reply. "He said he saw the man as he was leaving for the day to come home. Said they talked for a bit and the guy was memorable, but for no reason he can think of. Just one of those people. And years of being a trained observer, probably," she added.

"So there wasn't—"

"Wait! Is he a suspect in the murder?" Shirley gasped. "You said you're working on getting evidence. Are we harboring a killer?"

"Put your panic to rest, Shirley. I'm sure there's nothing to worry about. It may have nothing to do with the murder at all," he said. And then, realizing his mistake, he muttered, "Dagnabbit." He'd let his guard down because it was Shirley. And he knew she'd noticed.

"So it is murder!" she said victoriously. "I knew it! Should we warn our guests?"

He shook his head and sliced his hand through the air. "For God's sake, no. All you'll do is cause an uproar. And like I said, this may have nothing to do with anything."

"George said he's in number 14. Keep me posted."

"I'll let you know what I can when I can."

Shirley snorted. "You cops are all the same."

Juan laughed quietly. "You've been married to one for forty-five years. Think you'd be used to it by now."

"Heh. I had my way of getting things out of him."

Juan had always suspected Shirley knew more about cases than she should. *Not smart on George's part*, he thought. Too many officers whose lives ended in divorce regretted that very thing the minute they were handed their walking papers because of a spurned spouse. "I'm sure you did, Shirley. I'm sure you did." He knelt beside the car, slush seeping through the knees of his slate gray 5.11 tactical pants. "Gotta go. I'll talk to you soon. And thanks."

He tucked his phone in his pocket and took out his flashlight, shining it on the undercarriage of the vehicle and saw what he expected—slush spattered the entire thing. He stood, inspecting the car with his flashlight. Clean as a whistle. Odd. Why would someone wash their car on a day like today? And if he was guilty of something, why would he make his license plate visible when he'd likely want to lay low?

He walked around the building that butted up against the parking lot and followed the sidewalk to building three. He walked around the back to unit number 14 and rang the doorbell beside the sliding glass door. The blinds were drawn, but the outside light was on, lighting the tiny concrete slab. Someone peered between two slats of the blinds before he heard the click of the door unlocking. It slid open, and a man stood before him in a pair of green and black plaid pajama bottoms and a black t-shirt with a logo for Guinness beer on the front.

"Mr. O'Shea?"

"Duncan," he said, extending a hand. "How can I help you?"

Juan held up his badge. "I'm Detective Robles with the Blue Mist Mountain Police Department. Do you have a few minutes?"

"Of course, Detective, come in." He stepped aside, creating space for Juan to enter the small room. "Something wrong?" He rubbed the stubble on his chin.

Juan stood with his back to the wall and with easy access out the door. "Can you tell me where you were today between the hours of three and now?"

"With my wife, a buddy of ours, and his wife."

"Here in town?"

"Heck no." He ran a hand over his hair. "We were in Denver."

"The entire time?"

"Yeah. What's this about?" Duncan asked.

"The plaid cap and pipe in your car. They yours?"

Duncan narrowed his eyes. "No, as a matter of fact, they're not. Why?"

"Whose are they?"

"My buddy's." His tone changed and he turned his head slightly sideways, not taking his eyes off of Juan.

"Does your buddy have a name?"

"Depends. Are you accusing him of doing something?"

"Depends if he did it or not."

"Look, Detective, we can keep dancing and get nowhere, or you can tell me what's going on and get somewhere."

"I have a few questions for the owner of that cap and pipe, that's all. Nothing more, nothing less."

"Well, good luck with that. My wife is taking him to the airport as we speak. He's flying back home tonight on the red-eye."

"Where's home?"

"Canada."

Juan studied him a moment then looked around the room while keeping his sights on Duncan. "Can I get your friend's name?"

Duncan shrugged then shoved his hands in his pockets. Juan stiffened, his hand on his weapon in a split second. Duncan chuckled and shook his head slowly.

"Relax, Detective, I'm getting my phone out of my pocket so I can get you his phone number. Whatever it is, I'm sure he can explain it."

Juan relaxed slightly but kept his hand resting lightly on his weapon. "Can you write it down for me please? I'd appreciate it."

"Anything for Blue Mist Mountain's finest. Beer?"

"No, thank you."

"Of course. Being on the job and all. Don't mind me. I'm not on the job." He picked up a long neck bottle from the coffee table and took a swig, the neck of the bottle between two fingers. He snagged an envelope from the table, looked at the front, the back, then scrawled with a pen.

"You work here in Colorado?" Juan asked.

"Mostly. I travel a lot, though."

"What do you do?"

"Oil business." Duncan held out the envelope with the number. "Here you go."

Juan looked at the scrawled number. "Do you have a name for me, too?"

"Shawn. Shawn Carnahan."

"Thank you." Juan took the envelope, glanced at the number again briefly, then tucked it into his pocket. "I'll let myself out." He slid the door open then turned to face Duncan. "What car did your wife use to take the Carnahan's to the airport?"

"Hers. We met here. She came a couple of days earlier than I did."

Juan nodded. "Thank you, Mr. O'Shea."

Juan slid the door closed behind him. Duncan clicked the lock into place immediately after. As soon as Juan sat down in his car, he scratched the Mazda's license plate number on the scrap of paper beneath the phone number followed by the name. *Shawn Carnahan. Sean?* Using the computer attached to the dash of his vehicle, he entered in the license plate number. It came back to a Carrie Appleton. He glanced at his watch, then punched in the phone number. It rolled into voicemail.

Hey, this is Shawn. I'm unable to take your call and won't have access to voicemail until Monday. Please leave a message and I'll get back to you. If this is related to business, call my office phone at 555-333-2020.

Well, that was easy. He started the car and drove onto the main road where Abby said the car followed behind her. Not expecting to find anything of significance, he didn't spend too much time there. He only wanted to get a feel for what happened. Tomorrow, when it was daylight, he would go out to the spot in the woods where Abby saw the man looking back at her to see if he could find anything of value.

He had nothing connecting any of this to the murder of Susan Ramirez, but he had a niggling suspicion they were tied together somehow. He just needed to figure out how so he could solve the murder and keep Abigail safe as well.

He drove the dark winding road back to town, the only light now coming from the stars twinkling overhead and lights from the resorts and motels that dotted one side of the road. The mountains rose up on the other side. Juan kept his sights glued to the road and along both sides, watching for any signs of wildlife. The last thing he needed was to crash another vehicle from a deer darting out in front of him. The chief ripped him up one side and down the other for that very thing last year, claiming he should have known to be more careful having lived here for so long. Since the chief had to answer to the town council for the crashed vehicle, he could understand where he was coming from. But it didn't make it any more enjoyable.

As he drove, he thought about his visit from Collin Miller. The man sure had it in for Abigail Sinclair. Juan had a hard time believing the things Miller told him. All the same, he knew he had to check all angles and go down every road to get to the truth. The plan was to start digging into the history of both as soon as he got back to the precinct. Since his daughter was with her mother, he wasn't hard-pressed to go home to an empty house.

Juan pulled into the parking lot of the police department and backed into his parking space. His phone buzzed in his pocket, indicating an incoming text message.

Hi daddy. I miss you.

His heart wrenched in pain. It was bad enough when his wife had left him for someone else, but when his daughter was gone, it was nearly unbearable. Juan had broken the rules when he found out the man's name and did a background check—grounds for dismissal if the chief caught him. But he hadn't. And even if he had, it would have been worth it to be sure his little girl was safe. With everything he'd seen in his time as a cop, he could never be too careful.

His thick fingers fumbled on the keys as he attempted to text back. *Miss u 2. Luv u squirt.*

Love you too, daddy.

The response came back almost before Juan pushed send on his own message. How she could text back so fast was beyond him. "Kids," he muttered, smiling.

He opened the front door to see Pearl had already left for home and the evening shift woman was in her place. As lively and colorful as Pearl was, Shonna was equally as dry and gray.

"Buenas tardes, Shonna. Como va?"

"Hi, Detective. You know I don't speak Spanish." She gave him a rare smile. It didn't quite reach her eyes, but he'd take what he could get.

"Good evening. How goes it?" He repeated.

"Same ole' same ole.'"

"That good, huh?" he said.

Without waiting for a reply, he pushed past her and toward his office. He plunked down in his chair and swiveled toward his computer, pushing the button to make it come to life. Abby first. He wanted to broaden the scope from the in-state criminal history he'd run on her earlier.

He typed her information into the database. While he waited for the results, he swiveled around to face his laptop on the credenza in back of him and ran her criminal history. Nothing appeared on either except a speeding ticket from Oakland ten years ago and a misdemeanor harassment charge seven years ago. His curiosity rose slightly. Harassment could be anything as minor as disturbing someone's peace, destroying property, or a minor threat. But he also knew it could be as serious as assault, stalking, or even plead down from a more serious charge.

Eyes narrowed, he studied the short criminal history and discovered it was an act of domestic violence and she was offered a deferred adjudication if she plead guilty to the charge in exchange for supervised probation. "Looks like you got it revoked, Sinclair," he said to the empty room, looking deeper into the history. Another harassment charge. *Dagnabbit!* Why hadn't she mentioned it to him? Surely she had to know he'd find out. She wasn't making things easy for herself. He picked up a pen and jotted on a piece of scrap paper, *Ask Abigail Sinclair about her criminal record.*

He searched some more, relieved when nothing else turned up, and then went on to look up the same information for Collin. This search yielded a bit more. The good doctor hadn't been so good. Juan took a deep breath and delved into the information the search churned up. He watched as it continued, bringing to light a whole new side of the doctor.

And then came something he hadn't expected at all. He blinked a few times, thinking he must be reading it wrong. But as many years as he'd been running criminal histories, he knew he was more than capable of reading them accurately.

He sat back in his chair, exhaled, and poked at the screen with his finger. "Bingo!"

16

As soon as Detective Robles left the house, Jeremiah retired to his room with a heated plate of leftovers. Gabe built an impressive fire in the fireplace while Abby heated spaghetti sauce from the freezer and cooked some pasta then joined him in the living room. Gus was sprawled out on his side on a rug in front of the fire. He lazily opened one eye and looked at her as she handed Gabe his plate, then closed it again, apparently deciding food wasn't on his agenda at the moment. She set her plate on the coffee table and plunked down beside Gabe.

Gabe set his plate on the coffee table beside hers and pulled her toward him, wrapping an arm tight around her shoulders. "I worry about you, Hermosa."

"I'll be fine." But she wasn't so sure. If the same person who killed Susan was after her, she wasn't sure she wouldn't end with the same fate.

"Don't bother trying to convince me. It won't work." He rubbed light circles on the back of her hand. "I'm not leaving until we catch this guy."

"Guy? You've just cut out fifty percent of the population."

"It was a guy that's been following you."

"It was. But that doesn't mean he's the one that killed Susan or that he's out to hurt me. In fact, I feel oddly certain he isn't." She sat up and pulled back, enabling her to look into his eyes. "He's had plenty of opportunities to hurt me if that was the plan. He hasn't."

"Well, I, for one, am going to make sure he doesn't have that opportunity."

Abby gave him a wry smile. "You can't be with me 24/7."

"Watch me."

"No, I mean you *can't*. I won't let you. That's no way to live."

"I don't mind."

"But I do." She looked deep into his eyes, begging him to understand. "As much as I care about you, I'm not a be-together-all-the-time kinda gal."

Gabe sighed and sat back again, pulling her with him. "I know. And I appreciate that about you. I do. But exceptions can be made in certain circumstances, can't they?"

Abby didn't reply but only melted into him further. Finally, she pulled away and sat up. "Food's getting cold." She picked up his plate and handed it to him.

"How much?" He elbowed her lightly and winked at her.

"How much what?" she asked.

"Do you care about me?"

"A lot." She grinned. "This much," she said, stretching her arms as wide as she could.

"Oooh, that's a lot," he said, his tone husky. "But I can do one better."

"Yeah?" she asked, grinning wider.

"Yeah." He looked at her, up to no good, before he set his plate back down and tackled her to the couch, tickling her until she begged for mercy.

God, this felt so good to laugh. Felt so good to laugh with *him*.

He stopped and looked at her, gentle and genuine, running a finger softly against the side of her face. "I love you, Abigail Sinclair. And one day you're going to say those words back to me. I know it."

The words she wanted to say so badly stuck in her throat. *I love you, too.* Instead, she swallowed, picked up her plate, and rested it in her lap, lifting her fork. Gabe did the same, and they ate in silence for a few moments. "So how did your conference go? You never did tell me," she said.

"It was good. Not a whole lot I didn't already know. By the sounds of things, I would have been much more useful here."

"You can't stop living your life because some idiot is intent on scaring me for some unknown reason." She wrapped strands of angel hair pasta around the tines of her fork. "Besides, I'm not helpless."

"I know that very well. But you're also stubborn enough to prove your point without fully realizing the consequences."

"Did you just say I'm reckless?" She pulled back and looked at him with narrowed eyes.

"Walking Gus along the back road at dusk wasn't exactly safe."

At the sound of his name, Gus lifted his head, looked at them, then lay back down.

"A back road that hardly anyone knows about. It's not even a road, really, but a trail only wide enough for a car. I just want to live my life in a normal fashion."

"Think of it as a few temporary restrictions."

She took another bite of spaghetti, followed by a drink of water, then set her plate down. "You know, that's what stinks about being a woman. If this were happening to you, you wouldn't have to implement restrictions, temporary or otherwise. It's just not fair."

"Well, first of all, no one would want to stalk my sorry butt. Second of all—"

"I'm serious, Gabe." She looked away, then back at him. Tears stung her eyes. "I'm tired of being bullied, and I'm not putting up with it anymore."

Gabe groaned and pressed a palm against his forehead before looking back at her. "Why don't I like the sound of that? Not that you're not going to be bullied," he added quickly, "but what that implies." He set his plate next to hers and turned to face her, taking both her hands in his own. "Please tell me you won't do anything foolish."

"I can't make any promises," she said. "I need to get to the bottom of this whole mess so my son can get back home and life can resume as normal."

"You know what they say about normal."

"Yeah, yeah. It's a setting on the washing machine."

"And who's to say what normal is anyway. One person's normal is another's insanity."

She picked up his plate and handed it to him before taking her own. "It's getting cold." For the next several minutes while they ate, it was quiet except for the crackling logs in the fireplace. Abby set her plate back down and tossed her paper napkin on top of it. "I almost forgot to tell you what I've decided to do," she said.

"By the sound of your voice, it's something you're excited about."

"Let's say *passionate* about." She smiled at him.

"Ooh! Passionate. I like the sound of that."

She giggled and took his hand in her own. "I'm going to start a women's support group for victims of domestic violence."

Gabe's eyebrows shot up. "How did this come about?"

She filled him in on the specifics of what she had so far. "It's in the embryonic stage right now, and I'm still looking for a place to hold it. Not to mention there's a lot of details I need to decide and tasks to do first. I asked Dr. Miller if we could use his office space since it wouldn't conflict with his office hours, but that was a flat no. He said he forbids me to do it. Forbids! Can you believe it? The nerve!" She continued to fill him in on her run-in with Collin.

"Man, Abby, I'm so sorry I ever recommended that guy to you. I feel responsible."

She looked deep into his eyes and squeezed his hands. "You have nothing to be sorry for, Gabe. He came recommended to you from a friend you trusted."

"Yeah, I remembered after we hung up that it wasn't Bob that told me about him. It was a friend and his wife who both saw him together when they were having some marital problems. He said Miller literally saved their marriage. I'll have to ask him more."

"I'm sure he's not *all* bad." She shrugged. "He just did wrong by Susan. And a couple of others. Probably more."

"And you."

"I think with me it's just that he feels threatened because of what I know. I'm sure he doesn't want his wife to find out."

"It's probably why they live so far out of town."

"I'd be interested in meeting his wife sometime. To see if he keeps her out there. I mean, does she have a car?"

Gabe lifted her chin with a finger so she met his gaze. "No, Abby. Promise me you won't get involved."

"I already am. The mother of his child—at least I'm sure it's his child—was found dead. By me. In my hot tub. But I'm not going to go find his house if that's what you're worried about."

He exhaled with relief. "Thank God."

"But I'm still going to find out if he had anything to do with the death of Susan Ramirez."

He closed his eyes and tipped his head back.

"Gabe—"

"I know. You have to." He groaned then looked at her. "It's who you are, and I love you for that. I just don't want to lose you because you're helping someone who's already dead."

"It's not just Susan." She silently begged him to understand. "It's for all women who are stuck in situations where they feel they have no way out. No hope. For the women who deserve to have a life free from fear. That's what this support group is all about. They need my voice to help make theirs louder."

"And I'll support you in any way I can. I will. I just don't want anything happening to you. Cooper and me need you. Your father needs you. And Gus."

At the sound of his name, Gus opened his eyes, sleepily wagged his tail, yawned, then went back to sleep in front of the fire.

"God spared my life for a reason," she said softly. "And I truly believe this is what I'm supposed to do."

He tucked a stray chunk of hair behind her ear, his fingers lingering against her cheek. "Have I told you how proud of you I am?" His voice was husky.

"You just did." She leaned into him, feeling the warmth of his body next to hers, his muscles tight against his flannel.

He stroked her hair. "You drive me crazy, Hermosa."

"As long as I don't drive you away."

"Never."

They talked until the fire died to the smallest ember.

"I have an idea," he said.

"Yeah?"

"Why don't I go get the heater going in my camper and we can make our way out there."

"Gabriel Coleman, are you trying to make me a dishonest woman?" she teased, batting her eyelashes at him.

"Call it whatever you want, but I call it romantic and fun. Besides, you already agreed. Remember?"

She chuckled and shook her head. "No, I don't think I remember that."

He stood and pulled her up from the couch and against his chest. He entwined his fingers in her hair, tipping her head back. He kissed her lightly, his lips lingering against hers, his breath warm. "Yes?"

"Yes," she breathed. "I'll pick up in here and let Gus out one more time. By then the camper should be warm."

"With you in that camper, it would be warm without the heater."

She giggled and pulled away and playfully swatted at him. "Go."

"Don't be too long. Just sayin'." He winked at her and walked out, closing the door behind him.

Abby locked the door and looked at Gus laying on the rug by the front door, his head on his front paws. He looked up at her with sad big brown eyes.

"It's only for the night, Gussie. Stop making me feel guilty." She reached down and petted his head, running her hand down his back. His eyes closed. "You need to go on a diet, big boy." His eyes blinked back open, and he stared at her. "If I didn't know better, I'd think you were cursing at me right now," she said, rubbing his neck before heading for the stairs.

She'd no sooner reached the first step when the business phone rang. She looked at the incoming number. *Private Caller.* She debated not answering it but then decided she'd better in case it was Detective Robles calling from one of the department phones. And if it was someone looking for a cabin, she didn't want to lose the business. Especially now.

"Hello?" she said as she picked up the dishes and carried them to the sink. "Hello?" she said again into the empty phone line. She pulled the phone away and looked at the receiver as though it was at fault for no one on the other end. She put it back to her ear and said again, "Hello?" She was just about to hang up when a woman's voice came on the line.

"Abigail Sinclair?"

"Who is this?" Abby asked.

"Dr. Miller's wife. Is this Abigail Sinclair?"

Abby's interest piqued and her heartbeat quickened. "Yes, this is she. How can I help you, Mrs. Miller?" She set the dishes down and leaned against the counter, giving the phone call her undivided attention.

"I was wondering if you and I could meet tomorrow."

"Um, well—can we talk on the phone?" Her eagerness to know what Mrs. Miller wanted to tell her battled having to wait.

"I can't take the risk."

"Risk? Are you in danger, Mrs. Miller?"

"Martha. And no, of course not. But it's private. No one needs to know we're meeting. No one."

"What's this about, Martha?"

"I have a few questions for you about my husband. I think you might have some answers I need."

"Mrs. Mill—Martha, I would like to help. Really, I would. But if you have questions about your husband, I'm not sure I have answers for you." The last thing she wanted was to get in the middle of their marital divide. She was already in the middle of something she was trying to get out of. If Collin was upset with her before, he would certainly be more so after learning she'd met with his wife. And yet she wanted to know if Martha Miller was abused and help if she was. She ran her hand over her hair and briefly closed her eyes. *Oh, what to do.*

"Please," Martha said, a slight hitch in her voice. "I desperately need to talk to you."

Abby felt her resolve begin to vanish. "I can probably get away for a few minutes tomorrow morning. Where do you want to meet?"

"There's a little out-of-the-way coffee shop on Devil's Canyon road. It's about a mile out of town. Do you know the one? Called Devil's Brew."

"No, but it can't be too hard to find. Ten?"

"That works. And Abby?"

"Yes?"

"Thank you."

For what? What exactly could Martha Miller want to ask her about? And what had Martha heard? Why would she think Abby had answers to her questions?

She pushed off from the counter and headed upstairs, smiling. Whatever it was, it wasn't her concern right now. All that mattered at this moment was letting her father know she wouldn't be in the house for the night and getting out to the camper where Gabe was waiting for her.

17

Juan Robles didn't sleep worth beans that night. Thoughts of his daughter pervaded every thought that the Ramirez murder investigation didn't. Blue Mist Mountain had been a safe town the entire time he'd been there. Murder just wasn't something that happened. In fact, not at all since he'd been on the investigations team. And that'd been almost ten years now. He couldn't help but feel his investigative skills for solving a murder were anything better than rusty. He just hoped someone else didn't get hurt or killed in the process during the time it took him to solve this one. Like Abigail Sinclair. Someone was clearly out to get her, whether it was life-threatening or just to scare her. But he couldn't rule either one out, risking something happening to her.

Finally, at four-thirty he got up and stumbled to the kitchen. A photo of his daughter stared back at him from the refrigerator door. With her long dark braids and freckles across the bridge of her nose, she was a spitting image of her mother. Pain sliced through him. Even after how long it'd been and how it all went down, he still missed his wife.

He reached for the bottle of Baileys and poured some in reheated leftover coffee from yesterday morning. He took a long drink and then refilled his cup, draining the last of the pot, this time no Baileys, and popped it in the microwave. He couldn't afford to cloud his mind with booze if he was going to solve this case before someone else became a victim.

Juan sat down at the table with his cup, a pen, and his notepad that contained notes from his interviews with Abby and Collin. Reviewing them thoroughly, he jotted additional follow-up questions beside each. On another page he made a list of names, Collin and Abby included, as well as more people he needed to speak with today. Martha Miller headed the list, then John and Carrie Appleton. Maybe they could shed some light on Collin's relationship with the victim. If what Abby said was true, that would give Collin motive to want Susan Ramirez dead and out of the way. Depending on how much Collin's wife knew, Martha could very well have a motive, too. Next to their names, he scribbled possible motives. He couldn't think of one for the others until he talked with them. As for Abby, he couldn't think of a single one. But she did have the two dings on her criminal history. He scribbled *CH?* under motive. Either way, Collin's accusations just didn't add up.

He wrote Duncan O'Shea's name as well as Shawn Carnahan. He'd need to call Duncan and ask him to come to the station for further interviewing as well as call Shawn Carnahan, who should be home by now. If not, he would try his office number conveniently given to him in Shawn's answering machine.

Juan took a sip of coffee and scribbled circles in the top right corner of his notepad while he processed what he knew about either Duncan or Shawn so far. Which was pretty much nothing. He stopped doodling and wrote Bob and Judy Lopez on the list, followed by Conrad Schmidt. He needed second interviews with them as well. Judy appeared to harbor a lot of animosity toward her sister. And Conrad—well, he hadn't even been able to locate Conrad yet. He would have to check if there was a missing persons report on him. If he didn't have family, he could be long gone by now. That man was hiding something. He was sure of it. It didn't take a genius to figure that one out. Next to Conrad's name, under the motive, he scribbled *Spurned lover?*

Juan downed the rest of his coffee, cold by now, grimacing as the bitter liquid slid down his throat. One more look at his daughter's photo on the fridge and he headed up to shower and dress. He had a lot to do today and sitting around here wasn't getting it done.

Thirty minutes later, showered, shaved, and dressed in a pair of black 5.11s, black turtleneck, black cowboy boots, and gray blazer, he locked the door behind him and headed into the police station. He was surprised to find the front doors already unlocked. It was only five forty-five. He glanced at Shonna, who looked exhausted. He scanned the lobby and saw a woman with long brown hair, wearing a light blue dress with tights and boots, a look his wife used to call shabby chic. He looked back at Shonna and raised an eyebrow, nodding discreetly toward the woman. Shonna motioned him over with her finger and got up from the desk, leading him through the doors toward the back.

"The name's Angie Zamora. She's been waiting—"

"Didn't one of the night shift guys help her?"

"If you'd let me finish, sir—"

"Sorry, Shonna. Go on."

"She's waiting for you. Says she has something she wants to tell you."

"At five forty-five in the morning?"

"She got here at five-thirty. I didn't want her waiting out in the dark and the cold, so I let her in. Says she was up all night until she was able to come in."

"Detective Wilson in yet?"

"No, sir. He won't be in today. Sick wife and kid."

Juan inwardly groaned. "Ok. Tell Ms. Zamora that I'll be just a minute. I need to put my stuff down and grab a cup of coffee. Get oriented." He started toward his office.

"Detective?" Shonna said.

He stopped and turned to face her. "Yes?"

"When you're done maybe I could talk to you for a minute?"

"Isn't your shift about done?"

"I'll wait. I promise it will be brief."

"Do you need to talk to me first? Before I speak with Ms. Zamora?"

"No," she said.

Juan studied her for a moment, then shrugged. "Ok. I'll be out in a minute."

When he turned the corner into his office, he saw a large manilla envelope propped up against his computer monitor. He zeroed in on the return address—the Coroner's Office. He snatched it up and tore it open, yanking the pages out. He zipped down to cause and manner of death. Homicide. Asphyxia, including strangulation. *That's a personal attack*, he thought. *Someone close to her.*

He continued reading. *The victim has defensive wounds on her forearms, a bruise beneath her left eye. Petechia present in both eyes and on chest…No needle marks present…No debris under the victim's fingernails…* "Yeah, cause it's in the water samples," Juan said into the empty room.

He continued reading until the final word, took a moment to digest what he'd read, then put the pages face down on his desk. He'd need to follow up on the lab results from the hot tub water samples. If they weren't done yet, he'd have to push them to get it done ASAP. But right now, he had someone waiting for him in the lobby.

Juan stared at Angie Zamora from across his desk as she fidgeted in her chair, discreetly tugging at a loose string on the sleeve of her dress. He struggled to process the story she'd just spilled to him. Why now? Coincidence? Somehow he didn't think so. Collin Miller's world was collapsing around him without the man even knowing what was happening. As odd as the story was and the timing of it, Angie had too many details for Juan not to believe it.

He leaned back in his chair, exhaled between pursed lips, and stretched one arm behind his head. He laid his pen down beside the pad onto which he'd just scribbled copious notes. He returned to an upright position and leaned forward, elbows resting on his desk, hands clasped. "So let me get this straight, Ms. Zamora. Correct me wherever I'm wrong. So that I'm on the same page. You saw Dr. Miller and—how long had you been his patient?"

"Two years."

"Two years," he repeated. "You first sought him out in an attempt to save your marriage."

"That's correct."

"Who referred him to you?"

"The Internet. He had some good reviews," she said.

Mistake number one. Anyone could put anything they wanted on the Internet. Those reviews could have come from Collin's friends for all anyone knew. He'd talked to his daughter about the evils of the Internet until he was blue in the face and yet she was on social media all the time. He'd friended her so he could see what she posted and who posted on her page. The perils of having a detective as a father. He jotted a note to himself to dig into Dr. Miller's website.

"Ok. So it was about six months into the therapist-client relationship that he began acting weird, as you described it."

"Yes." Her voice was so quiet he had to strain to hear her. "As I said, it began by him sitting too close."

"And then he began giving you a hug when you arrived and again when you left."

"Yes. And they lasted too long."

"Did you tell him to stop?"

"At first I attempted to pull away, and he'd just hold on tighter, then let go."

"And it progressed from there," Juan added.

"Yes. Rapidly. He—he—he told me he knew it was wrong, but he couldn't help it, that he was falling in love with me. With my marriage falling apart, it was flattering that someone found me attractive." A tear rolled down her cheek. "It's my fault."

"Listen to me, Ms. Zamora," Juan said, his tone startling even himself, "this is not your fault. Do you hear me?" His gaze met her own, her brown eyes shining with unshed tears, pain etched in them. "Dr. Miller took advantage of you." He silently chastised himself for the annoyance he felt when he walked in that morning to find her waiting for him.

She wiped her cheek with the back of her hand. Juan slid a box of tissues toward her, and she snatched one up, then a second. "My husband left me because of it. Ironic, huh? I went there to save my marriage and ended up losing it for real."

"Because of nothing you did. Because of what *he* did. This is all on Dr. Miller." Juan's temples throbbed. He could sure use a cigarette right now and wished he hadn't promised his daughter he would quit. "Have you told anyone else?"

"No."

"I have to report him."

"I know." She looked down, her coal-black eyelashes wet.

"Can I offer the assistance of a victim advocate? We have one on at all times. One call and an advocate could be here in under half an hour."

"No." She shook her head. "No, thank you."

"Here," he said, lying a pamphlet on top of the tissue box. "In case you change your mind, here's the number to call." She picked it up and glanced at it briefly before sliding it into her purse. "Have you found another therapist to help with this?" he asked.

"I meet with one later this afternoon. It's a woman this time. I just feel—you know—more comfortable with everything that's happened."

"I completely understand."

As Angie stood and smoothed her skirt, Juan walked around his desk and opened the door for her. He held a business card between his thumb and forefinger. "If you think of anything else, Ms. Zamora, please call me."

She took it from him, studied it, and looked at him. "Thank you, Detective. I feel such a sense of relief."

"You're welcome. You did the right thing, you know. Coming in and reporting it."

"I just don't want him doing to someone else what he did to me."

I'm afraid he already has, Ms. Zamora. He already has. "Ms. Zamora, I have to ask. What has caused you to come in this morning, and at this hour." *Had she heard something?*

She shrugged then looked down at her hands wringing in her lap. "It's a small town, Detective. People talk."

"Who?"

"I can't remember."

Juan didn't need to see the color rising in her cheeks, her avoidance of eye contact, to know she was lying. "Ms. Zamora—"

"I have to go, Detective," she said in little more than a whisper. She stood, slung her purse over her shoulder and turned toward the door.

Juan watched as she disappeared from his office, and then he quickly got up to follow her. When she pushed open the front doors he turned his attention to the desk. "Mornin' Pearl."

"Back atcha, Detective Robles. Shonna said she'd be back in a few. She just went to get a cup of coffee down the street."

"We have coffee here for free. Why would she go get it somewhere else and pay for it?"

Pearl snorted. "Yeah. You all call this coffee, but it's really not. It's sludge."

Juan looked at the cup in his hand and shrugged. "Does the trick for me."

"Which tells me what a sad life you lead, Detective. We need to get you back on the horse. You need a date."

Now it was Juan who snorted, nearly choking on his coffee. "No, thank you. Not me. My horse is dead."

"You'll change your mind eventually, sir. Trust me."

"Stop playing mother, Pearl. I'm too old for that."

"No disrespect intended, but you're never too old to have someone care about you. And as long as I'm taking up space behind this desk, that's how it's going to go down."

Juan looked at Pearl, her bright yellow blouse and yellow-framed glasses brightening up the place. "You have glasses that match every blouse you own, Pearl?"

"Pretty much, sir." She grinned. "Thanks for noticing."

He chuckled. "Send Shonna back when she gets here. I'll be making some phone calls."

"Will do. And, sir?"

"Yup."

"I almost forgot. There was someone who called for you. Didn't want to be transferred to your extension though. Said they'd just call back later."

"Did they leave a name?"

"Nope. Was a man, though."

If it was someone he'd already spoken with they would have had his direct number. That meant it was someone else. Or perhaps it had nothing to do with this case at all. If that was possible. His life had become so wrapped up in this case, he had a hard time remembering life before it. He lifted his cup. "Guess I'll wait for him to call back."

Juan went back to his office, leaving his door open ajar for Shonna whenever she came back. In the meantime, he had some phone calls to make. The first to Abigail Sinclair. He flipped to the page with the list of numbers and called her cell phone. She answered on the fourth ring.

"Hello?"

"Abby?"

"Yes."

"It's Juan Robles. I'm sorry to call so early, but do you have a minute?"

"Um, sure. Hold for a minute, though, please." He heard muffled voices, hers and a man's. A moment later, she was back on the line. "Okay, I'm back. Did something happen?"

"What can you tell me about the harassment charge against you back in 2007? And again in 2008."

She gasped. "It was a deferred."

"A deferred that was revoked. What can you tell me about it?"

"I can tell you that I didn't do anything wrong."

Says everyone in the jails. A pang of guilt pricked his gut. When had he become so cynical? "Tell me how it came about." There was silence until he thought he'd lost the connection. "Are you there?"

"Yes. I'd be more than happy to talk to you about this but in person. Not on the phone."

"This morning? Say…ten-thirty?"

"Just a minute please." More muffled talking and then she was back on the line. "I have an appointment at ten but—well, I guess I can reschedule it. Ten-thirty it is. At the PD?"

"That would be perfect."

"I'll be there," she said.

The line went dead, and Juan held the phone in his hand a few moments before replacing it back in its cradle. The next call was to the American Psychological Association. When he'd asked to file an ethical complaint against Collin Miller, the voice on the other end asked, "Collin…Miller?"

"Yes, that's right."

"Hm. First name with two Ls or one?"

Juan heard the sound of a keyboard clicking on the line, then what sounded like the fast tapping of what he assumed was the delete button, then clicking again. His instinct told him he wouldn't be successful in filing a complaint.

"I'm sorry, sir," she said, "he isn't a member with us. We can't file a complaint against a non-member."

Yup. His instinct had been right. "Ok," he muttered, "the state medical board it is." He didn't think a psychologist would have a medical license. He wasn't that kind of doctor. But this was well above his pay grade as a simple detective. To be sure he covered all bases, he looked up the number on the Internet and called. As expected, another dead end that resulted in no answers and more questions. Once again he replaced the phone in its cradle and sat back, exhaling long and slow. He had a feeling he was stepping into a gigantic mess and opening a stinking can of worms. "I'm not paid enough to deal with this bureaucratic bull crap," he mumbled.

Yet, he reached for the phone again, hanging it back up when Shonna's head peeked around his door. He waved her in. "Come on in, Shonna. Have a seat."

"Is this a bad time?"

"Nope. What can I do for you?"

She sat on the edge of the chair opposite his desk, the one Angie Zamora had just little more than an hour ago occupied. "It's about Dr. Miller."

Suspicion pricked his senses. "Ya don't say."

By the time Shonna got done, Juan was sick to his stomach. How many women had this guy been messing with? He was just glad as hell that Shonna hadn't fallen for Miller's moves. What an idiot of a human being. Not to mention a scumbag.

"Shonna, did he know you work at the police department? Did you ever mention it?"

She appeared to think then shook her head. "No, not that I can recall. It never came up. I was there to talk about something personal."

Juan knew the something personal was probably about the battle with her ex. He didn't know details, just that there was a custody fight for her daughter. Happy relationships weren't available to anyone anymore. And Pearl wanted him to get back on the horse. *Not a chance, Pearl. Not a chance.* "Let me ask you something else," Juan said. "Did you ever see a license of any sort on the walls in his office?"

Shonna mentally disappeared for a moment, then shook her head again. "Not that I remember. But I didn't look for one either. So even if there was, I probably wouldn't have noticed." She narrowed her eyes. "Sir, do you think he's practicing without a license?"

"I can't talk about it at this time, Shonna. Especially since you're now part of the case."

"What do you mean, part of the case? You mean with Ramirez and Sinclair?"

"As I said, I can't discuss it." He attempted to smile. "I'm sorry."

She stood, the chair scraping against the floor. "That's okay. I know how these things go. I work here, remember?"

He watched her leave, closing the door behind her. He had a few more phone calls to make before Abigail Sinclair got there. He had a feeling the saga surrounding Collin Miller was going to get a lot uglier.

18

At ten o'clock sharp Abby pulled open the door to the Blue Mist Mountain Police Department, greeted by a cheerful and colorful Pearl.

"Hi, Pearl. Love the ensemble you've got going on there." Bright orange baubles that matched her lipstick and nail polish adorned the yellow blouse.

"Ms. Sinclair," Pearl said, beaming, this time without the smudge of lipstick on her teeth. "A pleasure to see you again, dear." She reached for her phone. "Detective Robles told me you were coming. Let me call him and tell him you're here."

"No need," Juan said from behind her. "I'm right here." He looked at Abby. "Come on back."

Abby followed him through the doors and down the hallway. "No interview room this time?" she asked.

"My office is more comfortable."

"I thought it has to be recorded," she said as she followed him into a small room. She looked around her. *How is this more comfortable? Looks like a bomb went off.*

"Don't worry. It will be recorded. Coffee?"

"No, thank you."

"Pearl's warned you about it, huh?"

"What?"

"About the coffee here."

"Can't be worse than the coffee my father makes." Truth of the matter was her nerves couldn't handle coffee right now. She hadn't thought about a background check until Juan mentioned the charges, but it made sense. She'd done so well at putting Hunter behind her that she hadn't even remembered the incidents until now. And now was the wrong time for it to pop up. Right in the middle of a murder investigation. A murder that happened on her property. And just when she thought things couldn't get any worse.

"Have a seat," he said, motioning to the chair opposite his desk. "I'll be right with you."

As soon as he was out of view, she looked around his office, taking in the mostly bare walls, the desk cluttered with stacks upon stacks of papers and files. More papers littered the floor, balls of paper surrounded his garbage can.

In the corner, right beside his phone, a dual photo frame peeked out between paper stacks. It held a picture of a little girl about six with long black braids, big brown eyes, cheeks covered in freckles, and a grin showing missing teeth. The picture beside it was the same girl, only a few years older. She appeared to be at least twelve. Rather than braids, she wore a ponytail, and her freckles were less noticeable beneath a beautiful, youthful tan. The biggest difference was her big, sad eyes. Abby wondered if the transformation came about because of the little girl's parents getting divorced. She noticed the detective didn't wear a wedding ring. And there wasn't any indication that it had been taken off just recently. She supposed that didn't really mean anything, though. Some men just didn't like to wear a ring. But she remembered seeing a difference in Cooper about the time of her divorce with

Hunter. The same sad look that was in the little girl's eyes on the photograph. At the thought of her boy, pain shot through her. She missed him terribly.

"Sorry about the wait," Juan said as he breezed past her to his chair, paper cup in his hand. He lifted the cup then set it on his desk. "Brought my mug home to wash it and forgot it," he explained. Abby forced a tight smile. He opened his notebook to a new page, wrote her name on the top and the date, then looked at her. "What can you tell me about the first harassment charge against you?"

Abby twisted the silver ring on her forefinger, then clasped her hands together. "It's all a misunderstanding." Juan started to say something, but Abby held up her hand. "I know. I'm sure you hear that from every person who has a record."

"That's not what I was going to say but go on."

"My husband—uh, ex-husband, but he was my husband at the time—went out with some of the guys after work. He was already mad at me from a fight the night before."

"What was the fight about?"

Abby hesitated, not sure it mattered, yet had nothing to hide at this point. "He was yelling at me in front of my four-year-old son when we were at the dinner table, calling me names. Cooper got up from the table and said, 'Let's go play, daddy. Mommy clean dishes.' My little boy pointed at me, then looked at Hunter, and said, 'Women's work, huh dad?' Hunter laughed and told Cooper, 'Don't ever get married, son. When women get married they get their hair cut short, get fat, and stop wearing makeup.' It was sickening." Abby shook her head, trying to shake free from the all-too-vivid memory.

"What did you do then?"

"What Hunter said didn't bother me so much. My hair was long, I knew I wasn't fat, and I never wore makeup before we were married, so that hadn't changed. What hurt and was unforgivable were the values he was teaching our son." Abby tucked the memory away in the corner of her mind, hoping to get rid of it permanently someday. "By the time he came home the next night in a foul mood, I'd had time to think about things. He sat at the table demanding dinner and a beer. I set his plate in front of him but refused to get him a beer because he'd already had too many. He ordered me to, I said no."

"Where was Cooper?"

"In bed by that time, thank God."

"And then what?" Rather than write down what she was saying, he listened intently.

"He stood up and came at me, I pushed him and he stumbled backward, tripped over his chair and landed on the floor. Guess you could say his pride was hurt. He told me I was going to pay and called the police. They charged me with battery. He told me I was lucky not to be charged with battery on a peace officer or domestic violence. Said he was giving me a break."

"But he wasn't on duty, right?"

"No." She shook her head, her chest heavy as memories infiltrated the moment. "But I was tired of it all. And scared."

"What happened in court? I'm assuming it went to court since you were offered a deferred."

"Yes."

"Why didn't you tell the prosecutor what happened?"

"Hunter was doing court security that day. I'm sure he arranged it that way. The prosecutor had always hated him and I never knew why until that day. He could see right through

Hunter. But with him—Hunter—right there, I just accepted my fate and wanted to move on." The pity she saw in his eyes was nearly unbearable. She squirmed in her chair from the humiliation. Might as well spill it all. "The second time was a mirror of the first. Honestly? I think he set it up that way. For me to get my deferred revoked. He was paying me back for not submitting to him." Tears stung her eyes but she fought them back. There was no way she was going to humiliate herself even further.

"I'm so sorry, Abigail."

"Don't be." She instantly regretted the sharpness to her tone, closed her eyes, and took a deep breath.

"Not all of us are corrupt like your ex. I hope you know that."

"I do," she said, her voice merely a whisper. "At least I'm getting there. Thanks in part to you."

"Your boyfriend's a very lucky man."

Abby blushed. "I'm the lucky one. Gabe is a good man."

"Seems to be." He leaned back in his chair. "After I left your place last evening I went for a drive on Walking Stick Trail to see what I could find."

"And?"

He explained the car at a nearby resort, finding the cap and pipe in the car, followed by his conversation with Duncan O'Shea.

Abby's eyes grew wide. "Do you think he was the one who's been following me?"

"At this point, I don't think so."

"Why not?"

"For starters, your guy has a mustache. Duncan doesn't. Coulda shaved easy enough, though. He said the cap and pipe belong to his buddy who flew back to Canada last night. He gave me this buddy's phone number. It's on my list of to-dos for today."

"Canada?" she gasped. "Collin Miller is from Canada. That can't be a coincidence."

"Tell me something, has Collin Miller ever been inappropriate with you?"

"He attempted to hug me once but I pulled away from him. It was uncomfortable for me."

"Anything else?"

"Other than sitting too close on occasion, no. Why do you ask?"

"Just making sure. We both know Susan wasn't a one-time indiscretion," he said.

"Hm. He's admitted to two of them."

"A couple have come forward to me. Course they may be the two he admitted to."

Abby shuddered, then said softly, "I guess I should consider myself lucky. How sad is that?"

"How are things at the resort?" he asked.

"Better now that Gabe is there for the weekend. Hopefully, my son will be back home in a couple of days and then everything will be perfect."

He glanced at the photo by his phone. "They can be complex little creatures at times and certainly not easy, but I couldn't imagine life without my daughter."

Abby smiled. "I know what you mean. So did Susan Ramirez," she said, her voice barely audible.

Silence fell between them until Juan stood. Abby followed suit. "I'll walk you out," he said.

"Detective?" He stopped and turned to face her. "Do you think he's responsible for the murder?" she asked.

"Let me just say that at this point, whether directly or indirectly, I wouldn't be surprised."

Abby thought about that for a moment then shivered. "Yeah, I guess I wouldn't be surprised anymore, either."

Abby jogged across the street to the coffee shop before heading home.

"Hey, Travis," she said when she walked in.

"Abby!" he called cheerfully. "How goes it? Same old thing or a Travis Special?"

Abby smiled, the feel-good endorphins not quite reaching her brain. "Depends what the Travis Special is today. The last one was enjoyable. Can you match that one?"

"I'll do even better."

"That'll be good then. To go, though. I need to get back to the resort. Thanks, Trav."

"My pleasure," he said, tossing a stainless-steel steamer mug behind his back with one hand, catching it with the other. "What's new? Other than finding a body that is." Travis shook his head. "Man, that musta been rough. You're looking a little worn out. Sleeping okay?"

"As okay as one could be after something like that." She watched him mix a concoction of milk, coffee, and syrups. "Hey, have you happened to hear anything about it? The murder. Overhear anyone say anything?"

"Nope. Not a word. Which that in itself is strange around here. Usually, you can hear anything you want to in a coffee shop. And a lot of what you don't want to." He winked at her. "People at a table talk as if they're alone in their own kitchen without realizing that everyone in the room just heard their business."

"But nothing about Susan Ramirez, huh?"

"Nope. Nada." He snapped a lid onto the paper cup, slipped the cup into a cardboard sleeve, and slid it across the counter toward her.

She handed him some bills and slipped one into the tip jar. "Thanks. Appreciate it."

"As always, my pleasure."

Abby got to the door, opened, and turned to face him again. "Hey, Travis?"

"Yup."

"If you hear anything, anything at all, will you call me?" She walked a business card over to the counter and set it down. "I'd like to know I'm safe again out there."

Travis picked it up and tacked it to the side of the cash register with a magnet. "Sure will."

"Thanks."

She turned to leave and saw a plaid cap duck between two buildings, a puff of smoke lingering behind. She walked toward the smoke, nearly dissipated by the time she got there. Though the scent of cherry tobacco was unmistakable. She ducked in and out of a few businesses to lose the guy. Confident she had, she twisted her blond ponytail into a knot and flipped up her hood. Then as nonchalantly as she could, she made her way to her car. She wasn't quite sure why she was trying to lose him. He knew where she lived anyway. Who was this guy, and what did he want with her? He had plenty of opportunities to get at her, and yet he hadn't. Yet. What was he waiting for? As she thought of the unsavory possibilities, she shivered.

Constantly looking around her in every direction until she was out of town, she breathed a sigh of relief when she was on the main road home. Keeping her eyes peeled on the rearview mirror nearly caused her to hit two goats grazing on the side of the road, but other than that the drive home was blissfully uneventful. It was sad to think that a happy day in her life had become based on whether there were no stalkers or lurkers. And no dead bodies.

Abigail, what are you doing here? She'd never had these issues in Oakland. For a moment, she yearned to go back to a time when life was routine again. When she and Cooper drove to the same school every morning and she went to her classroom to teach for the day and him to his first class. The days when he sporadically came to see her throughout the day. Back to the time when she had her friend Holly, and they met for breaks and lunch. When she and Cooper drove back home together. Even the times he rode the bus home, the babysitter staying with him until Abby got home from work. Back to the evening routines of homework, a little TV time, and bed. And especially back to the time Henry was alive and well and Hunter was in prison. Although, that's exactly where he was again. In prison, where he belonged.

And yet, those days seemed so far away. The tagline from the old soap opera her mother used to watch ran through her mind—"Like sands through the hourglass, so are the days of our lives." *No truer statement had ever been made*, she thought.

And yet she couldn't imagine going back to those days. In fact, if she truly thought about it, life hadn't been so simple there either. Routine, yes, but in some ways it was even more dangerous with a man like Hunter, even though he was in prison. She wasn't so naive as to think he didn't have ways of getting to her if he wanted to. And routine just made her more complacent and easier to track.

Suddenly, her heart started beating fast. Too fast! Her hands gripped the steering wheel. Is that who the Sherlock looking man is working for? Hunter? A knot formed in the pit of her stomach. She pulled over and reached for her phone.

"Hey, Abs," her sister answered. "Did they find the guy? Is it safe to bring Cooper home?"

"Piper, what if this guy following me is one of Hunter's hired goons?"

"Dang, sis! I hadn't even thought of that." Her voice was grim. "Did you tell the detective?"

"He knows about the guy following me, yeah. Not about the part I just told you."

"You need to tell him."

"I know that. You're just the first person I thought of telling. Don't tell Cooper, though, okay?"

"Of course I won't. I'm not an idiot, you know."

Abby felt a semblance of relief at hearing her sister's sarcasm back in its normal place. She hated to admit it, but when her sister was concerned about something, it caused Abby herself to worry even more.

"Thanks, sis. Gotta go."

"Keep me posted, Abs. I mean it. We all know what that man is capable of."

"I will." She clicked off and dialed the number that had become all too familiar.

"Detective Robles."

"Hi Detective, it's Abigail."

"Did something happen?" The concern in his voice was palpable.

"I saw the Sherlock guy again when I left the police department, and—"

"Where?"

"Well, I didn't see him, just his cap as he ducked between two buildings. When I got closer, I could smell pipe smoke."

"Wait! You went closer? Why didn't you call me immediately?"

"Honestly? Because the only thing I thought of was to see who it was."

"Abby, I could have been out there in a split second and found the guy."

"I know, I'm sorry. I blew it." She hadn't planned on the scolding and it rattled her, though she knew he was fully justified. "What if my ex-husband hired this guy?"

"I've already thought of that. I have some guys checking into it."

"Oh."

"You have to trust me, okay? This isn't my first day on the job. But you need to let me know the minute these things happen, not an hour later."

"But it hasn't been an hour," she said defensiveness creeping in.

"You know what I mean. Now, please, if anything like that happens again, call me immediately. We don't need another homicide to investigate. Until Susan Ramirez, Blue Mist Mountain hadn't had one for decades."

"I understand. And I will. Thank you."

Abby tossed the phone on the seat beside her and lay her head back against the headrest while she collected herself. After a few moments, she sat up straight, adjusted her seat belt, and prepared to pull back onto the road. She glanced in her side mirror and saw a few cars and waited for them to pass before she pulled out. When the last one approached, it slowed to a near stop beside her car, a piece of white cardboard covered the entire passenger side window. Written in red marker was, *Mind your own business or it will be your day to die like Ms. Ramirez.*

Abby gasped and reached for her phone, keeping an eye on the car as it passed. Slowly. She struggled to see from the back passenger window who the holder of the sign was and felt a sharp punch to her gut. Collin!

19

Juan hated lying to Abby. When she inquired into investigation details, he'd had no choice. It was an open investigation, and he couldn't tell her the truth. He was just relieved she hadn't fallen for the man's shenanigans.

As soon as she left his office, he called the number for Shawn Carnahan.

"Carnahan Carnahan and Sibley," a woman's voice said.

"Shawn Carnahan, please," Juan said.

"He's in a meeting. Would you like his voicemail?"

"That'll work. Thank you."

Juan waited for the transfer then left the appropriate voicemail, giving a brief description of the reason for his call and asked Shawn to call him as soon as he had a moment. He hadn't expected Shawn to be in the office at all. Not on a Saturday and not when his voicemail said he wouldn't be back in the office until Monday. He hadn't known what to expect. He just knew he needed answers. And he just got some.

He sat back in his chair and stared at the phone. So Shawn Carnahan is an attorney. That put a new spin on things. Not that attorneys couldn't be dirty. Just like cops, most were good, but there were a few sleazeballs. Like Abby's ex-husband in the pool of good cops. Juan decided a Skype visit would better help him determine whether Shawn was the party responsible for stalking Abby. But the fact that Abby saw the

Sherlock-looking character when Shawn was in Canada brought even more questions.

He was still staring at the phone when it rang. Apparently, the meeting didn't last long. Or Shawn hadn't been in a meeting at all. He reached for the receiver.

"Robles."

"Something has happened."

He bolted upright in his chair. "Abby? Where are you?"

"On the side of Elk Ridge Road. The one that goes to the resort. I can't—"

"Abby, I need you to take a deep breath, okay? I'm on my way." He grabbed his blazer from the chair. "I'm going to hang up and call you back on my cell phone."

"Okay. Please hurry."

Juan slipped his arms into his jacket and punched in Abby's number as he hustled through the lobby, but it went to voicemail. "Crap! Pearl, I've gotta run. Johnson!" he called to the officer who was pouring a cup of coffee in a travel mug. "Come on. We're going to Whispering Pines Resort."

"You got it, jefe."

"Your Spanish is terrible, dude," Juan said. "Speak English until you can do it right." He playfully cupped him on the back of the head as Johnson passed him. "Now come on!"

"What are we headed to?" Johnson asked, smoothing the hair on the back of his head.

As they jogged to their respective cars, Juan briefly filled him in on the most critical details. "I don't know exactly what's happening now, just that Ms. Sinclair called in a panic. Go!"

Juan stuck his police light on top of his car and peeled out of the parking lot and onto the road, going through the red light as cars stopped to let him through. Johnson was already ahead of him. He tried Abby again.

"Hello?" she answered, her voice trembling.

"I told you I was calling you right back from my cell phone."

"I'm sorry. Gabe called. I'm headed to the house to meet him and my father. I'm almost there now."

"Well, stay on the line with me until you get there. We're about two minutes out."

"We?"

"Me and Officer Johnson. Tell me what happened."

Abby filled him in. "It was Collin Miller. I saw him."

"That doesn't sound right. Why would Collin Miller let you see him?"

"I don't think he meant to, but I did. The sign covered the entire front passenger window. I saw him from the back in the rear passenger window."

"So you didn't get a clear look."

"It was him. I'm telling you."

"Okay, okay. Was it the same car?"

"No, it was a black Kia."

"Plate?" He held his breath.

"FXY-533."

Juan's eyes popped wide, surprised. "Good job." He keyed the plate into the computer mounted on his dashboard, keeping one eye on the road. "Well, well, well. It's registered to Collin Miller."

"See? It was him. He killed Susan! I know it now. The sign said it would be my day to die like Ms. Ramirez. He did it."

"I'm turning onto your road now."

"Officer Johnson just pulled in behind me, so I'm going to hang up."

When Juan pulled into the driveway, he saw Johnson, Gabe, and Abby through the kitchen window. Gabe's arm wrapped tight around Abby. Juan caught a glimpse of Jeremiah in the background, the concern of a father for his daughter etched into every line of his face. He knew how Jeremiah Jordan felt. He'd be worried sick if this was his daughter. Juan had been forty-seven when his daughter was born. He just hoped he'd live long enough to protect her from all the evils in the world. Man, he sure could use a drink.

After getting the last details from Abby, Johnson stayed at the house with Jeremiah and Gabe while he and Abby, along with Gus, trekked out to the site where she saw the Sherlock look-a-like watching her through binoculars.

"Keep Gus away from the area so he doesn't disturb any evidence," Juan said.

Abby kept him on a short leash away from the scene, scanning the surrounding area. Juan took photos of any footprint remnants, some surprisingly intact in the shaded snowy areas not yet melted by the sun.

"Gus found something," Abby called to him.

Juan stopped and looked over at them, the dog nudging something with his black nose. "Coming over. Pull Gus back." Carefully making his way to them, taking in everything in his path, he looked at the small black patch on the ground then snapped a photo before slipping on a glove and picking it up. "Looks like a fake mustache." He turned it over between his fingers. "One of those Halloween-style peel and stick ones."

Abby bent over him, looking at it.

"That means—"

"That this guy made an effort to look like Sherlock Holmes."

"So do you think he's a detective of some sort?"

"Yes, I do. But I think he's some cheesy guy playing at it." He scanned the area still in his squatted position.

"But why? And who? I mean, why would he be watching me?"

"That's what I need to find out."

"Hunter!" she gasped. "It's gotta be."

He watched as fear transformed her face. "Don't jump to conclusions. We don't know that." But he was worried about the same thing. Yet he suspected it was all related to Collin Miller. The timing of it all was too coincidental.

He reached in his pocket and unfolded a photo he'd printed earlier that morning. The beauty of the Internet. You can find anything on anyone, down to an up-close picture of the house a person lives in. "Do you recognize this guy?"

Abby studied the photo. "Umm...yes! He's a spitting image of the man who's been following me but without the mustache."

"That's because, my dear Watson, your Sherlock's mustache is right here in my hand. And he's a Mr. Duncan O'Shea. Looks like me and Duncan need to have another little chat."

He stood, wincing as his knees complained about squatting for too long. After another brief look around, they trotted back to the resort.

"Well?" Gabe met them at the door. "Find anything?"

Juan held up the baggie that contained the mustache. Gabe's questioning look made him explain.

"The photo of Duncan O'Shea matches the guy who's been following me and who was watching me from the woods," Abby said. "Minus the mustache in that bag." She nodded toward Juan.

"Why?" Jeremiah asked, voice steady and quiet. "Why is this man stalking my daughter?"

"I don't know, Mr. Jordan, but I intend to find out. I'll go have a chat with Mr. O'Shea right now. Johnson," he said, "I want you to patrol this area frequently. And you three," he looked at Abby, Gabe, and Jeremiah, "if you see anything at all, call 9-1-1."

"Not you?" Jeremiah asked.

"9-1-1 first. Then call me. And Abby," he said, looking at her, "Stay put, will you? Do not leave this house without Gabe or your father."

"For how long?"

"Until I tell you otherwise." Now wasn't the time for her to pronounce her independence, and he silently prayed she wouldn't push it. Prayer answered. As he walked out the door, there wasn't a word of argument.

Once again, Juan drove down Walking Stick Trail. Unlike yesterday, he knew exactly who he was looking for. He pulled up to the resort Duncan was staying at and ran into George in the parking lot.

"Juan!" George called, clapping him on the back when he reached him. "What brings you here?"

"Looking to speak with Duncan O'Shea again."

"Gone. Took off early this morning. Wife's still here, though. She's not leaving until tomorrow."

"Guess she'll have to do for now, then," Juan said. "I can find my way. Thanks, George."

"Pleasure's mine. Let me know if you need any help. It'd feel good to do a little work in the field again."

"And have Shirley jump me about causing you undue stress? Don't think so, pal. I'm scared of her." He grinned.

"Doesn't hurt a man to try," he said, chuckling.

Juan wound his way around the sidewalks leading to the condo he was at the previous evening. He rang the doorbell and waited. When he turned to walk away, assuming no one was there, he heard the lock click. A woman in her late thirties stared at him through the screen door. She tightened the belt on her robe, her black hair messed up.

"Can I help you?" she asked.

"Sorry, didn't mean to wake you."

"No problem. What do you need?" Her tone spoke loud and clear that she wanted him gone yesterday. That she had much more important things to tend to.

Juan heard a door close from somewhere behind her. "Detective Robles with Blue Mist Mountain PD." He held up his badge. "You alone? I thought Duncan left this morning."

"Yeah, he did." She looked behind her. "The wind from opening the front door must have caused one of the doors to shut."

"Can I come in for a minute? Just a couple a questions is all."

"Now's not a good time. I can come down to the station later if I need to."

"Nah, that's not necessary. I can ask you from here." She shifted her weight from one foot to the other, her gaze darting behind her, then back at Juan. "Can you tell me what your husband does for a living?"

"Oil business."

"Anything else?"

"Why?"

"Curious."

"I'm not an idiot, Detective Robles. There's a reason for your questions. Now if you're not going to be honest with me, then I don't have the slightest interest in being honest with you." She started closing the door.

"Wait," Juan said before she closed it all the way. "You're right. There is a reason I'm asking."

She opened the door again, this time only halfway. "And?"

"I know he works as a PI. Private investigator."

"I know what PI stands for," she said, rolling her eyes and acting as if she couldn't be more bored. "What's this got to do with me?" There was another sound from the back room, followed by a muffled curse.

"I think this is the part where I tell you I'm not an idiot, Ms. O'Shea. Is he here?"

"No. And that's the truth. My marriage and what happens in it is none of your business. But I can assure you my husband is not here."

"Who hired him for the job here in Blue Mist Mountain, Ms. O'Shea?"

"How would I know?"

"You don't care who he works for?"

"As long as he's getting paid, no, I don't."

"Do you know who paid him?" Juan asked.

Her eyes hardened. "No. If I knew that, I'd know who he's working for, now wouldn't I? If you don't mind, I have to be going."

"Of course." He scanned the area behind her before she slammed the door closed in his face. But not before he saw the pair of men's black dress shoes beside the sofa and a dress jacket hanging on one of the kitchen chairs. Juan jotted down on his notepad the details of both for later reference.

He'd no sooner said goodbye to George who was still in the parking lot and got into his car, fastening his seat belt, when his cell phone rang.

"Detective Robles." He put the car in reverse and began backing out of the parking space.

"This is Shawn Carnahan returning your call."

Juan pulled back into the parking space, turned off his car, and retrieved his notepad. "Thank you for calling back. I understand you're a friend of Duncan O'Shea's. That's who gave me your number."

"That's correct. Duncan and I went to college together."

"I wouldn't have guessed that with you going to law school and Duncan working in the oil industry."

"I didn't start out wanting to be an attorney. Long story."

"What can you tell me about his job as a PI?"

"It's not a job. A hobby of his is all. Nothing serious. How did you even find out about it? He doesn't tell anyone."

"How long has he been doing it?"

"Maybe five years or so. As I said, it's nothing more than a hobby. A paid hobby, but a hobby, nonetheless. Some people play video games for fun. Duncan takes gigs as a PI."

"Do you know who he was working for just recently?"

"No. I never asked him."

"The cap and pipe in his car. He said they were yours. But he's been seen wearing them."

Shawn laughed. "Yeah. I got those for him as an inside joke. He's seriously been wearing the cap and mustache?"

"Yes."

"Smoking the pipe, too?"

"Yes."

He laughed again, louder this time. "What a joker. What's this all about, Detective Robles? I'm sure you didn't call me to talk about Duncan's Sherlock getup."

"Do you know Collin Miller?"

"Why do you ask?" The change in his tone was palpable, almost a growl, an intense dislike apparent.

"Well, with you both being from Canada and wintering here and all..."

"There's a hell of a lot of people from Canada, Detective. And there's still a lot of us here. Thank God Collin's not one of them."

"I take it there's no love lost there."

"No comment."

"Did you represent Collin as his attorney when he lived in Canada?" He was met with silence. Silence that spoke what he needed to know. "What did you represent him for?"

"As much as I'd like to, you know I can't answer that. Attorney-Client Privilege. But you can find out some of this on your end."

"And I will. I do know this much, that he lost his license to practice for misconduct." Juan knew he was treading on thin ice. He knew of no such thing. It was mere suspicion. He just hoped it wasn't wrong, causing Shawn to stop from telling him anything else.

"So you've done some of your homework already. I'm sure you can understand when I tell you I refused to represent him in the United States then. My specialty is business law, not family drama. And forgery doesn't fall within business law."

Forgery? Juan pumped his fist in the air, stating as calmly as he could, "I understand completely. If you think of anything you can tell me, I'd appreciate you letting me know. You have my number."

"Indeed I do." He cleared his throat. "If I could help you, I would. Collin Miller is a piece of trash that needs to be taken out."

"Just one more thing. Have you ever heard of Susan Ramirez, Mr. Carnahan?"

"I might have heard the name."

"That's all?"

"That I can think of right now."

"What about Abigail Sinclair?"

"Yes. And that one I can tell you about because it has nothing to do with me. My buddy was hired to follow and watch her. The guy told him—Duncan—that the woman was doing something shady that was destroying him."

Juan's heart rate ticked up a notch. "Do you know who it was that hired him?"

"No, but I can find out if it would help you."

"That would be huge. Thank you. I just spoke with his wife and—"

"Amy? Let me guess, she wouldn't help you."

"Said she didn't know. That she knew he was doing a job but didn't know for who."

"Duncan wasn't there?"

"No, he left early this morning."

"Was Amy alone?" Now it was Juan who cleared his throat. "No need to answer that," Shawn said. "My guess is she wasn't."

"I didn't see anyone, but, you know..."

"Yeah, I do. I know, that is." Shawn exhaled loudly on his end. "I've suspected for a long time. When she took me and my wife to the airport, she said more than she should have. I'm Duncan's friend, not hers."

"Thank you. And like I said, if you know anything else..."

"Good luck, Detective. I hope you catch the little weasel. And you might want to check into Collin Miller's whereabouts during the time frame you were speaking with Amy O'Shea."

Juan's eyebrows shot up. "Collin Miller and Amy O'Shea?"

"That didn't come from me."

When Juan hung up, he drove his car to the far corner of the parking lot, across from Duncan and Amy's condo. He tucked it behind a panel van that belonged to the grounds crew and waited. Sure enough, twenty-five minutes later, out came Collin Miller, pants perfectly pressed, a matching blazer that had been hanging on a kitchen chair in Amy O'Shea's condo, and the black dress shoes he'd seen there as well. Juan snapped some pictures with his cell phone. "Looks like Mr. Miller has a problem that's going to bury him," he mumbled as he watched Collin drive off in a new sporty red car. "How many cars does the man have?" he muttered again. "Sheesh!" Then he noticed the dealer plates. "Collin Miller has a side job." He watched until the car was out of sight.

When Juan got back to the office, he submitted a new records request for Collin Miller from Canada's Criminal Records Information Management Services. He'd had to run one on someone else a few years back, so he was familiar with the different levels of a standard criminal record check. For Collin, Juan chose to run the level four so he could get insight into any sexual offenses and convictions. He stopped typing and leaned back in his chair, tapping the tip of his pen on his desk as he thought about it. Maybe he should extend the reach and do a check in the vulnerable sector. These women could qualify as being harmed by a person in a position of authority or trust. Yes. The women of whom Collin potentially took advantage deserved the time and effort. He sat back up, fingers on the keyboard. Juan had a strong hunch he was onto something. Collin Miller's past was quickly rolling into his present and was about to run him over.

20

Abby opened the door to Devil's Brew coffee shop, waving a final time to Gabe who sat waiting in the car for her. His concealed weapon he'd purchased last summer, a little Taurus 360 handgun, was tucked under his seat.

Martha waved at her from a little table in the corner across the room.

"Hi, Martha," Abby said, extending her hand. She looked at the woman, trying to match her with Collin Miller, but was unable to. She was a mousy, timid-looking woman with thin walnut-colored hair. Her jeggings were snug against her full thighs, her blouse tugging against her ample bosom. "Thank you for agreeing to meet later than originally planned," Abby said.

"Of course. I have to admit when you called I was afraid you were calling to cancel. So when you said you wanted to push it back to two o'clock, well," she shrugged a shoulder, "imagine my relief. I know I don't know you, but you sounded a little out of sorts when you called. Everything okay?"

"Yes, it's fine." Divulging her business to a stranger, especially Collin's wife, wasn't tempting in the slightest. Gabe had warned her of that very thing before she got out of the car. Right before she told him she was a big girl who didn't need him to tell her what to say and not to say. And that right before she apologized profusely for being on edge.

"I got here a little early and ordered already," Martha said, motioning toward her half-empty cup. "Their cappuccinos are the bomb here."

The bomb? Abby hadn't heard anyone much older than Cooper use that term. "Excuse me while I go get something," she said, making her way to the counter. After reviewing the menu posted on the wall behind the counter, she decided on a vanilla latte. A real treat for her. She typically had tea or black coffee. *Boring stuff*, as Travis had told her numerous times. While she waited, she watched Martha out of the corner of her eye. The woman appeared lost somehow, like she was searching for something or someone to befriend. By Martha's fear of being seen, Abby wondered if Collin was abusive to her. She fit the stereotype of the abused woman. Abby pitied her. She could very likely benefit from the domestic violence support group she planned to start. She turned away, chiding herself for jumping to conclusions and being so judgmental.

Drink in hand, she swerved through several tables packed into the small space and pulled out the chair across from Martha. She hung her purse on the edge of her chair.

She looked at Martha, who was staring out the window. "So what's up?"

Martha peeled her gaze away from the mountainside and looked at Abby. "How well do you know my husband?"

Abby leaned forward, her brow furrowed. "Why do you ask?"

Martha looked away momentarily and crossed her arms, leaning on the table. She focused on Abby again. "Because what I'm about to tell you...well, you might think I'm crazy. And if you're a fan of my husband's—"

"Martha, whatever it is, you're safe in telling me. I would be the last person in the world to go back to him with anything you tell me. For one thing, I'm no longer his patient. Whatever you tell me is strictly between us." Abby leaned forward a bit more, closing the gap, letting Martha know she had her undivided attention.

"I think my husband was seeing that woman you found on your property. You know," she whispered, shielding her mouth with her hand so Abby had to struggle to hear her, "the dead one."

Abby fought to keep any element of surprise at bay. She lifted her cup to take a drink but quickly set it back down when she noticed her hand trembling. "Seeing her?"

"Yes. Having an affair."

"What makes you say that?" The murder and her stalker had completely consumed her time and energy. Oddly, it caused her to second-guess her conclusion that Susan's child was Collin's. What if what Collin had told Detective Robles was true? What if Ryan truly was his nephew and she'd made a gigantic mistake in her assumption? If it was a blood relative, heterochromia would still make sense. Things seemed to move in slow motion as she processed what Martha had just told her. Blood pulsed in her ears.

"I've been noticing large chunks of money missing from his account, and—"

"His account?"

"Yes. We have separate accounts. When we got married, my father insisted me and Collin have separate accounts or he wouldn't give me my inheritance. Daddy owns several car dealerships, and I'm an only child. So you can guess who gets the money when he's gone." She thrust her thumb toward her chest.

"Is he? Your father—is he gone?"

"No, but it won't be long. He has stage IV liver cancer."

Her heart ached for the woman. If Abby lost her father, she'd be devastated. She crossed her arms, elbows on the table, and lightly rubbed her biceps. "I'm so sorry, Martha."

She waved a hand. "You know what they say," she said through a tight smile, "nothing in life is guaranteed except death and taxes."

"Yes, but that doesn't mean it's easy."

Martha's eyes brimmed with tears, and she looked down at her hands now folded around her cup. "No. No, it's not," she said quietly.

"So what did you find in his bank statements?" Abby said.

"Significant amounts of money missing, checks written out to Susan Ramirez."

"How much money are we talking about?"

"Ten thousand a month. It's taken from the account that has the income from the only car dealership daddy has agreed to give him." She looked deep into Abby's eyes. "Daddy has never liked my husband. Not from day one."

"Martha, I have to ask—well, how did you get access to his account? I can't imagine he'd let you see it or give you the password."

Martha scoffed. "Heck no! I watched from behind him one time as he logged in. He was so engrossed in what he was doing that he didn't know I was there."

"Pretty careless on his part," Abby said as she took a drink.

"Right?" Martha chuckled bitterly, what came out like a snorting sound. "I never said my husband was a smart man."

She appeared to ponder whether to continue. Abby stayed quiet, letting her decide. "She had a kid, you know. Susan."

"Yes, I did know that. Did you ever see him?"

"Once." Her eyes took on a faraway look and for a moment Abby thought she'd lost her. "I followed him into town one day. Collin, not the kid. I saw her coming out of his office with the little boy."

"How long have you and Collin been married?"

"Five years. He'd just moved here the year before. We met and—well, it was love at first sight. For me, at least."

"And for him?" Abby asked.

"The first time we went out, we talked and got to know each other, and, well, the rest is history. He fell in love with me. I just don't know when he fell out of love with me." She picked up her cup to take a drink, but decided against it apparently, because she set it back down on the table and looked out the window again.

She looked so pathetic sitting there. Abby almost wanted to hug her. Almost. Instead, she reached over and placed her hand gently over Martha's. Martha's hand twitched.

"Martha, has Collin ever hurt you? Physically," she added. It was becoming more obvious by the minute that the man emotionally abused her.

Her eyes widened, the tip of her nose turned pink. "Why would you ask such a thing? Collin loves me."

"You just said you think he's fallen out of love with you."

"He's just—well, he's confused right now," she stammered. "He'll come around. Marriage isn't something either of us takes lightly."

Abby almost choked on the drink she just swallowed. This woman was in denial with a capital D. "I'm in the process of planning a support group for victims of domestic violence. Maybe you could come see what it's all about when I have it up and running. It could be a while, though. There's a lot I have to do on my end."

"Why would I need a group like that? I'm afraid you've got the wrong impression." A gleam of defiance flickered in her eye but disappeared just as quickly.

"Martha," Abby said, "Collin is going to be found out. It's just a matter of time. Please protect yourself."

"What do you mean, *found out?*" Her eyes were haunting yet flat and lifeless.

"I think you know what I mean. You may not be ready to hear it, but it's out there. People know. He will be found out. I would like to help you." Abby watched as Martha tried to process what was said. After a few moments, Abby looked at her watch. "I need to get going. My boyfriend is waiting for me in the car. But please, I'm begging you, think about what I said. You don't have to live this way."

"Your boyfriend is waiting for you?"

"Yes."

"How long have you been going out?"

"A while."

"He doesn't trust you to come alone?"

"He trusts me, yes. He just doesn't—" she stopped herself before saying anything she knew she shouldn't. "We're just doing some shopping and thought it'd be easier to do both at the same time rather than making two trips."

"Oh. He must be a good man."

Abby genuinely smiled for the first time since coming into the coffee shop. "Yes, he is. He's a keeper, for sure."

"Well, make sure you're good back to him. My husband left early this morning. Long before his office even opens." Her lips twisted in a sad attempt at a smile. "He's a hard worker, you know."

Abby cocked her head to the side and studied Martha a moment. "I am good to Gabe. Thank you for your concern." She stood and slipped her purse strap over her shoulder. "Take care, okay? And if you change your mind and decide to visit the support group when I get it going, you're more than welcome. It's going to be called A Future Without Violence. Watch for the flyers I'll hang around town."

"Thank you, Abigail. But I'm sure I don't need no such thing."

"I hope not, Martha. I hope not. I'll pray for your father." With one last look at her, Abby turned and left.

As soon as she shut her car door, Abby turned toward Gabe. "Well, I know why Collin married Martha. For money." Gabe's questioning look encouraged her to go on. "And she knows about Collin and Susan, Gabe. She's seen his bank statements. Collin was paying Susan ten thousand a month. Probably a combination of child support and hush money."

"All hush money after he took the child away from her," Gabe said, scowling. "What a pig." He started the car. "We need to get this information to Detective Robles."

"I promised Martha what she said would stay only between us. That I wouldn't tell anyone."

"Detective Robles isn't just anyone. This could be critical information."

Abby felt torn between doing what she promised and what she knew was right. "I don't know, Gabe. I need to think about it."

"Babe, there's no time to think about it. We need to get to the bottom of this so Cooper can come home."

At the mention of Cooper, she swayed toward doing the right thing, but hesitated again. "What kind of facilitator am I going to be for a support group if I can't keep what people say confidential?"

"This isn't your support group. It's a murder investigation. Besides, when a murder is involved and your life is in danger, safety trumps confidentiality." Gabe's tone was solid, unwavering.

"I know you're right, it's just that—well, I made a promise."

"Unfortunately, a promise you're unable to keep. Think of it this way, by telling Detective Robles, you're probably keeping Martha alive. If Collin has killed once, he can kill again. You said it yourself that Martha appears abused, at least mentally. Collin will only escalate. You know that. We can go see him right now. Detective Robles, not Collin," he added quickly. "I'll be with you."

That was all it took to persuade her. "I'll just call him. But drive somewhere else so when Martha comes out she doesn't see me on the phone. This parking lot isn't big enough to hide." Abby clicked her seat belt into place before Gabe pulled out and onto the road. Comfortable she was far enough away, she punched in the detective's number programmed into her phone. As she mentally prepared what to say in the voicemail she was sure she would have to leave, he picked up, sounding distracted.

"Detective Robles."

"It's Abby. And Gabe. Is this a bad time?"

He cleared his throat, and there was shuffling of papers followed by a loud crash. "No, no. Are you okay? What happened?"

"I just met with Martha Miller."

"Abby—"

"It was okay. We met in a public place and Gabe came with me and waited in the car. When she called asking to meet, she sounded desperate. I was worried about her. I couldn't tell her no." She heard him exhale and grumble something unintelligible.

"And?"

Abby filled him in on the entire conversation. "That proves Collin killed Susan Ramirez, right? Ten thousand a month?"

"It doesn't prove anything except that he probably has an illegitimate child with her. And he's an unethical therapist who is practicing without a license."

"But it gives him motive—wait, what? He's practicing without a license? How did you find that out?"

"I don't know that for certain, but I'm fairly confident. I ordered his criminal history from Canada. And I spoke with Shawn Carnahan and Duncan O'Shea. And that's all I can tell you, which is more than I should have."

"His license was revoked?"

"My guess is, yes, for sanctions placed on him in Canada."

"And yet he practiced here."

"As I said, I've told you too much already. We'll have to wait for the records request to come back to know for sure. In the meantime, I'll check into the information you just gave me."

"Thank you."

Abby hung up as she looked out her side window. Martha looked at her through her own car window. The light turned green and Gabe took off but not before Abby saw the pained look on Martha's face. It was unmistakable. Abby's stomach lurched. Martha would never trust her again.

21

After speaking with Abby, the dealer plates on Collin's hot new red sports car made sense. As well as the number of other cars that came back registered to him. The first thing he needed to do was to get a court order for Collin's bank records. But he needed something strong enough for the judge to sign a warrant. Something concrete. He was getting closer and closer to tying Collin to the murder of Susan Ramirez. He could feel it.

He puffed his cheeks and blew air through pursed lips, making a whistling sound.

"Boss?" He looked up to find Officer Johnson standing in his doorway, one hand on either side of the door frame.

"Yup. Come in."

Officer Johnson was already across the small office and sitting in the chair opposite Juan's desk. "Got somethin' for you. It's good."

"What is it? I could use good right now."

"Pearl said that after Shonna talked with you, she agreed to file charges."

"Pearl told you that?" Juan raised an eyebrow.

"She did."

"Was Pearl supposed to tell you that? Shonna's business is Shonna's business."

"Relax. Shonna already told me about it anyway."

Juan's eyebrows shot up. "Something you want to tell me, Johnson?"

Johnson's smile told him more than he wanted to know. "Walk carefully. You know how the Chief feels about dating in the workplace."

"Yeah, but I don't supervise her so it shouldn't be a problem."

"My suggestion is to have that talk with the Chief now so it doesn't become a problem."

Johnson's grin grew. "You worry too much, sir. Shonna's going to come back today and let you know."

Johnson left and Juan shook his head. He wished them both the best but knew all too well the perils of romance in the workplace. Had seen it blow up far too many times during the course of his career, ruining too many people. He'd almost been a casualty of one of those blow-ups with a fellow female officer before he'd married his wife.

He shook his head again, clearing his mind of the disturbing memory, then picked up the phone. The man answered on the second ring.

"Dr. Miller. Can I help you?"

"This is Detective Robles."

"Nice to hear from you, Detective. Are you calling with news on Ms. Sinclair? She was following me again earlier today. The last I heard stalking is illegal."

"Maybe you should come to my office so you can tell me about it." It wasn't exactly the way Juan had planned to ask him to come in, but the opportunity was too perfect to pass up.

"I have a patient due in fifteen minutes. It'll have to wait," he said.

"Where were you when this so-called stalking occurred?"

"Is that cynicism I hear in your voice, Detective?"

"Not at all, Doctor." Juan bit his tongue from saying something inappropriate. *Doctor* wasn't exactly what he wanted to call the man. "You can tell me about it when you come in." He wanted to talk to him in person. He'd always been particularly good at reading body language and was usually spot on no matter how hard someone tried to hide it. The Chief told him it was his gift. Juan could think of other things he'd like as a gift, like full custody of his daughter. Or heck, someone to pay off his mortgage. Reading body language didn't qualify as a gift as far as he was concerned.

"Have you looked into Abigail Sinclair at all? You haven't, have you?"

"I've looked into a lot of people, Dr. Miller." *Especially you.*

"You haven't answered my question."

"This isn't a game. I'm the detective. I ask the questions. Now you told me that Abigail Sinclair has been following you. I'm asking you to stop by and tell me about it. If you want me to look into it, you need to answer my questions so I know what it is I'm looking into."

"It was on Elk Pass Road. Earlier today."

Apparently over the phone would have to do. For now. "Yeah? What were you doing on Elk Pass Road?"

"That's none of your business. I'm not the one who's in the wrong here."

"Well, actually, it is. My business that is. Elk Pass Road is right by Ms. Sinclair's house. She has to drive that way to get home. So my question remains, what were *you* doing on Elk Pass Road, out by Ms. Sinclair's house?"

"Visiting a client who is staying at one of the resorts. She was ill and not able to make it out."

"Amy O'Shea?" The question was met with dead silence. "Collin?"

"You know I can't divulge the names of my clients. Besides, what does it matter who it was?"

You were making a house call all right, but it wasn't for therapy. Juan swallowed his retort. "Of course not. Do you have any openings in your schedule this afternoon to come by the station? You can tell me about your incident then."

"I can be there about four."

"Perfect. You sure stay busy, huh?"

"Word of mouth is the best advertisement there is. That's why Ms. Sinclair needs to stay out of my business. Literally. I must go. I just heard the door to my patient waiting area open."

"See you in a bit," said Juan.

Juan held the phone in his hand long after the line went dead. He wondered how far Collin Miller was going to push the whole issue. He may very well be burying his own business by working so hard to blame Abby for his woes. Juan could only hope it happened sooner rather than later, sparing any further victims.

His cell phone pinged with a text message. *Hi daddy. Can you pick me up from Shannon's house about five?*

Where does she live? He texted back.

Out on Mountain View. 19153, came the response mere seconds later.

Juan's interest piqued. Mountain View was the road that the Millers lived on, about ten miles out of town. Looking at the address given by his daughter, it was only a mile or so from the Millers. If luck was on his side, he'd have an opportunity to speak with Shannon's parents to see if they know Collin and Martha. If not, he'd have to make it happen somehow.

Daddy? Can you?

~~Patience kiddo. It takes your old man a while to type with his big fat~~ *fingers. Yes. I can pick u up.*

Awesome! Thanks!

Wait! He added. *Did you ask your mom?*

What do you think?

An answer please.

Yes. She's busy and told me 2 call you.

See you soon.

Juan smiled. Seeing his daughter was exactly what he needed to brighten his day. And hearing from her was exactly the motivation he needed to make sure Collin Miller was found out before he victimized more women. If anyone ever took advantage of his daughter, well—he shuddered at what he might be capable of.

Collin breezed through the front doors of the police department while Juan dropped off a file for Pearl.

"Detective," he said harshly, "I've only got about ten minutes. Let's get this over with."

Pearl looked at Juan with raised eyebrows then glared at Collin over the rims of her reading glasses. Juan placed a hand on her shoulder and smiled, calming the protective side of Pearl. "It's okay," he murmured.

"Careful, Detective. Touching a female employee like that will land you in a hot mess of sexual harassment," Collin said.

Pearl attempted to stand, and Juan gently pressed her back down. Angry heat radiated through the yellow blouse.

"Doctor," she said tightly, "you'll have a seat and wait your turn like any other person who comes in here."

"It's okay, Pearl. I was expecting him. I just forgot to let you know."

Pearl relaxed a bit but didn't take her eyes off Collin. The man didn't know what he'd just done. Pearl was the most loyal, kind-hearted woman on this side of heaven, but when someone was rude to her friends, all bets were off. And somehow, with just two sentences, Collin had managed to make it on her list of enemies. And that list probably only contained one name.

"Come on back, Mr. Miller," Juan said, standing between him and Pearl as he passed through the front room. "We'll head on back to room one."

Juan led the way, Collin close on his heels. He opened the door and Collin strode through, taking a seat at the old, worn table. Juan turned one of the straight-backed chairs around and straddled it. He flipped on the recording device on the table and rested his arms across the chair's back.

"I assume it's okay if I record our conversation?"

"Of course. I have nothing to hide."

Juan suppressed another retort. "Of course not. Start from the beginning." The fact that Collin wanted to talk with him made it easier to get the information he needed with less chance of the man becoming defensive.

"I was driving down the road to my client's house, minding my own business," Collin said, "when Abigail Sinclair pulled up on the side of the road beside me. She mean-mugged me and sped off."

Juan struggled not to laugh. "Mean-mugged you?"

"Yes. You know what I mean."

"And you felt threatened?"

Collin frowned. "Of course I did, wouldn't you? I mean, we don't know what Ms. Sinclair is capable of. Ms. Ramirez's body was found in her hot tub after all. And that only a day after she saw her leave my office."

"You think there's a connection there." It was a statement rather than a question.

"Of course! Don't you? How could you not think there's a connection?" Collin scoffed, apparently shocked that Juan didn't come to the same conclusion. "It's not unusual for a patient to develop feelings for her therapist. Happens all the time. I didn't reciprocate those feelings and look where we are. She's angry and vindictive and will stop at nothing to get back at me. Including murder."

The man's arrogance yielded Juan speechless. Though he wasn't sure why it surprised him. Collin was a narcissist and this was simply a fabricated story made up by a narcissistic person. He should be used to dealing with the narcissistic personality. Up until five years ago when they'd finally reached an understanding, he'd had years of practice with his ex-wife. And yet, here he was. He pitied Martha.

"So what is it you want us in the police department to do? We can put detail on your house and office. In fact, I can get it approved by the Chief today." *Please, oh please, say yes.* But he knew it wouldn't be that easy.

"Absolutely not," Collin boomed. He slammed his fist down on the table. "I will not have your goons following me around like I'm the criminal."

"No one said you're a criminal, Mr. Miller," Juan said. *Well, not out loud.* "But if you feel threatened, that's the best way for us to be sure you're safe."

Collin sat on the edge of his chair. "No, I won't hear of it."

"We can't help you if you won't let us."

"Follow *her*. Keep her away from me." His words were clipped.

"With all due respect, Doctor, we don't just follow people. We can offer you protection if you feel you need it."

Collin sat back in his chair with a loud exhale. "With all due respect to *you*, Detective, you guys are worthless."

"I'm sorry you feel that way. We offered you protection and you refused." Juan met Collin's gaze, neither wavering. A competition of the wills. "Do you have any children?" Juan asked.

Collin's face reddened. "My wife can't have children. It doesn't seem to be a secret around this town."

Juan shrugged. "I don't get involved in town gossip. But I did see a child that looks an awful lot like you the other day."

"You did? Or Ms. Sinclair did? Because that's exactly the gossip that can destroy my livelihood as a marriage and family therapist. And that's the kind of gossip that will get her in the same hot water as Susan Ramirez. No pun intended."

"Is that a threat against Ms. Sinclair, Mr. Miller?" Juan's eyes darted to the recorder, making sure the red light still shone.

Collin stood up, rested both hands on the table, and leaned toward Juan. "Keep an eye on that woman, Detective. She's a menace and she's dangerous."

Juan stood and followed Collin as he stomped out of the room, through the doors to the lobby, past Pearl, and out the front doors into the cool air.

"Guess you peed in his Wheaties, huh, sir?" Pearl said with a grimace.

"Guess you could say that, Pearl." He looked at her and grinned. "And it was fun."

"He's on Santa's naughty list this year and it's only March." She clucked her tongue and shook her head.

At 4:45, Juan left for Shannon's house to pick up his daughter. He was so wrapped up in his thoughts of the conversation with Abby and her meeting with Martha that he nearly missed the driveway. He understood Abby's need to help the woman, but he didn't want her to give Collin any more ammunition to use against her.

His daughter bounded down the steps as soon as he pulled in the driveway. She whipped open the car door with a burst of energy. "Hi, Daddy!" she said with a huge smile, showing new braces. She leaned over and kissed him on the cheek.

"Hi, pumpkin. Got your braces yesterday, I see."

"Yup. Mom said she'd call you about the bill. I told her to pay it with the money you give her every month."

"Amy Rae—"

"No, Daddy, you cover me on your insurance and you pay her enough money every month to cover the rest."

He squinted and studied her. "How do you know all of this? And how do you know how much I pay her?"

"I heard her talking on the phone to Scott. She said what it was and that it's hardly enough to live on." The statement rifled his nerves. He paid through the nose but as long as Amy Rae's needs were met, he'd never complain.

"Sweetie, that's nothing for you to worry about. And please don't disrespect your mom."

"She was disrespecting you, Daddy. I don't know why you let her get away with it." She rolled her eyes and gave an exasperated sigh.

"I know you and your mom are struggling right now, but—"

"But nothing," she pouted. "She's wrong and you know it. I don't know why I can't just come live with you."

"There's rules at my house too, pumpkin." He reached over and took her hand. "In the meantime, I need you to make an honest-to-God effort, okay?"

"Fine." Her sullen posture let him know she was not all too happy with his request.

"Are Shannon's parents home?"

"Her dad is. Why?"

"Wanted to talk to him about something." He began to open his car door.

"Why? Are me and Shannon in trouble?"

Juan chuckled and touched her shoulder. "Has nothing to do with you guys. I'll be right back."

"I'll come with you."

"I'll only be a second. If you get in there, you guys'll start gabbing again and I'll never get you back out." Before the words were out of his mouth, she was already on her phone.

"Shannon's letting her dad know you want to talk to him."

"Really? You had to text her that?"

She looked over at him, eyebrows knit together in confusion. "Well, yeah. Duh!"

"Amy Rae, watch the attitude."

"Sorry."

Juan got out and walked across the front yard. Shannon's father opened the door before he reached it. He held his hand out and Juan shook it.

"Good evening, Mr. Robles. Come on in."

Juan entered and closed the door behind him. After some small talk, the how-you-doing and sure-glad-we-didn't-get-all-the-snow-that-was-predicted small talk, Juan asked, "Do you know the Millers? They live that way about a mile." He tipped his head to his right.

"I know of them, but don't know them, if that makes sense. Everyone knows they live out this way but the Millers pretty much keep to themselves. Why do you ask?"

"Just something I'm looking into."

Shannon's dad shoved his hands into his front pockets and rocked on his toes then down again. "Yeah, they seem nice enough but anyone can seem nice in public, right? Don't think I've ever seen them for the past coupla months, though, now that I think of it. But when I have, he's the one that does the talking. She just smiles but doesn't say anything. Quiet gal. Heard she's been taking care of her niece or something along those lines."

"Her niece?" Juan asked. "Have you seen her? The niece."

"Nope. Just a rumor through the rural neighborhood."

Juan shrugged. "All right, thanks. I hope Amy Rae was no trouble?"

"No trouble 'tall. She's a good girl."

"I think so, but being her father and all, I can be somewhat biased." Juan chuckled and Shannon's dad followed suit.

"Never had a problem with Amy Rae. Thanks for letting her spend time with Shannon. Those girls sure do have fun together."

"It's our turn to have Shannon over to our house next time."

"Deal." The two men shook hands and Juan cut across the lawn to the car where Amy Rae was still on her phone.

"Put that thing away and talk to me." He watched as she put the phone on the seat next to her.

"About what?"

"You." He looked over at her and smiled. "What'd you girls do?"

"Instagram mostly. And watched a movie."

"Which one?"

"A kid-tested-mother-approved one." Her phone pinged. She looked at it, appeared to read something, giggled, then looked back up at him.

"That doesn't tell me which one, now, does it?" He winked at her.

She rolled her eyes and smiled. "The Princess Diaries."

"Wow. Now that sounds like a movie I would like to watch. Not!" They both laughed.

"Hey, why are you going this way? Home is that way." She pointed behind them.

"Need to check something out."

"Work?"

"Why would you ask that?"

"Duh!" She rolled her eyes. "You don't have anything else in your life. Why would I think it was something other than work?"

He cocked his head to the side and half-smiled. "Well, that paints a pretty grim picture of my life."

"Truth sometimes hurts, daddy."

"Yes, that it does," he mumbled as he looked into the rearview mirror and then forward again. She blew a giant bubble, then popped it by sucking in.

The sound made Juan jump. "Amy Rae," he warned.

The girl giggled. "You're not very good at sounding mad, daddy. Now, mom—well, she has it mastered."

Juan fought from laughing. When he and Amy Rae's mom first got married, they never fought. It was everything he'd always hoped it would be and everything his parents' marriage wasn't. After Amy Rae was born, though, things began to slowly change. It's not so much that they argued. But it seemed there was a silent undercurrent that threatened to sweep his feet out from under him. And it became more and more palpable. He nearly flinched as he remembered the day she'd thrown a stainless-steel slotted turner at him, narrowly missing his head. All because he'd gotten home late after an intense investigation, forgetting about their date that night.

"Earth to daddy," Amy Rae sang. She tucked a strand of hair behind her ear, turned the visor down to look at her reflection.

"Don't worry. You're beautiful," Juan said with a smile. She had a way of making everything better just by being in the same room.

"You have to say that. You're my dad."

He chuckled.

Coming up on the Miller's driveway, he slowed and looked at the enormous three-story log house, taking in the expanse of the yard and a garage that would make most men jealous. Off to the side of the house, tucked partially behind the garage, enough that he would have missed it had he not been looking closely, was a Backyard Discovery cedar swing set.

Alongside it sat a couple of pink snow sleds and a large pink innertube for sliding. And a pink Power Wheels Jeep. Odd that they would buy so many big things when they were simply watching a niece. Especially when they can't have children to play with it, too. And pink? Perhaps Shannon's father was right. It was Martha's niece and Juan was off target.

"What are you looking at?" Amy Rae leaned forward and peered around her father.

"Admiring the swing set. Would have been nice to have one of those for you when you were little." *Wasn't exactly a lie*, he reasoned. He drove down another few blocks and turned around in a driveway, heading back to town.

"That's what you wanted to see? A swing set?" She screwed up her face.

"Yup. that's exactly what I wanted to see," he said.

Amy Rae sat back again. "Um, weird."

He smiled at her and looked back at the Miller's again when he passed back through, slowing when he saw an older woman walking to a car with a little boy who was undoubtedly the child of Susan Ramirez.

22

Abby and Gabe got back to the resort just as Cody and Roxanne were in the checkout process. Jeremiah handed them their paperwork with a final send-off.

"Thank you for staying despite the chaos of unfortunate events. I hope you come back," Abby said.

"Oh, we'll be back alright," Cody said, laughing. "Rox caught the biggest fish, and I can't let that rest."

Roxanne laughed. "Not that he's competitive or anything."

"No, I can see that," Gabe joined in. He wrapped an arm around Abby's shoulders as they watched the two climb into their jam-packed car. As soon as their car turned onto the road and out of sight, Abby and Gabe strolled back into the store. Abby made a visual sweep around the area, chilled that someone might be watching her.

"Pops, thanks so much for picking up the slack around here so much this week," she said, as she gave him a side hug. "I don't know what I'd do without you."

"Someday you'll have to, but you have Gabe here."

"Don't talk like that," she scolded.

"Circle of life," Jeremiah said. "Seasons come and seasons go."

"What's gotten into you?" she asked, frowning.

He gave her a half-smile and winked. "Just the facts, ma'am, just the facts."

Abby scowled and shook her head, then glanced at Gabe, who was trying furtively to suppress a smile. She narrowed her eyes. "Don't encourage him."

Gabe laughed and held up his hands, palms forward, "I didn't say anything."

"Didn't have to." She looked at Jeremiah. "Any word from Pip today?"

"They started out and will be here day after tomorrow." He chewed on the toothpick held between his lips.

Abby gasped. "What if the killer isn't found out by then?"

"Can't keep the boy away forever." He looked out the window, his eyes revealing thoughts far from where he was at the moment.

"My head knows that. But my heart is a bit behind," she said quietly, looking out the window at what held her father's attention. "He needs to get back to school. I just wish answers were easier to come by."

"And I wish your ma was still here. Neither is." His voice was quiet from lingering grief.

She took comfort in the warmth of Gabe's hand on her lower back.

"I'm gonna go do some work around the yard. Snow's melting fast, and there's some things need doing." He tucked his hands in his pockets and left, leaving grief hanging in the air.

After the door closed, Abby said, "I don't think he'll ever get over my mom passing. He'll go to his grave with a broken heart."

Gabe wrapped his arm around her waist, and he pulled her close. "He's got you, Hermosa. That's keeping him as happy as he can be right now."

Abby wiped a stray tear from her cheek with the back of her hand. "I just want so much more for him. It would crush my mom if she knew this is what he was doing with his life, pining after her like this. Drinking his sorrows away."

Gabe cocked his head to the side. "Funny. That's what he said about you last summer. That he wanted more for you. And look at you now. You're happy, aren't you? I mean, despite the crap that's happening at the moment."

"I am. Happier than I ever was in California. As you said, though, without all of this stuff," she flung her hand up in the air. She looked up into his eyes and smiled. "And happier than I've ever been with anyone."

He bent his head and planted a kiss on her lips. "Ditto, my love." He looked around him, then back at her. "Hey, why don't you go spend some time in your studio? Writing or painting would do you some good. I'll take care of things here."

"I don't know, Gabe," she said, hesitating to accept his generous offer. "I've been gone more than I've been here."

"And now's the time of year to be able to do that. Come later spring, and especially summer and fall, you won't be able to get away. As it so happens," he said, pulling her close to him, "now is the time you need it most." He patted her behind. "Go. Enjoy yourself. Trust me to know what I'm doing here."

She grinned, thoughts of being alone in her studio with her art and her words won. "Okay. If you're sure."

"A hundred percent. I wouldn't have offered if I wasn't."

"What if someone wants a coffee? You don't know how to run the machine."

He tilted his head back and sighed dramatically. "Oh, Abigail, you have such little faith in me."

Laughing, she reached up on her tiptoes and planted a kiss on his cheek. "Okay, I'll go."

"Whoa, whoa, whoa!" he exclaimed, grabbing her hand as she walked away. "On the cheek? Really?"

She melted in the twinkle of his bluer than blue eyes, wrapped her arms around his waist, stood on her tiptoes again, and slowly, drawing out every move, kissed him on the lips.

"Wow! Much better," he said. "Now go before I won't let you out of here."

"Won't let me?" She laughed. "Won't *let* me?" she repeated, grinning. "Oh, Mr. Coleman, I do what I want to do. No one *lets* me do anything."

"Don't I know it," he mumbled.

"What was that?" she asked, laughing again, her hand cupped behind her ear.

"You own it," he said louder.

"I thought that's what you said."

Both laughing now, she slowly disentangled her fingers from his, fingertips lingering for a second longer. "Take Gus with you," he said.

"Yes, master," she teased him. "Come on, Gussie," she said, the big black lab rising to his feet, eager to go on an adventure. She fished his leash out from under the counter, ready to snap it on in the blink of an eye. Gus trotted after her toward the door.

"Got your phone?" he called out after her. "I mean, just in case."

She held her smartphone up for him to see and closed the door behind her.

Abby slopped through the slush to her studio, vigilant of every movement, every sound. Since Detective Robles told her Duncan O'Shea had been a private eye hired to keep watch on her, supposedly by Collin, it helped her relax a little. Knowing it probably wasn't Hunter behind it was a relief. And yet, even though it *probably* wasn't Hunter…well, not knowing that for sure, she'd be lying to herself if she didn't admit she was still a little spooked. Hunter frightened her more than anything or anyone ever could. Collin she could handle. He was nothing more than a white-collar wanna-be who couldn't keep his hands to himself, landing him in trouble. And now that she'd learned his license was revoked due to sanctions for misconduct—or the likelihood thereof—it all made sense. If Collin killed Susan, he had motive. However, she believed Collin was only out to intimidate her. Regardless, she remained on high alert. She'd been wrong before. Oh, so wrong. But with her father and Gabe watching out for her and with Detective Robles hot on Collin's trail, she was reasonably certain she was safe.

Most of the snow on the short trail had melted, patches of bright green grass peeking through. Spring was all about new growth, fresh starts, and she couldn't wait for this to be over so she could fully enjoy it. She longed to take walks by herself deep in the woods, with or without Gus, and to have Cooper back home safe and sound. She wanted to sit on the dock by the lake in the early morning light, as the sun rose above the mountain top. And she wanted to enjoy her hot tub as dawn broke, when all was still and silent, without remembering why she'd stopped. New life. Susan would never see another spring. Abby was going to make sure Collin paid for that.

She glanced at her watch as she unlocked the door to her studio. Five-fifteen already. Guilt sliced through her. She'd been terribly neglectful lately from her duties at the resort and making meals for her father. And tonight Gabe would be at the receiving end of that neglect. She was torn between heading back and taking care of her responsibilities or doing what Gabe told her to do. As soon as the doors to her studio opened, the smell of her paints convinced her to stay. "Thirty minutes," she said in the silence of the room. "Just thirty minutes and I'll go back and whip something up for dinner."

She tied Gus's long leash to a tree within feet of the studio, poured some water from a bottle she'd left in the little mini fridge into a dog bowl she kept there and then closed the French doors behind her. She tugged the chain on her desk lamp, and warm light filtered through the small area, creating shadows. She looked at the painting she'd started and the manuscript on her desk she'd written longhand. *Which to do*, she wondered. The manuscript. She didn't want to waste a minute of the little time she had with cleaning up paints. The simple rustic weathered pine writing desk with matching two-drawer filing cabinet beside it seemed to beckon her.

She shivered from the cool evening air. Sitting down on the wooden chair, she bent over and reached below her desk to turn on the small space heater to take the chill out of the room. As she did, movement from the floor in the corner of the room to her left caught her eye. The corner was eight feet from where she'd just planted herself. She caught her breath and froze. The hair on the back of her neck and her arms stood up. It seemed like she saw everything through clear molasses as she turned her head to see what was there. A long, thick snake, coiling itself, lifted its head as if ready to strike.

She'd heard about rattlers in Colorado but had been fortunate never to see one. Panic raced through her as her blood turned cold. Slowly, she put one foot on her chair, then the other. Next one foot on her desk and then the other. She clutched her phone, her knuckles white, and dialed Gabe's number. She spoke before he could utter a word.

"Snake," she whispered urgently. "Snake. There's a snake in here."

"On my way."

Abby kept her gaze glued to the reptile that remained motionless except for its head which moved slowly, watching her. She struggled to stay completely still. Within seconds but what felt like hours, Gabe was at the door, opening it slowly, quietly, leaving it open. He took two steps forward and looked at the point of Abby's fear. The snake looked at him, then back at Abby, its tongue slithering in and out. Abby shivered. "What do I do," she whispered.

Gabe held out his hand, and she reached for it, slowly, clutching it tightly when she grasped it. "Come this way, slowly," he said, keeping his eyes on the snake.

As slowly and quietly as humanly possible, she stepped off the desk behind Gabe and then out the door. She frantically searched for Gus, who'd wandered around the corner and bedded down, napping peacefully. *Some watchdog you are.*

"Come out of there," she issued to Gabe in a harsh whisper. "Is it a rattler? Looks like a rattler. But I didn't think they're out of hibernation yet. Are they out yet?"

Gabe took a step back but kept his focus on the snake. "Typically they're not. Especially with the snow we just had."

"Maybe it's confused since we've had such warm temps before this snowfall." The snake began uncoiling, its tongue still slithering. "Get out of there!" she said again.

In one swift move, Gabe took a giant step backward and slammed the door. Abby watched, unable to move, unable to look away from the impending train wreck. She looked through the window. It was uncoiled entirely now and slithering toward them. Despite the closed door, Abby's heart rate sped up, and she jerked back. "I didn't hear a rattling sound," she said, trying to regain her breathing to a normal state as she frantically looked around her feet for any more of them.

"They don't always rattle like people think they do," Gabe said, still watching it through the window. "They're sometimes quiet to protect themselves."

"To protect themselves?" she squealed. "Between us and him, he's the venomous one of the three. Why didn't it move until I sat down? You'd think my movement would have irritated it."

"It was cold enough in there, I suppose. Until you started the space heater and probably startled him." Abby shuddered. Gabe continued to watch it. "It may be a bull snake," he said. "They're too similar for me to tell the difference without getting close. And I've no intention of doing that." He took out his phone. "What's Detective Robles's number?"

"Why are you calling him? I can't imagine he can do anything about a snake."

He looked deep into her eyes, conveying the seriousness of it all. "I'm calling him because this snake didn't just open the door and crawl in here. It was planted."

The statement was a punch to her gut. "Planted?"

"Someone really wants to quiet you. I'd bet my bottom dollar it's Collin. If it's a bull snake, we'll know he's trying to intimidate you. If it's a rattler, we'll know he wants you out of the way permanently."

Abby's memory reflected on the sign that was held up in the car window as it crawled by her. Once again her blood ran cold.

The white Wildlife Control panel van rumbled up the driveway, followed by Detective Robles's police cruiser.

Jeremiah left to meet them. Abby watched through the kitchen window as the Wildlife Control tech shook her father's hand. A long metal tong-looking apparatus hung loosely in the man's other hand. Detective Robles followed the sidewalk to the door. Gabe opened it for him before he could knock.

"What are your thoughts?" Gabe asked when he'd finished the story. "I think it's Collin."

The detective inhaled long and slow, exhaling in the same manner. "If I had to guess, I would say the same. I was just out by the Miller's house to pick up my daughter from a friend's house, and his car wasn't there. At least it wasn't in the driveway. Could have been in the garage, I suppose. He was, however, conducting an at-home visit of a client of his out this way earlier today."

"That can't be a coincidence," Abby said, wrapping her arms around herself. "Guess I shouldn't have let down my guard."

"I take the blame here," Gabe said, his hand on Abby's shoulder. "I'm the one that suggested you go out there."

Abby said, "That's right, you did. It's a good thing I know you don't like snakes." She pulled back, looked at him, and narrowed her eyes. "You don't, right?"

"It's not that I don't like them," he said, "I have just never had a reason to interact with them. And I'm okay with that."

She cocked her head to the side, her eyes locking on his.

"Oh, come on!" he said when he realized her train of thought. "You can't seriously think I would have done this."

She nudged him with her shoulder. "Of course not. We know who is responsible. And it's disturbing to think he's willing to go to such lengths to shut me up."

"If he killed Susan, which I'm convinced he did," Gabe said, "vowing to avenge her death was a threat to him. We know Collin doesn't like to be threatened or inconvenienced."

"I think I tried to convince myself he was only trying to intimidate me," she said. "I'll bet Susan threatened to spill the beans about their child."

"To who?" Gabe asked.

"His wife? The Psychology Ethics Board? Who knows? Someone." She shrugged then crossed her arms around her waist. "But I bet he felt threatened. And Collin would never allow anyone to get away with making him feel threatened."

"And that," Juan said, pointing at her, "is exactly my thought. He shut her up, and he's fixing to shut you up, too."

The door opened, and Jeremiah came in, stomping the slush from his boots, the Wildlife Control man right behind him.

"Where's the snake?" Abby asked.

"In my van."

"Well?" Gabe asked. "What kind was it."

"I hate to tell you this, but it was a rattler. A Western."

"What's the chance it got there organically?" Abby asked, knowing the answer before he spoke.

"Zero to none," he answered, shaking his head. "It's rare to see Western rattlers up here to begin with. The higher elevations are too cold for them. And it's been a cold and snowy March."

"So it was intentional," she mumbled, swallowing hard.

"I'll go have a look around your studio and hopefully find something to seal the deal on Collin's arrest," Juan said. "If not, I'll have a chat with Martha. I think she knows more than she feels safe to admit. After that—well, Collin's fate is getting closer and closer. Which means he's going to be about as dangerous as that rattler in your studio. He will strike. No going anywhere alone," he said, looking at her, at Gabe, and back at her again. "I mean nowhere. I'll make sure there's security detail on your house."

He pulled on a pair of gloves and left, closing the door behind him. Abby stayed frozen in place. "A prisoner of an egotistical maniac once again."

"Yes, but a safe prisoner," Gabe said in an attempt to make light of things.

She looked at her father. "Regretting moving out here with me, Pops?"

"Nope." He gave her a half-smile, toothpick in place between his lips. "You cook like your ma. That's worth it all by itself."

She smiled at him. "Subtle, Pops. I get it. You're hungry. She looked from him to Gabe. "You two go take a load off and tend to the store if someone comes in. I'll whip something up in no time at all."

She shooed them out of the kitchen, eager to have the room to herself, making dinner as if it was the same as any other evening. Except she knew it wasn't. Tonight she was reminded all too well of her mortality and how close she came to not making another dinner.

23

Juan's disappointment weighed heavy that there was nothing last evening at Abby's studio to tie the event to Collin. At the very least, he'd hoped to find *something*, but there was nothing. Nada. It was as if the snake had been placed there by a ghost. Not a single fingerprint. Not that a fingerprint is something he would have expected. It's not like Collin would have handled the snake with bare hands. And yet Juan expected to find something, *anything*, to somehow tie it to him. He wouldn't be in the least bit surprised if Collin knew people in the industry, in his perverted circle, that would know how to get the anti-venom for a rattlesnake bite in case he had been bitten during the planting.

He pounded the top of his desk with a closed fist in a rare display of anger, cursing out loud. Another rarity. Collin Miller was as slimy as the snake Juan was sure he'd planted.

Pearl's head poked through his doorway, followed by Officer Johnson. He sensed the presence of other officers hanging out behind them.

"You okay, sir?" Johnson asked.

"No," he growled.

"You need some fresh coffee?" Pearl asked, her glasses dangling from the chain around her neck.

"I need something a heck of a lot stronger than that," he said.

"Not while on duty, sir," she said, shaking her head. "But you know that," she quickly added when she saw the scowl he gave her. "Fresh coffee coming right up." She scurried off, leaving Juan feeling terrible for taking out his frustration on her. A whiff of her perfume billowed into his office, assaulting his sinuses. Johnson stayed put, a few sets of eyes from the troops looked through the door at him.

"What?" He grumbled, throwing up his hands. "I have a right to get upset too, don't I?"

"Yes, sir," one of them said. "But it never happens."

"Well, now it has. Now get." He flung his hand toward them.

All left except for Johnson who dared to sit across the desk from Juan. "What gives, sir?"

"Johnson..." he warned.

Johnson gave him a wry smile. "Yeah, don't try that with me. I know better. What're you gonna do, throw a stapler at me?"

Juan leaned back in his chair, his gaze leveled on Johnson. "Collin Miller isn't the brightest man in town. Why is he always one step ahead of me? If I can't find something to pin on him fast, like this murder I know he committed, there's going to be another one. Abigail Sinclair's." He rested his head against the back of his chair. He stared absently at the blinking red light on his desk phone, toying with the idea of listening to the voicemail. If it was an emergency, whoever it was would have called his cell number.

"If anyone can catch him, sir, you can. But telling yourself he's ahead of you is admitting defeat. You can't do that."

Juan met his eyes and growled an illiterate response. "I don't know, Johnson. I'm missing something. Something huge."

"What about the practicing without a license thing? Can you get him put in jail for that for at least a couple a days? While he's in the clink, you can do your thing to pin this murder on him without worrying about him prowling around the Sinclair's. It'll give you some space to work without worrying about what he's doing out there. And stop just looking at the blinking light and listen to the darn message."

Juan narrowed his eyes at the almost rookie and picked up the handset. He punched in his security code and listened to the message. Suddenly he bolted upright in his chair and dropped the handset back on the switch hook. "Johnson, you're a genius."

Johnson frowned. "I am?"

"Yes. And if you weren't seeing Shonna I'd give you a big kiss."

The man chuckled. "You're not my type, sir."

Juan stood, sending his chair wheeling from under him, hitting the credenza that sat behind his desk. He grabbed his jacket off the chair and strode toward the door. "Come on, we have to go."

"We? Where?"

"Call Shonna and see if she can be at the PD in half an hour."

Johnson cleared his throat. "Sir, she worked all night, so she's sleeping. She turns her phone off when she's sleeping. As soon as she wakes up she's going hiking."

"At least try, dagnabbit," he boomed. "You can call her on the way."

"On the way where?"

"Collin's office," Juan tossed back over his shoulder.

"Why wouldn't we just walk there?"

"Because we're not going to walk him back here in handcuffs on the street for all to see. Think, Johnson. We'll park out back and take him that way."

"But we had nothing a minute ago. What changed?" Johnson asked, hurrying behind him.

As Juan got to his cruiser, he pulled out his phone and the small notepad he kept in his jacket pocket. He flipped through the pages until he found the one with the name of the outcry victim. Angela. He punched in her phone number.

With no answer on Angela's end, he left an urgent detailed voicemail. He could only hope she would get it in time and be at the PD when he got back from bringing in Collin.

Juan grinned and said to Johnson, "That voicemail in my office was the key. Miller lost his license in Canada and falsified documents to keep practicing in the U.S.!"

Juan and Johnson pulled into the parking lot behind Dr. Miller's practice simultaneously. Despite their effort to not draw attention, a few onlookers developed from the neighboring businesses. Juan went in first, hand on the butt of his gun holstered on his hip. Johnson was close on his heels.

Juan entered through the outside door and put his ear against the interior door of Collin's office. The last thing he wanted was Collin in the middle of a session. He didn't trust that he wouldn't take a hostage in an attempt to get away. Hearing nothing, he crept a few feet further to the door of the patient waiting area. He turned the knob and pushed the door open slowly. It was dark and stripped of any furniture.

"Looks like he's not using this room anymore," Johnson whispered, flipping on the light switch.

Juan looked under the door to the office. Darkness. He slowly turned the knob and opened the door, gun at the ready. Light from the waiting area filtered in through the open door, revealing another vacant room.

"It's as if he's never been here," Johnson said as he put his gun back in its holster.

"Except he has," Juan said. "Get a team over here to go through every inch of this place. You and I are going to the Miller's home. He can run, but he can't hide."

"Lights and sirens, sir?"

"Lights. No sirens. I don't want him to hear us coming."

By the time they sped out of the parking lot, a growing number of people dotted the sidewalk, looky-loos, eyes wide. Not that he could blame them. Nothing this exciting in Blue Mist Mountain had happened in decades. Before Susan was found, that is.

Juan fixed his light to the top of his car as soon as he was on the main road, Johnson following him with his own red, white, and blue lights flashing.

Right before he reached the Miller's driveway, he cut his police lights and Johnson followed suit. The back end of Juan's car slid a few feet as he turned, a billow of dust appearing in his rear window.

Juan spotted Collin tossing a suitcase into the trunk. He stopped and stared at Juan's car, appearing to contemplate whether he should run or stay. Juan jumped out of the car.

"I wouldn't if I were you, Collin."

"Wouldn't what?" He finished stuffing the suitcase and slammed the trunk, looking squarely at Juan.

"We both know there's nowhere you can go. You'll never get away." He looked at Johnson and nodded his head toward Collin. Johnson pulled his handcuffs from his duty belt.

"Not in front of—"

"In front of who?" Juan interrupted him.

"Martha."

"Uh-huh. She's a big girl who has a right to know who her husband *really* is."

From the corner of his eye, Juan saw a little boy run down the front steps of the house, Martha right behind him.

"Ryan, get back in here!" Martha called behind him.

"I want my daddy," Ryan said, his little chin thrust outward.

Martha looked at Juan, then took in the handcuffs in Johnson's hands. Her eyes grew wide. She caught up with Ryan and put an arm around his little shoulders. "Come on, honey. Let's get a jacket first. You'll catch a cold."

The little boy looked from her to Collin, unsure of what to do.

"Go with your mom, son," Collin said. "Go."

Ryan sulked back into the house, holding Martha's hand.

Once the door closed behind them, Juan looked at Collin and said, "And here I thought Martha can't have children. Don't know where I coulda ever got that notion. Any idea *Dr. Miller?*"

Johnson grabbed hold of one of Collin's hands, then the other, placing them behind his back, slapping handcuffs on and clicking them in place. "I didn't know we have a doctor in our midst, sir." He slapped his palm against his forehead. "Oh wait! That's right, we don't," he said, tightening the handcuffs as Collin winced.

"Collin Miller," Juan said, "you have the right to remain silent. Anything you say can and will be used against you in a court of law. You have a right to have an attorney. If you cannot afford one, one will be appointed to you by the court. With—"

"Yeah, yeah," Collin grumbled, "I know what you're—"

Juan continued with the rest of the Miranda warning, ignoring Collin's objection. No way was he giving this white-collar monster a way to squirm out from under these charges.

When Juan finished, Collin said, "Is all of this necessary, Detective?"

"If you would have acted like a civilized human being, no, it wouldn't have been. But you didn't do that."

"I didn't kill Susan Ramirez, and you'll find that out. I'll be back out before your chief can say 'You're fired!' "

Juan smirked. "Yeah, I don't think so. I'm not arresting you for Ms. Ramirez's murder, although that'll happen soon enough. I'm arresting you for fraud, impersonating a doctor, sexual assault on one in a position of trust. I'll see what else we can come up with."

Collin's face turned red. "Fraud for what?"

"Forging documents to practice mental health therapy in the States when you lost your license in Canada. We don't take well to that here. Especially when you abuse female clients who trusted you when they were most vulnerable. Need I go on with what you already know?"

"I did no such things," he spat.

"Really? Cause, Fraud Miller, we have victims of your abuse stating otherwise."

"Their word against mine."

"You're right. At this point, anyway. But your word doesn't hold much weight anymore."

"Anyone claiming I did anything is lying. Those women came on to *me*. I turned them down. This is retaliation! They're retaliating against me!"

"Keep kidding yourself," Johnson said. "I'd have said 'with all due respect,' but you don't deserve any respect." With his big palm, he shoved Collin's head as he guided him into the back of the patrol vehicle.

"Johnson," Juan warned.

"You're getting sued," Collin said simultaneously, his teeth clenched.

"Can't wait," Johnson said.

Juan glanced at the house. Martha watched closely from the window. Thankfully, there was no sign of Ryan. Juan didn't want to be responsible for making this memory in the little boy's mind. Especially so soon after losing his mother.

"Take him in, Johnson. I want to talk to the wife."

"Make sure she knows we did her a favor," Johnson said before slamming the car door shut.

"Don't screw this up, kid," Juan warned him, leveling his gaze on the younger officer.

Juan watched as the squad car drove out of the driveway. Collin turned his head and looked squarely at Juan.

When he climbed the wooden stairs that led to the front porch, the door whisked open before Juan had a chance to knock. Martha stood in the doorway looking solemn and defeated. Tears stained her cheeks.

"What are you doing here?" she asked.

"Where's the boy?"

"I managed to redirect him and got him to stay in his room for a while. At least until the fiasco in the front yard got done. Thanks to you and your partner." Words that should have been an accusation came out flat and lifeless.

"Can I come in?"

"Why not." She stepped aside and extended her arm, closing the door behind him. "What's going on? Have you plum lost your mind arresting my husband like that in front of his child?" A spark of emotion cut through the surface.

"Thank you for taking him into the house."

"Thank goodness one of us had the presence of mind to think of Ryan." Tears threatened to spill again. "What's this all about?"

"Mrs. Miller, two women have come forward, claiming unethical behavior by your husband. Do you know anything about that?"

"I know someone did in the past, but Collin said it was all a misunderstanding. That women get confused when they're getting treatment and sometimes fall in love with their therapist."

"And you believe that?"

"Why wouldn't I? I trust my husband, Detective. It's easy to fall for my husband. He's a loving, family man."

"Speaking of family—"

"Guess the cat's out of the bag on that one, huh?" she interrupted.

"Out of the bag?"

"About Ryan."

"So you admit Ryan is Collin's?"

"Collin's?" she said, creases taking residence in her forehead. "Ryan is Collin's brother's kid. He couldn't take care

279

of him so Collin adopted him. We're Ryan's family now. I can't have kids, so…" she said, her words trailing off.

"John?" Martha looked at him with questioning eyes so Juan continued. "Ryan is John's and Susan's?" Could she possibly be so gullible as to believe that hooey? Or was she covering for her husband? But why would she cover for him if he had an affair? He could see that Collin had done a real number on her.

"Yeah. Not that it matters. That's all in the past."

"All?"

"Yes." She squared her shoulders and jutted her chin, cues that Juan knew to be false bravado.

"Did your husband ever talk about Susan Ramirez, Mrs. Miller?"

"Just once. She was one of the women who had an unhealthy attraction for my husband. Not her fault, really. I mean, look at the man. He told her he was a married man and suggested she find a different therapist. He said he insisted on it."

"Huh." Juan studied her. He knew without question that Martha was covering for her husband. He could tell by the way she twisted her wedding ring and offered too much information in an effort to get him to believe her. His assessment was interrupted by Ryan.

"Martha, you said you were coming to play with me. You promised." The little guy tugged on her hand.

She pulled him in for a side hug, his arm wrapping around her leg. She pulled back and stooped over to look at him, lifting his chin with her fingers. "Just a minute longer and mommy will be right there."

Ryan's eyes clouded with confusion. "Mommy? Where is she?"

Martha looked from him to Juan, back to Ryan, her cheeks flushing. "Right here, silly boy." She placed her palm on the boy's back and gave him a gentle nudge. "Go back to your room. I'll be right there. Promise."

Juan watched as Ryan gave her a disbelieving scowl and then his back, shoulders slightly rounded, as he retreated to his room.

"Odd, don't you think?" Juan said when Ryan was gone. "He has the same two-color eye that Collin has." He hoped the spoken observation would net him something.

"Not odd at all," she said with the briefest of smiles. "More people than you'd think have that. Collin's brother, Ryan's biological father, has that same thing. It's hereditary, you know."

Juan nodded. "Yes, I'm aware. Mrs. Miller, do you know why Collin quit his practice in Canada?"

"Of course I do."

Juan waited for her to go on. When it was clear she wasn't going to, he asked, "Mrs. Miller, where was your husband the night of Thursday, March 24th, and the early morning hours of Friday, March 25th?"

She appeared to think back, tapping her chin with her finger, then looked at Juan. "He was here. With me."

"You're sure about that?"

She nodded. "Completely. I know because that's the night we started discussing adding me to the adoption papers. It was a special night for us."

"And he was here all night?"

"He was."

"Are you a heavy sleeper?"

"Unlike my husband, yes. I could sleep right through a tornado. Now, Collin, on the other hand, he wakes up if I so much as roll over."

"Okay, then. I guess that's all I have." He tucked his notepad and pen into his shirt pocket.

"Detective?" Juan turned to look at her. "These women who say my husband has been inappropriate with them. Do you believe it?"

He saw the pain, the fear of his answer, reflected in her eyes. "It doesn't matter what I believe. The only thing that matters is the truth."

She began to wring her hands, then toyed with her wedding ring again. "Collin can be a devil. I'm not stupid. But what kind of marriage would we have if I didn't believe him unless I had a reason not to?"

What kind of marriage, indeed. "I wish I had answers for you, but I don't yet. I assure you, though, we will find out." He tipped his head toward her and turned for the door.

When he got to the top step, Juan turned to look at Martha. "Just one more thing. Did it ever occur to you that social services would never allow a child to just live with anyone? That they would search out the boy's father? If the father doesn't want him, they'll look for next of kin. They won't just let him stay with anyone."

"John can't keep him so Collin is next of kin. And apparently, they've already decided because they're letting me and Collin raise him."

"Were you there for the meetings between Collin and Social Services?"

"No. They took care of all that while Collin was in town at work. That's why I'm not on the adoption papers yet."

Spoken like the boy was a puppy instead of a child. Juan didn't even know what to say. Except Collin sure picked him a wife that believed every lie that spilled from his mouth. He shook his head slowly.

"My husband is a well-respected man. Ryan will be well cared for here."

"We'll see, Mrs. Miller. We'll see," he said. The insecurity emanating from her haunted him. He hoped Abby would be able to convince her to join her support group once it was up and running.

As he headed across the yard to his car, he looked back toward the window, but Martha wasn't there. No doubt she went to be with Ryan. As he turned, a glare from something caught the corner of his eye. He glanced in the direction of the source to see sunlight bouncing off a glass object partially hidden behind a shed. Seeing the window still empty, he went to investigate and found a two-by-four acrylic cage with a tightly sealed cover, slatted to allow for air. A device perfect for transporting a snake. Collin the snake.

24

That afternoon Abby's hands shook as she hung up the phone from Juan. He'd filled her in on Collin's arrest.

"And be careful," he'd said. "Shonna had a hiking accident earlier today. Supposedly fell from a cliff."

"Supposedly?" Abby asked.

"Johnson insists it wasn't an accident. Apparently, she's an avid hiker and climber."

Abby gasped, comprehending the full weight of it. "You don't believe it was an accident either. How is she doing?"

"I can't go into any more detail. Just be careful." His voice was grim. "It doesn't look good for her."

Abby trembled as she cruised the road to Martha's house. With Collin in jail, she would have time to safely talk to Martha again. Too many women were getting hurt by this lunatic. Now, more than ever, Martha would need support. Just because the planning phase had roughly started for the support group and it hadn't officially begun yet, well, that didn't mean she couldn't reach out. Not to mention the perfect timing to help Martha realize there was more to life than what she had endured at the hands of her husband.

Her ringing cell phone interrupted her thoughts. She fished it from the coffee holder in the center console and glanced at the caller ID, reflecting a number rather than a name. Not a number programmed into her phone, so it wasn't anyone she knew. Contemplating for a moment whether she should answer, she finally did a half a second before it rolled into voicemail.

"Hello?" She said, pulling off the road and onto the graveled shoulder.

"Abby?"

"This is her." The voice was familiar, but she couldn't put a name to it.

"It's Travis. From the coffee shop."

"Oh," she said, stunned. "Hi, Travis. How did you get my number?"

"You gave it to me a few days ago, remember? In case I heard anything you'd want to know. Which is the reason for my call."

Duh! She now recalled handing Travis the business card. She was losing her mind! "Of course, I remember. I swear sometimes it's hard to remember what happened this morning, much less a few days ago." She chuckled, attempting to pass off the growing discomfort in the pit of her stomach.

"I can only imagine how difficult it's been for you lately," he said.

She heard laughter and a few voices in the background. "Sounds busy."

"Not very."

"So you heard something about the murder?" she asked, fingers crossed.

"Not exactly about the murder, but it could have something to do with it."

"What'd you hear?"

"A man and woman were talking about Collin Miller. Supposedly he's been arrested for misconduct and fraud.

Something about forging a license. I didn't understand the whole thing."

"How in the world would someone have gotten that information already?"

"So it's true? Because you know how it is in small towns. More often than not, people don't rumor correct information. That's why it's called gossip."

"Do you know who the two people were?"

"Nope. The man was older. The woman about your age. The man said he wasn't at all surprised and said he believed Dr. Miller killed the Ramirez woman."

"He said that?"

"Yup." He mumbled something on the other end. "Hey, hold on, K? I have a customer." Without waiting for her to answer, Travis set the phone down while Abby listened to the entire transaction. Finally, he picked the phone back up. "Sorry about that."

"No problem. So what else did you hear?"

"The man talked about how the doctor's wife needed to get the heck outta that marriage before he killed her like he killed the Ramirez woman."

"What'd the woman say?"

"Saw her nod in agreement, but I couldn't hear what she said. Her voice was too quiet. I could have sworn that I saw her say your name though. I've been a barista for long enough to be good at lip-reading."

A chill rippled down her spine. "But you don't know who they were? You've never seen them before?"

"Nope. The woman looked familiar, but I can't place her. The man I've never seen. Hey, I got a few more customers that just walked in. I gotta run."

"Thanks, Travis. For everything. The next time I'm in I'll leave you a giant tip."

"Well, take *this* tip, Abby. Be careful. I know a little about the law. This Miller guy won't stay behind bars for long just on the charges I heard about so far. He'll bond out in no time at all."

"I'll be careful. Thanks."

If she was going to talk to Martha, she needed to hurry it up. It was hard telling how long before Juan called her with the news that he had arrested Collin. He said 'earlier.' Earlier could mean anything from the moment before he called to hours before. She hadn't thought of asking him an exact time. For safety sake, she dialed his number, but it went to voice mail. She hung up without leaving a message. He'd get the text before any voice mail she left him anyway.

Abby pressed down on the accelerator, quickly reaching the Miller's house. Juan said he didn't have the authority to give her the address, but it hadn't been hard to put it together.

Turning in the driveway, she saw three cars: a red Corvette and a white Honda Civic parked off to the side of the yard and a black Enclave in the front. As she got closer, she saw the Corvette and Honda both had dealer's plates. The Enclave had what appeared to be a vanity plate: MRGRN.

MRGRN? Mr. something. She took a moment to try to figure it out, so she knew what she was about to walk into. *Mr. Green?* She didn't know anyone with the name of Green. Family? Or could Martha be in trouble? Her adrenaline picked up. Maybe this was a dumb idea to come all the way out here by herself. With Collin behind bars, she'd assumed the threat was over. She'd left Gabe running the resort so her father could run to the hardware store. What if Collin had an accomplice? Her adrenaline kicked up another notch.

She sat in her car for a moment longer until a little boy opened the door and bounded down the steps, Martha behind him. Abby instantly recognized the boy as Ryan Ramirez. She watched for someone else to follow them out, but when no one did, she opened her car door.

"Hey!" Ryan called out, running over. "You're the lady who knows my mommy."

"I am," Abby said, forcing a smile.

"I wish she'd come back," he said, his smile fading. "My daddy and Martha said they don't think she's comin' back. But I know she will. Just wait and see," he said, his chin jutting out defiantly.

"Are you having fun with your daddy?" Abby asked.

"Yup. Daddy's not here though."

"Do you know where your daddy is?" she asked, fishing for how much the little boy knew.

"Uh-uh. Martha said he had to go to work."

"Ryan," Martha interrupted him, "Sweetie, why don't you go play on the swing set. I bet Ms. Sinclair will come and play with you after we're done talking." Martha looked at Abby then back at Ryan, her eyes sparkling with delight at the boy.

Ryan ran off with the raw energy of a four-year-old, both women watching his retreating back. When he was out of hearing range, Martha looked at Abby. "What brings you out here?"

"I wanted to check on you."

"So you've heard what happened with my husband earlier today."

"I have."

Martha's eyes brimmed with tears, and she looked off into the distance. "We're probably the talk of the town."

Abby didn't know what to say. The last thing Martha needed to hear was that, yes, they probably were. But not so much her, as her husband. She suspected most talked about Martha with pity. And, according to the people in the coffee shop, they feared for her safety.

Abby shut her car door. "I think more than anything, Martha, they worry about you."

"They don't know me. Whoever *they* are. Collin doesn't think it's a good idea for me to go into town too often, so I don't. Only when I need to. He said he's seen a lot of bad things in his career, seen people do unspeakable things. He didn't want me to be exposed to that. He's just protective is all."

"Sweetie, he's isolating you. Taking you away from people who care about you. That's what perpetrators do."

"Is that what yours did to you?"

Abby noticed Martha's arms, crossed in front of her, loosen a bit. Her body became visibly less rigid. An emotional wall Martha kept erected appeared to partially come down. Abby nodded her head. "He did."

"Is that what happened? Why you left?"

Abby thought Martha's tone was too flat. Had she taken some kind of medication? "That's a very small part of it."

"Collin kinda told me what happened. Said it was partially your fault and that's why you're trying to pin this murder on him."

Practicing without a license, assaulting his clients, and now betraying client confidentiality. Nice. Her stomach churned. Just when she thought she couldn't dislike the man anymore than she already did.

"Martha, Collin has brought all this on himself. He's the one who was practicing without a license. He's the one who initiated relations with his clients. He's the one who fathered a child with Susan. And I believe with all my heart he's the one who murdered her. I'm pleading with you; please get out while you still can. Before you end up the same way Susan did."

"Ryan needs a family. He deserves a family. Collin and me, we're all he's got."

"Thanks to Collin, that little boy is without a mother."

"*I'm* his mother," she said, her eyes flashing with a renewed spark. "I can be exactly what that little boy needs. I *am* what he needs."

"Martha," Abby said, her tone slow and steady, "that little boy didn't deserve what happened to his mommy. Susan has a sister who wants to raise him. He has a grandmother who wants to see him."

"No! He's mine," she said, her tone hard. "Mine and Collin's."

"Martha—"

"Don't!" Martha said, teeth clenched, visibly shaking with rage. "Don't you take what's mine." Abby gasped as Martha, seemingly out of nowhere, produced a 360 Glock, the muzzle trained on Abby. "I'm sick a people taking what's mine."

Abby sucked in her breath, and instinctively her hands went up, palms facing forward. The gun might be small, but she was well aware of the damage it could do. "Don't do this, Martha. What about Ryan?"

"That's why I'm doing this. Why I've done what I've done. Don't you see? That little boy is half Collin. With Susan out of the way, he's mine and Collin's. We can raise him. Be a family like we always wanted."

With Susan out of the way? Why she's done what she's done? Abby began piecing it together and her heart sunk, heavy from the weight of what she'd just now figured out. She had been so wrong! She swept the area around her, looking for an escape. Her car was so close, but she didn't have the time to open the door before Martha stopped her, much less get in and drive away. She frantically scanned the yard for someone, *anyone.* Her gaze landed on a pair of snake tongs, gloves resting on top.

"You killed Susan and you tried to kill me," she said quietly, all of it making sense now. "But why? Don't you see what you've done will only take Ryan away from you?"

"No, *you* tried to take Ryan away from me. Why couldn't you just have minded your own beeswax? None of us would be in this predicament if you'd just left us alone."

"Shonna," Abby said.

Martha's eyes were hard, the gun unmoving. "Yup. She had the nerve to come on to my husband. Working at the police department was her misfortune."

"But—but—how did you—"

"How did I know?" Martha said in disbelief. "That woman called to tell *me.* She thought I had a right to know." She laughed cynically. "A right to know? *A right to know?*" Martha's voice raised an octave. "She had a right to know I couldn't tolerate her doing what she was doing. Trying to take my husband away from me."

Abby's head reeled. "Why my hot tub? Susan. Why my hot tub? And how did you get her body into it?" Abby's gaze flickered between the gun and Martha's eyes.

"That woman had the nerve to come see me and tell me she was going to turn Collin in for doing to other women what he did to her. He didn't do nothin' to her! He told me so himself."

"So you killed her."

"I did."

She said it as if she was proud. How could Abby have been so wrong? Her cell phone buzzed and Abby moved one hand slowly.

"Don't even think about it," Martha warned.

Abby put her hand back in the air. "What if it's Gabe or Detective Robles? They'll wonder where I am. They both know I came out here and will know something's wrong if I don't answer," she lied.

"You're bluffing."

"I'm not. But you can think what you want." Abby struggled to remain calm. Cooper flashed through her mind and she fought back tears.

"I'm calling it anyway. Your bluff." Martha jerked the gun's muzzle toward the shed. "Move."

Abby began backing up slowly, Martha matching her step for step.

"Where you going, Martha?" Ryan called. "You said you'd play with me. You, too, lady," he said to Abby.

"Martha, think about what you're doing. You don't want him to see you doing this. I know you don't."

"Shut up and keep moving," she said, too calmly. "Ryan, honey," she called over her shoulder, "stay there. I'll be with you in just a minute." She looked back at Abby. "A minute is all it should take."

"How did you do it, Martha? How did you kill her?"

"We fought, she fell and hit her head."

"See?" Abby grabbed her chance to help Martha see reason. "It wasn't your fault. It was an accident. Killing me will only make matters worse."

"You're wrong. It was my fault. The fall didn't kill her. It knocked her out for a bit but then she came to and threatened to go to the police. I panicked, and before I knew it, my hands were around her neck. I saw the life go right out of her. Do you know what that's like, Abby? Do you?" Her voice was steel. She swiped her sleeve across her face, keeping the gun pointed at Abby. "Of course you don't know. She was going to take my family away from me. Collin said so."

"Collin was here when you did it?"

She looked at Abby as though she was a sandwich short of a picnic.

"No. He told me about her. He told me that she was trying to destroy us and that if she came at me I was supposed to do whatever I needed to do to stop that from happening."

"He used you, Martha. He used you to do his dirty work."

"No," she said, shaking her head. She unlatched the door to the shed with one hand and shoved Abby with the gun. "Get in there."

"Ryan will hear the gun and come over here. Please don't do this. Not in front of Ryan."

"I'm not stupid, you know. Collin says I am but I'm not. I'm not going to kill you yet. Not when Ryan is around. Now get in the shed."

Abby stepped over the lip of the door. Martha snatched up a rope from the seat of the lawnmower and tossed it to her. "Tie this around your ankles."

With trembling hands, Abby did as she was told as slowly as she could. "How did you get Susan's body in the hot tub? Did Collin do that? And why mine? Why *my* hot tub?"

Abby's feet tied together, Martha snatched a piece of twine from a hook on the wall of the shed, with surprising strength pushed Abby to a sitting position, and tied Abby's hands behind her back and to the lawn tractor, making it impossible should she try to run.

"Guess it doesn't matter much if I tell you. It's not like you're getting out of here alive to tell anyone." She paused and tilted her head slightly. "Collin wasn't home. I called John and told him what I did. Him and Conrad—"

"How do John and Conrad know each other?" Abby said, stalling for time. *Keep her talking.*

"Because of Collin. My husband is always getting Conrad out of trouble for something or other. Conrad owes him a ton of favors." She chuckled bitterly.

"What kind of trouble?" She winced as Martha tugged the twine, biting into her skin.

Martha shook her head. "What do you care?" she sneered. "Anyhow, they came out and took care of it so Collin and me wouldn't get in trouble. But you—you just couldn't stay out of it. You and your do-gooder attitude, always wanting to help women in trouble."

Martha knelt next to her and tied her bound feet to a metal bar next to the lawn tractor. Seeing her only opportunity for escape, Abby butted her head against Martha's, making contact with her nose. Abby heard bone crush followed by a loud yelp as Martha cursed a blue streak. Crimson gushed through her fingers.

Abby's phone chimed with an incoming text. "It's probably Gabe. He'll be coming out here."

"Well, he won't find you, I guarantee you that," she spat through a spray of blood.

Holding her nose with one hand, Martha grabbed her phone with the other, punching in a series of numbers.

"It's me," she said. "I need your help again. It's Abby Sinclair this time." She listened as the person spoke, then answered, "I had to. She was going to take my family away. She was going to make sure Ryan didn't stay with me and Collin." She was silent again, then, "Uh-huh. Yeah. Okay." She hung up.

"Let me guess, John?"

"Conrad. He's out on the lake fishing. John and Carrie left to go back home."

"The car in your yard. That's his?" Abby wasn't sure if that thought terrified her or gave her hope.

"Yup. Now stop talking. I don't like having to do this, you know. But you give me no choice. Just like Susan Ramirez. And that Shonna chick."

"When Shonna regains consciousness she'll tell the police, Martha. You know that."

Martha shook her head. "No, she won't. I gave her just the slightest little push over the edge. She didn't even know what happened. Quick and easy."

"Martha, please—"

"This is your own fault. When Conrad gets here, I'll take Ryan for a drive while he takes care of you."

"Martha, please," Abby said, trying to think of something, anything, to keep the inevitable from happening. Thoughts of Cooper invaded her head again and she began pleading.

"Please, I have a son. Don't make him grow up without a mother."

"Like I said, you did that yourself."

"Please," she cried, tears springing to her eyes. "Mother to mother, I'm begging you."

She thought she saw Martha waver for a moment, but that moment gave her the hope she desperately needed. "I know you don't want to do this."

"Stop. Talking."

Martha scooped up a dirty rag from the seat of the lawnmower and shoved it in Abby's mouth before she pushed open the door. But as the door opened, Abby heard the unmistakable sound of sirens from a distance. Martha's panic-stricken face looked from the door to Abby back to the door. "No!" she yelled, before she bolted outside, slamming and locking the door behind her.

The sirens got closer and Abby heard tires screeching on the pavement, then in the front yard. A car door opened, then another.

"Martha Miller, you're under arrest!"

Abby slumped with relief and tears spilled. Detective Robles. She couldn't utter a sound with the rag in her mouth but he'd see her car. She thought of Ryan and her heart grew heavy. The poor boy had seen more than any child should have to see in a lifetime. All because of a therapist who preyed on women. Including his wife.

Abby listened as a scuffle ensued outside. She attempted to scream, a sound that was snuffed out by the dirty rag in her mouth and the noise of the commotion. Then a gun shot. *No!*

"Abby!"

Gabe! The sound of his voice gave her a new burst of energy. She struggled against the restraints, twisting in ways she didn't know she could until she was able to pull the dirty rag from her mouth.

"Gabe!" she yelled. Her lungs screamed. "Gabe! In here! I'm in the shed!"

Someone fumbled with the door and then the lock. "Abby? Stand back, I'm coming in," Detective Robles hollered. Like she could go anywhere anyway. A boot crushed through the door, splintering the wood as Abby covered her head the best she could with her arms. Gabe fell to his knees beside her. "Abigail Sinclair, you get yourself in the worst predicaments. You scared me to death."

"You're one lucky woman," Detective Robles said as he cut the rope that bound her feet. Next he cut the twine around her wrists.

Abby rubbed her burning wrists.

"How did you know?" she asked. "How did you know it was her? I totally missed it."

"The snake cage I found had Martha's prints all over it."

"Martha's the one who hurt Shonna. She pushed her over the ledge," Abby said.

"Shonna woke up about half an hour ago," Robles said. "She's going to be fine."

Abby shuddered with relief and the possibility of what could have been. A fresh wave of tears spilled down her cheeks. "How did you know I was out here?"

"That'd be me," Gabe said. "I know you. I knew you would want to support her after Juan arrested Collin. When Detective Robles called for you and you didn't answer, we figured it out."

"Thank God," Abby whispered as she melted into his arms.

"Literally," Gabe said. "Thank God." He pulled back and looked at her, cupping her chin in his hand. "Speaking of God, He said you're taking up all of His time and would appreciate it if you stayed out of trouble for a while." His eyes flickered with hope and concern.

She laughed softly and loved how it felt. Minutes ago, she didn't think she would ever be able to laugh again.

25

"I still can't believe you drove out to Martha's without telling me," Gabe said. He and Abby cuddled in his camper as the early morning sun began to rise above the mountain, casting a warm glow over the campground and what remained of the snow. "But what's more disturbing is that I'm surprised at all."

"I didn't lie to you. I'd never lie."

"Lie by omission," he countered.

She chuckled and snuggled in closer. "Not so. I just don't tell you everything that I do, every move I make."

"Well, when it comes to putting your life in danger, I wish you would."

"Had I known that, Mr. Coleman, I wouldn't have gone now, would I? My only concern was getting out there to see her before Collin bonded out."

Gabe groaned with exasperation and held her tighter. "Hermosa, you're going to kill me one of these days."

"I don't think Martha is fully to blame."

Gabe twisted around to look into her eyes. "How can you say that? She was going to kill you."

"She wasn't going to kill me. Conrad was. What I don't understand, though, is that she killed Susan and tried to kill Shonna, but she wasn't going to kill me. Until now, anyway. Why?"

"I think it's because you tried to help her. Deep down, she likes you. And you didn't succumb to her husband's crap."

Abby shuddered. "Thank the good Lord she likes me. We've seen what happens to the people she doesn't." They lay in silence for a moment. "The call I got from Travis, he said it was an older man and younger woman he heard talking. That man and woman were Conrad and Martha. They tried to disguise it though, talking as though they were someone else, in case someone overheard them." She shrugged. "Which they did. He—Conrad—believed Collin was capable of murdering her."

"So, what are you saying?"

"I think Conrad has a thing for Martha. And Martha is a victim of Collin's manipulation and abuse as well as her own low self-esteem, which was only crushed into a million pieces by her scum-bag husband. A woman like that—well, women who go through that kind of abuse, it can do things to them that—it can make them do things that they normally would never dream of doing."

"She's a killer, babe. She took the life of another person. Almost more than one. Twice."

"I'm not disputing that. It's just that—" Abby looked deep into his eyes, searching for understanding. "I thought about killing Hunter so many times. Thought about how it would solve all of mine and Cooper's problems."

He stroked her cheek with his finger. "But you didn't act on it. There's a big difference."

She leaned back into him again. "What if I would have? What if—"

"You didn't. You wouldn't have."

"Battered women's syndrome is very real. It's a legit mental disorder." She sat up straight and turned to face him. "Domestic violence is a cycle. For a while, everything is hunky-dory. Then something happens to build tension, it could be something as minor as dinner late or the house not picked up, saying the wrong thing, and it will set the guy off. Or woman. In Martha's case, I don't have any proof that he physically abused her, but the mental abuse was severe. In a typical case, the guy will ask for forgiveness, be all sweet and loving, give her gifts—it's called the honeymoon phase. I came to know it as the hearts and flowers stage. That's what a therapist once told me. After so many cycles of this, the victim becomes helpless in a way, believing that she can't live without him. She becomes so depressed and defeated that she feels she can't leave. Oftentimes, she still hangs onto hope that the abuser will stop, and each honeymoon phase gives new hope. So the cycle continues."

"But—"

"She stays, even believes the abuse is her own fault." She paused, swallowing raw emotion. "He continues the cycle of violence, making the syndrome even worse. Martha didn't blame Collin for anything. In fact, she praised him. But according to the conversation Travis overheard, Martha believed Conrad when he told her Collin would end up killing her. And to top it all off, she believed all of Collin's lies as if they were fact. Those are all symptoms of Battered Women's Syndrome. And sometimes these women have been known to kill their abuser." Her voice was hoarse. "Probably more than you wanted to know."

Gabe's voice was thick with grief. "You know all of this so well because you had this when you were married to—"

"My punk of an ex-husband."

Gabe's jaw clenched. "I can think of a word far more appropriate than punk."

"I can't stay mad at him, Gabe. If I do, it only lets him keep my power. It's not easy and I'm not always successful, it's a work in progress. Probably for the rest of my life. And that's what you're getting into with me." She pulled back and looked at him. The words kept pouring out like the tears that wet her cheeks. She couldn't stop them. "That's the damage you will have to deal with for the rest of your life. I'm not sure you fully realize the extent of that. And Cooper? Hunter damaged him as well. And that is what I have the hardest time getting past. That my son was a casualty of such horrific things. I worry that as he gets older, he might display symptoms of the abuse he saw. Do you want me to go on? To tell you how difficult a life with me and Coop could be?"

"Oh, Hermosa," he said, gently pulling her back to him, then holding her at arm's length so he could look deep into her eyes. "Nothing you can say will make me want to get out of this relationship. I love you not because I think you have this perfect life and no baggage. I love you for all of you. I love Cooper. And I would never in a million years do anything to hurt either of you. I know it's hard for you to trust, but I think I'm gaining some headway." He smiled gently. "Yes?"

She sniffled, gave him a half-smile, and nodded.

He continued. "And I won't stop until I've earned your trust completely. And then I still won't stop."

His voice was so gentle it almost hurt to hear it. "Gabriel Coleman..." She swallowed hard, ready to say it. "I love you. With all my heart."

An hour later, as they sat around the kitchen table, Abby poured coffee into Juan's cup, then refilled Gabe's and Jeremiah's before sitting back down.

"Aren't you having coffee?" Juan asked.

"I'm on the wagon," she said, looking at her father pointedly. She'd found two empty vodka shooters on the bottom of the trash not half an hour earlier when she was looking for a document that had found its way into the trash instead of on her desk.

"How's Shonna?" Abby asked Juan.

He chuckled. "Johnson popped the question. The Chief isn't happy but he'll get over it."

"And?" Abby could tell there was more.

"I didn't tell you before, but the autopsy results came in," Juan said.

"Let me guess," Abby said, "asphyxia consistent with strangulation."

"That's right. Martha already told you." He took a sip of coffee. "Well, the autopsy confirms what we already knew."

"What I never found out is why John and Conrad put the body in my hot tub? I mean, why mine? I asked Martha more than once but she never answered me."

"For no other reason than convenience, according to Conrad. If the body was here, they assumed no one would look at either of them, also assuming no one would think they were that stupid. They were though. Stupid."

"What about John?" Abby asked.

"Canada is one of the countries the States has a treaty with for extradition. He'll be brought back here to stand trial."

Abby reached for Gabe's hand. "Does anyone else see the irony that Susan, a victim of Collin's, was murdered by Martha, another victim of his?"

"Abby was educating me earlier on Battered Women's Syndrome," Gabe said. "Think Martha will get off if she's found to suffer from that?"

Juan shook his head. "Don't think so. Battered women sometimes kill the abuser but I haven't heard any cases where they've killed someone else and gotten off. I could be wrong, I guess."

"The man makes me sick," Abby said, shaking her head slowly. "Several of his clients were more than likely abused. I hope they come forward when the news breaks." Gabe squeezed her hand. "He took advantage of them, magnifying its detrimental effects by hundreds."

"Glad you weren't one of 'em," Jeremiah said, his voice barely audible.

"Bob and Judy are adopting Ryan," Juan said.

Grief weighed on Abby's heart. "That poor boy has a long road ahead of him. He lost both his mother and father in a matter of a week. What do you think will happen to Collin?"

Juan shook his head. "Unauthorized practice is only a Class 2 misdemeanor for a first offense. A second or any subsequent offense thereafter is a Class 6 felony. He had a license in Canada and moved here when he lost it. So this is his first offense. That'll only get him a fine and a few months in jail. He's already bonded out at this time, though."

"You're kidding!" Gabe exclaimed.

Abby felt as though she'd been sucker-punched. "That's just not right. What did he say about Martha killing Susan? Did he know it was her?"

"Eventually he figured it out, I guess. He was more concerned about keeping his reputation intact."

"Sicko," Abby said, shaking her head slowly.

"He'll get slapped with more serious charges of aggravated sexual assault on a client by a psychotherapist. As for how many charges, we won't know until it's been more thoroughly investigated and we see how many victims we have. Even then, he'll potentially plea to a lesser charge and might only get probation. That's our wonderful justice system. But since he posted bond right away, he won't get credit for time served if the judge does impose a jail sentence."

A heavy silence fell around the table until Juan spoke. "On a lighter note, the Chief is asking the town council for funding to provide a meeting place for your support group. A room of your own."

Abby smiled, finally able to see the possibility of light amid the darkness. "That's amazing news. Thank you so much, Detective."

"Juan," he reminded her. "I think we've all moved far beyond the formality of 'detective'."

"So what are you going to do with yourself now that this isn't hanging over your head anymore?" Gabe asked him.

Juan leaned back, stretching his legs out in front of him, crossing his boot-clad feet at the ankles. "Thinking of retiring. I want to spend more time with my daughter. I had her late in life. I want to enjoy time with her before it's too late for me."

Abby smiled, understanding exactly how he felt. The moments she spent with Cooper were the best part of her days. "I feel so fortunate to be able to work here at the resort and have my son with me full time." She looked at Gabe and squeezed his hand. "I'm so blessed."

As if on cue, the sound of a car pulling into the yard, followed by a honk, sent her heart soaring. She ran to the kitchen window in time to see Cooper jump out of the car, leaving the door open. Ignoring the scolding from his aunt, he bolted for the house, his long blond skater hair blowing in the breeze. He threw open the door, wrapped his arms around his mom in a rare display of affection, then Jeremiah, and lastly Gabe. He looked at Juan then headed for the refrigerator.

"Man is it good to be back home. I miss anything?" He turned to look at the four sets of eyes looking back at him and stopped, holding a pitcher of juice. "What?"

Abby shook her head and wrapped her arm around his shoulder. "Not a thing, son."

"Nope," Jeremiah said.

"Nada," said Gabe, all in unison.

Cooper looked at Juan, who simply put his hands up, palms facing forward. "Hey, I'm just a friend here for the coffee."

Jeremiah chuckled, followed by Gabe, then Juan. Suddenly laughter erupted throughout the kitchen, and Abby's heart warmed. She looked upward. *This is for you, Susan. May you rest in peace.*

Dear Reader,

Thank you for reading *Abby's Redemption,* book two in The Whispering Pines Mystery Series. Though the series is only a duology (two books), it's a subject that is close to my heart—Domestic Violence. I work with domestic violence victims in my job and it's a nightmare too many women experience and not all survive. Though this is a work of fiction, my goal is to help educate as well. Here are some staggering statistics:

Statistics from domesticviolencestatistics.org:

❖ Every 9 seconds in the US a woman is assaulted or beaten.

❖ Domestic violence is the leading cause of injury to women—more than car accidents, muggings, and rapes combined.

❖ Based on reports from 10 countries, between 55 percent and 95 percent of women who had been physically abused by their partners had never contacted non-governmental organizations, shelters, or the police for help.

❖ Studies suggest that up to 10 million children witness some form of domestic violence annually.

❖ Men who as children witnessed their parents' domestic violence were twice as likely to abuse their own wives than sons of nonviolent parents.

Facts and Statistics from The National Coalition Against Domestic Violence:

❖ 1 in 3 women and 1 in 4 men have been physically abused by an intimate partner.

❖ 48% of women and 49% of men have experienced psychological abuse by an intimate partner.

❖ Domestic violence hotlines across the country receive approximately 20,800 crisis calls a day.

❖ Domestic violence (DV) accounts for 15% of all crime reported to law enforcement.

If you, or someone you know, is in need of resources, please reach out to the following:

❖ National Domestic Violence Hotline: 1-800-799-SAFE

❖ National Sexual Assault Hotline: 1-800.656.HOPE and online.rainn.org

❖ National Suicide Prevention Hotline: 1-800-273-TALK www.suicidepreventionlifeline.org

❖ National Center for Victims of Crime: 1-855-484-2846 victimsofcrime.org

Also, word of mouth is the best promotion for an author. Please consider leaving a review on Amazon and Goodreads. A sentence or two all that is needed. By doing this, it helps me as the author as well as other readers.

I would love for you to connect with me at:

Website: rhondablackhurst.com
Email: rjblackhurst0611@gmail.com
Facebook: www.facebook.com/rjblackhurst/
Twitter: @rjblackhurst
Instagram: Rhonda.blackhurst

Best,
Rhonda

Acknowledgements

Sometimes thank you is not enough. And sometimes thank you is the biggest gift we can give. With all my heart, thank you to:

Bridget Dyson—You've opened my eyes and my heart in more ways than you can ever know. Your story has changed my life. Your energy, zest, and passion for life. You're always looking at the glass as half full when it was so close to empty. You, my friend, are an inspiration to me and so many. Thank you for sharing your life with me. I am grateful for you.

My Parents—You've modeled a healthy relationship through my formative years and beyond. And when I decided to take a few detours, it was the example of your relationship that brought me around and landed me in the beautiful one I have now. I am grateful for you.

Clint—My husband, my soulmate, my gift from God. No woman anywhere could ask for a better husband or partner in life than you. I am grateful for you.

Sandy Camphilger—Your feedback is invaluable. You take beta reading to the next level and I am grateful for you.

Jessica Cornwell—Your editing skills make me a much better writer. I am grateful for you.

Karen Whalen—My soul sister. Your positive "get-back-to-it-girl" pep talks when I didn't think I could, are what pushed me through. I am grateful for you.

And my God— You took this wayward girl, picked me up every time I fell, and You have given me a life I never dreamed possible. I am eternally grateful for You.

About the Author

Rhonda was born in northern Minnesota but now resides in Colorado with her husband, dogs, and close to her children and grandchildren. She loves the Rocky Mountains, but a piece of her heart will always belong to the woods and lakes of Minnesota.

Her love of writing took flight at the tender age of four when she was caught writing with her crayons on the knotty pine walls of the family home. In her teens, she tested her hand at journalism by writing an article or two for the city newspaper about school events. She completed an online Journalism/Short Story Writing course and was a stringer for another local newspaper, writing about school and community events. It was then she realized writing fiction is her first love and true calling.

When she's not at her day job at a District Attorney's Office, she can be found hibernating in her home office creating characters, settings, and stories. When she's not writing, she's reading books on the craft of writing, and is typically reading more than one fiction book at a time. Mostly mysteries, of course.

Made in the USA
Middletown, DE
17 July 2020